Daniel
A
Reyes

Library of Congress Control Number: 2016907412

ISBN:	Hardcover	978-1-5144-9188-1
	Softcover	978-1-5144-9187-4
	eBook	978-1-5144-9186-7

Print information available on the last page.

Rev. date: 09/21/2016

To order additional copies of this book, contact:
Xlibris
1-888-795-4274
www.Xlibris.com
Orders@Xlibris.com
739503

Dareyesauthor.com
Twitter: @DannyFigEssence
Facebook: Daniel.Reyes.7505
Instagram: DannyEssential
Snapchat: DannyEssential

THE ESSENCES

BOOK 1 OF THE EPIC SERIES

BY

DANIEL A. REYES

BOOK COVER BY CARLOS QUEVEDO
CHAPTER ILLUSTRATIONS BY ANTONIA LOWE

TO MY THREE FAMILIES,
THE HOLY FAMILY,
MY EXTENDED EARTHLY FAMILY,
AND MY FAMILY IN OPUS DEI,
WHO I LOVE AND CARE FOR VERY MUCH

Contents

THE ESSENCES

BOOK 1 OF THE EPIC SERIES

Chapter 1

The Four Gallants

How could it have come to this? Not so long ago things were very different in Heaven, but now, I just witnessed *the fall*… Fire, ashes, perdition, and many of my brethren lost to this cliff of eternal abyss… the rebellious one calls it hell… Now I know what is meant by the very profound message of warning, *"The road to hell is paved with good intentions."* Indeed it is! I cannot help but think that my own good intentions are also cemented, here, on this path!

This is where defiance to God leads… Many would call this the wrath of God, but God did not do this, we did! This is the saddest, most devastating, episode in my angelic existence. Tears of excruciating grief running down my face… The dark prophecy, foretold by the choirs of angels, is fulfilled! But who has won in this civil war? God's faithful, angelic, Hosts? Or the rebel ones? It is unclear, but it is done! I think I know where this all started… I think I know where it all went wrong...

The Almighty God summons his four Archangels to His Palace in Heaven. It is for a very special occasion, a celebration. Today is the day in which the universe is created. I have just witnessed with amazement how matter is put into existence; call it the big bang, if you will. Particles and spectacle of pure, inconceivable, energy in the air… It is power, colors, and indescribable love, flying, all over a blank canvas.

For me, especially, it is a day of great importance, a day of great honor and privilege, because I have also been summoned to the house of the Lord. How could it be that, I, an angel with no particular stature, have also been summoned to the meeting with God's most important angels? I ask myself, what could be the reason that I may be included in such an exalted gathering? Soon, I will find out and no doubt it shall be glorious!

Until that moment comes, I diligently prepare my Archangel's armor and weapon for this meeting with God. I always spend many hours polishing his sword, leaving no precious, blue sapphire without luster. No golden or silver edge left unpolished and deprived of gloss. I take my time to inspect it in the gleaming light. I know this is no small feat, paying attention to detail, taking special care of the ordinary things. Even now, when I know that this weapon is by no means small or lacking importance. This lofty sword, that I hold, is no ordinary sword, it is a well-known super weapon, crafted by God, in which He shares His inalienable powers with His angels. It belongs to my commander, the Archangel or Gallant, Michael. The weapon even has a name; it is called, ***"The Sword of Justice and Mercy."*** And it is inscribed in the blade.

How many can say that they have been in the presence of such greatness? I can! I cannot emphasize, enough, how I am so lucky to be honored with the position of being the best friend, and apprentice, to an Archangel! I give thanks for this position of supreme nobility. I strive to serve faithfully with every breath of my soul and existence!

My commander's black armor is also within reach... the stamp of a blue sword, branded, on the chest protector has also been given special care, thoroughly cleaned and polished. No crack or crevice of the, deceivingly light, breastplate left impure.

In just a few moments, he, my good pal, my mentor, the Archangel, Michael, shall enter this room and will be covered with this armor from wings to toes. The armor and weapons of an Archangel are especially important because they are what differentiate them from us, Cherubs… angels of lesser superiority and stature, (In both rank and size).

Under the tutelage of my master, Michael, and this sword, I was once taught the art of battle just as all angels were. This is fitting because both Michael and this sword jointly created the art of combat.

Not too long ago, I recall my commander's words of wisdom in Heaven's training arena, imparting to everyone, with his curious accent, "Peace above all! Restraint, self-c'ntrol and submissive behavi'r! Our acts wilt always be ones of strife and struggle, especially with oneself…

"Avoideth conflict at all costs, but sometimes c'nflict and resolution is needed! The key of c'mbat shall always be strength and weakness! Expose thy opponent's weakness and attacketh with all thy strengths! It will maketh thou both improve…"

We would all recite and repeat his words of wisdom in astounding legions, in gang chants of thousands… These phrases always resonate in my head and are words that I attempt to live up to.

Under Michael's care of infinite wisdom, the two virtues of justice and mercy never conflicted. "Aft'r war comes peace… Aft'r combat comes f'rgiveness," he preached to us all.

With his sword of justice and mercy, he taught us many other virtues as well and how they are applied in warfare.

He announced, "Clemency wilt always be ex'rcis'd!"

I remember vividly and with a smile that no one would dare spar with him, not even I, even though I knew he would take it easier on me because I am his friend and confidant. Even so, Michael would teach and train, showing his might and fervor, against many opponents, thrusting on, and hurtling forward, elevating his trainees into the sky, slashing and thrashing with each stroke of his sword. He would brandish his weapon, using his, mighty, fighting skills, just as I am, playfully, role-playing with it right now. He could use his entire being, wings included, to thwart his pupils and all challengers. All onlookers were also awed by his display of valiant swordsmanship. He also had the power to shock his adversaries with blue, lightning-like, bolts, jolts of energy exuding from his electrified sword, which would magnify his fighting skills. Leading by God's example he was, and is, always, both just and merciful.

Lucky for us, when we train with him, we improve our abilities, daily, and there is no limit to the heights our skills can reach. We try our hardest to one day be on par with him, but this realization is much easier said than done…

As a good Commander, Michael is always there for us, like

a father, and especially for me, never with one moment of his own... His love for all his students is selfless. In Michael, I see and admire the characteristics of the one he serves, directly, *The Father* and *Almighty God*.

With him, I always knew I was in good hands, that God had tasked him specifically for this purpose, to keep peace and enforce His will in Heaven. It is no coincidence that the Gallant, Michael, was chosen to be one of the four Supreme Commanders of us angels, serving a very specific role in God's plan.

Now, I carefully put his sword of justice and mercy in its sheath and attach it to Michael's armor. It is now ready to be worn by a General of God!

Just as I predicted, with the punctuality of a Gallant, Michael enters the hall, he gives me a glowing stare and a heart-warming smile… I do the same, except mine is accompanied with a simple bow of respect to my superior. The mystifying light that exudes from his black complexion is inspiring. It shines from his skin and illuminates all it touches.

We both keep to ourselves, not saying anything. He likes to keep to himself because he knows he is about to meet with God, that the Lord commands respect and deserves to hear the first words of the day.

With reverence, he first kisses the hilt of his sword. With the finest touch of his lips, it automatically becomes activated and lit with an electrifying, glimmering, blue, light. Then he quickly, but methodically, dresses himself with the armor, which I have carefully placed on the table. Now, I am delighted to say, he is worthy of facing the Lord…

All four Gallants have heard the calling of our Lord, and now exit their palaces simultaneously. I am there to accompany my master, Michael, every step of the way. Well, maybe it isn't steps we will be taking… A flight cannot be characterized as such…

I follow my friend, closely, to the outskirts of his palace. I can tell he is happy for me, that I will also be joining-in on the meeting. I am sure he is already briefed on what the Lord beckons from me at this gathering, but he will not give me a clue, wishing it to be a surprise, which adds to my excitement.

My gaze is entirely focused on his armor and sword, attentive to its perfect placement on my Gallant's back, right in between his two wings. But now, we are finally ready to go... I am eager to take flight…

As Michael strongly grabs ahold of my waist, I am swept off of my feet. He easily does this with his mighty strength, even though we are of comparable size. I am just a little smaller than he is because I am pretty big and tall for a Cherub.

He takes off flying, first with me in his right arm, and then I climb onto his back, on top of his sword of justice and mercy. We are propelled into the very blue, Heavenly skies. I am like a child, completely trusting in the stability of my master. I can honestly say that I enjoy this too much! Flying is always my favorite part of the day!

Even though I also have two wings, my wings are more aesthetic than functional for flying. Only the four Archangels' wings are made for flight. And, so, I have the gratification of being carried by Michael through Heavens' spheres. My friend indulges me on this guilty pleasure. I think it is because every time we do this, he sees the joy that exudes from my soul. Maybe, it is because, otherwise, I would have to find a more mundane mode of transportation to arrive at Paradise Palace…

Right now it is the crack of dawn, when God's light begins to shine its brightest. You cannot beat the view from my perspective. The scene is beautiful… Heaven is as stunning as promised, more astounding than your wildest dreams. It is nothing like you have ever seen before. It is as striking as a pristine jungle-beach and has the look of a brand new technologically modern city. There are towers, turrets, and castles in the horizon. Architectural wonders are everywhere…

Workshops specialized for building all types of artifacts, big and small. These are the most prominent sights... It is truly a fusion between nature and technology. Everything is alive and vibrant, all part of a hybrid creation. For instance, edifices of metal and skin, yet, everything is elegant and aesthetically pleasing to the senses. The smell is of delightful freshness. The sensation on my tongue is of sweetness and it lingers freshly on my breath. The sounds are of peace and clarity. The sights are colorfully vibrant, shiny and sensational. Both nature and our nurturing care are the themes…

Very soon after lift-off, in the skies, another flying angel joins us. It is the Archangel, Gabriel, who appears out of the blue. His extremely fast flight pattern now mimics our own, as we soar parallel to one another. Gabriel's beauty is astounding! He too is wearing a matching, black, armor to that of Michael's, except his chest is stamped with the image of a green shield instead of a blue sword. He does not carry anyone on his back. Like I said, I am very lucky to be in this unique position…

Gabriel too is fasting in silence before the conference with the Lord. Their concentration, in preparation, for the meeting with God is exemplary.

Just a warm smile says it all to both Michael and I, no need for a formal greeting. I can tell by his expression that he never gets tired of seeing my enjoyment when traversing through the skies. You never see a Cherub fly!

I wish dearly to break my silence because one cannot squander the opportunity to be heard by the Archangels. Not just that, but the thrill I am experiencing remains unrivaled and has to be expressed… Still, I remain quiet and simply smile back at Gabriel. I really wish my smile could match his!

As we soar through the skies, I begin to reminisce on my past experiences with Gabriel. I fervently cherish these memories, remembering how after long days of weapons training in Heaven's coliseum with Michael; I would look forward to what followed, a chance to unwind and spend time with another of God's General's, Gabriel.

In the coliseum of Heaven, Gabriel's smile and tales of optimism would gather thousands of angels before him. This coliseum is the location, which we now fly over. It is enormous and oval, meant to fit all angels inside its perimeter.

In that moment, I have flashbacks of Gabriel's grin, gathered around my brothers and sisters, all trying to learn from his leadership and positivity. A word from his mouth could cheer the saddest, and he could make any angel see light in darkness.

He can turn rotten apples into the sweetest of nectars. Inspiring and moving, he is the best storyteller, intriguing, suspenseful, comedic. My story telling cannot even compare to Gabriel's.

Gabriel always keeps morale high in Heaven by laughing and sharing stories. After intense, but fulfilling, combat training, he sometimes accompanied us on our walks home. We all listened to his tales, as he was projected in majestic sounds and images in the skies. Most vividly, I remember his voice amplified, recounting the stories and anecdotes of all four Archangels' creations, his included. Telling us how fortunate we are to see God and to know He exists. How lucky we are to be in His presence and share in His omnipotence. Even though he was projected for all to see, he would always make the experience feel very personal, speaking to each one of us uniquely just as God does.

"Those who have a good father do not need to worry about anything because a good father always takes care of his children. What better father than God!" He would also say, "Angels are not blinded or short sided by anything material. We know the full truth."

In all his stories, Gabriel's, green, weapon, ***"The Shield of Good News,"*** was the focus of attention and awe. He is definitely the shield of Heaven and the one who brings high morale to the kingdom, protecting God's creations.

So imagine me now, in even more awe than before to be in the presence of he who possesses the shield of good news. I usually get to spend a long time with the sword of justice and mercy, when I polish it, and pass quality time with my pal, but never long periods with Gabriel's shield. Even though the weapon is on his back, covered, in its semi-transparent sheath, I can still see the glimmer of the green sapphires and the shining of the gold and silver outlining.

I know in my heart that Gabriel was created to serve God as a good son would, honoring his father, being obedient, being humble, but also complementing the father. Lead by his example, I too try to be like this, in a constant state of joyous improvement.

As we soar through the firmament, in the distance, I can see two more paths of flight approaching our direction. One of the airborne body's leaves a red trail of fire and the other leaves a trail of purple gas. When Gabriel and Michael see these flying objects approach, they quickly accelerate, as if racing...

I love every exhilarating instant! Picture my face of joy once we reach the most incredible speeds. Even so I grab a better hold of Michael's back, whereas before my hands were free from attachment. They were previously extended on both sides of my torso, only bound to the pure air that trespassed my complexion... My hair flowing backward with the intensity of the fresh wind...

The red and purple objects flying in the distance are now closer, they resemble, vivid, shooting stars, like us, they are airborne at incredible speeds.

Below, I can see many angels in the streets of Heaven who stare up at the Gallants as they are flying. The Archangels stare back at them and admire God's creation. The distance that we travel seems very short because of the incredulous speeds that are reached, but it is really quite long, having flied through almost all of Heaven's spheres.

Then we land almost simultaneously in the courtyard below Paradise Palace. Our landing is as though we were wearing jet-propelled backpacks. In our wake, as we all place our feet firmly on the ground; we have formed ripples of wind. The impact is epic, bionic!

Now I am released from Michael's firm support and am able to walk about freely. Acknowledging each other, the two, Michael and Gabriel, now embrace, but remain silent. I quickly step aside to allow my Gallants to attend to their rituals and duties.

The two red and purple objects that we just saw, at a distance, while flying, now descend and land right next to us as vortexes of light. Their playful but fierce landings also create, intense, ripple-tremors that shake me to my core.

The colored objects soaring in the sky were the final two Archangels left to be introduced, Satan and Raphael; they now join us, overwhelming me with ecstasy, if at all possible, at this point. Satan, the oldest of God's Gallants and Raphael the youngest, are just a few steps away! Both have magnificent weapons of their own that are being carried, in sheaths, on their backs, inside the plumage of their wings.

It is my duty to clear a path for these embodiments to land as if my location were a landing strip. It is they who are the guests of honor at the palace, not I. I am just a secondary guest. Besides, I can always rely on this alternate spot and angle to get a marvelous glimpse of the Archangel, Raphael, landing, and the beautiful staff he carries, and today my spot does not disappoint! Too many favorite instances to choose from!

All four Gallants are now present. These Generals of Heaven are such a great taste of the grandiosity in God's creations. None higher than them, except the Almighty Himself.

Here at the base of Paradise Palace, I am one step closer to finding out why I have been summoned. If I had only known that this is the day it all started, this is the day it all began to go wrong, for me and for all the angels, things might have been different!

Chapter 2

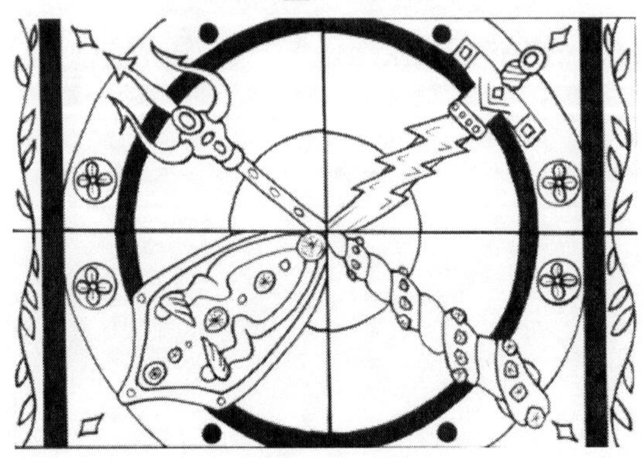

The Four Essences and The Dark Prophecy

Now the Gallants begin to walk side-by-side, heading towards a flight of stairs. Oh how majestic they are in entirety, from wings to toes! I humbly follow at a distance, trailing from behind.

Many crowds of angels always gather to the presence of their Gallants entering the Palace. Some try to touch the Archangels armors and weapons, attempting to receive special graces as their powers always, residually, rub-off. Today is no exception. Multitudes of our brethren approach the area to get a glimpse of their leaders and cheer them on with praises. This welcoming is more epic than any victory parade. This is the sense of belonging and community in Heaven because we are all loving brothers and sisters.

None are jealous of my position of importance at their side. They are happy for me. I can sense their unconditional support as they wave at me with the joy of children. I simply wave back.

But, ever since Raphael and Satan landed, my gaze has mostly been focused on Raphael's staff, which he carries partially covered on his back. Let me be clear… It is not a fixation on precious objects that I have, which you may be thinking… It is the power of God and His craftsmanship that fascinate me.

Raphael has the same black uniform as the other Gallants, but has a bright, purple staff, symbol encrusted on his chest armor. His weapon, ***"The Staff of Souls,"*** resembles a simple, silver and gold walking stick, adorned with purple ametrine stones. It looks as though it has been cut from a tree branch and spun around itself on an axis.

I notice that the staff has been leaning a little too far to the right, on his back, so I cannot help but approach and straighten it out for him. Raphael felt my corrective action. He simply turns around, winks one of his eyes at me, and does so with a smile. He is known for doing exactly this, always winking his eye in approval and encouragement. His silent appreciation for what I have just done speaks louder than words. I wish desperately to answer back, but still do not. Now, I can go back to admiring the near perfection of the Archangels…

This staff is one of the very first things I remember seeing on my birthday. Yes, I too had a birthday! I cannot tell you the exact date or moment because that is not how things work here. What I can tell you is that on the day of my creation, God gave me life, through a touch on the forehead, by Raphael's staff. I remember suspiring as if I would have never tasted oxygen, and right then, I was given my spirit, unique and childish as you might have noticed, but it was a spirit nonetheless. Perhaps this was the very instant where I got my silly and competitive nature, always wishing to outshine others. My goal is not to be better than everyone else, but to simply perform to the highest of my abilities, and in doing so, raise the bar for everyone.

As I awoke into existence, Raphael was there to greet me with a warm embrace. He put down his staff and said to me in a raspy voice, "Suscipiat ad caelum, Uriel! Welcome to Heaven, Uriel!"

If you were wondering, that is my God-given name, Uriel, it means, God is my light… If only everyone could be greeted in such a fashion! That would be a sight!

Since then, I have been a witness to the marvels of the staff of souls and how it can cure the ailments of the soul, mind, and body. But more so, I can attest to its defensive powers. Raphael infused me with strength, encouragement, and healing when I fell in the training arena, and boy did I fall, over and over…

I remember clearly, soon after my creation day, Raphael approached me, and very reverently said in angel-talk, "Constare Deum posse decreverint perfom multa signa per virgam meam quæ vocabatur... God can perform many miracles, through my staff, but the true miracula, miracles, are those I have no part of, those that come as gifts straight from the Omnipotens, Almighty." He said this to encourage me to perform my own miracles…

It is with him that I learned to praise with my singing. I do not have a very melodic voice, but I try to sing with my entire being.

He said to me, "Gratias tibi Deus! Thank God! Give Him the praise and gloria! Honorem and proclaim God's deeds and do not be lackadaisical in praising Him!

"Before all the existing, acknowledge the many good things He has done for you by benedictionem, blessing, and extolling his name in canticum, song..."

The Gallants continue to walk up impeccable, white, steps that are a mix of clouds and sunlight beaming through. One must traverse this staircase, on foot, to enter Paradise Palace. Only the worthy and full of grace may enter.

In my current trance, walking up the staircase, I trip on a step and nearly fall on my face, "Concentrate!" I say to myself. I am forcefully awoken from my day dreaming to now focus on my surroundings. It is not polite to stare, or least, to obsess on any particular topic, so I apologize… I forgot how hard and tiring it can be to walk up hill!

From up close, the palace's detail is now more visible. It is a majestic, white, temple, with four obelisks, that can be seen, standing proud, from all places in Heaven. On the outside, there are Corinthian style columns. It is simple, but grand, modern, but antique looking, made to represent the simplicity and grandiosity of God.

The light of Heaven glistens in the Archangels' complexion, glowing in entirety. The blackness of their armors makes a sort of chessboard contrast with the white steps that they climb. Everything happens as if in slow motion. Their importance makes one savor the moment just a little longer, but not too long because I can barely keep up with their enthusiastic pace…

As the Gallants reach the end of the very long staircase, two gray angels similar in appearance to me are holding long, golden, spears, and they open enormous wooden doors for us to enter.

When the Archangels walk by, they are greeted with their titles, *"GALLANTS,"* and *"SERVIAM,"* the second term meaning, "We will serve." This refers to an angel's duties to serve God the Almighty, to work for the increase of His glory, and to see that His will be done.

With jittery smiles on their faces, much like my own, the guards salute, raising their spears to the sky, and continue to bow their heads, in reverence.

The Gallants walk into a great, Greek style, edifice, reminiscent of a Pantheon building, which sole purpose, in this case, is to pay tribute to the *One, True, God.*

The inside is specially adorned with bright lights like the stars of the newly created universe. The walls contain enormous murals depicting the vivid stories of creation. The Archangel's images are engraved and painted with vibrant colors throughout. Some of these murals illustrate and narrate the stories that I have just told you, and many more of the creation of the Gallants and their weapons.

My gaze turns to one of the murals, which vividly contains Satan below a majestic, golden, tree. It is incredible artwork! Definitely one of my favorites, but it is an unfinished painting! Which means the events in the masterpiece are not yet completed or have not yet unfolded... So, I stay a moment to admire the painting, speculating how the mural's story will develop. I have always wondered what, that, my favorite painting, will be about…

Now, I can see the flawless, white, marble, walls, along with bright chandeliers, throughout, which give additional glow to the stories depicted on these paintings.

Entering an opening where there is no ceiling, lies a resplendent, white fountain. The angels casually wash their foreheads and hands. I do the same. We all do this as a tradition, to cleanse, and so that we will be presentable in front of our Lord. Think of it as a very refreshing bath of the spirit.

With water from the tips of his fingers, Raphael swiftly splashes my face. If only he had done this sooner, before I almost fell to the ground on the stairs, I would have awoken from my daze and not stumbled. The others laugh at this playful joke. By the time I try to get him back, their determined strides had already left me behind. This water lights a fire in our souls, which is clearly visible in their demeanor and hopefully in mine too.

Now, the Archangels continue to traverse in a straight line, side-by-side, as equals in the eyes of God. On occasion their footsteps become synchronized and the sound of their trotting is as if they were marching.

Our destination, within reach, an enormous hall awaits us…

Finally, after all the poetic displacement, they reach the main hall of the palace where God is more intimately present.

I say more intimately present because God is everywhere, omnipresent. If you do not believe me, turn around… Smile! He is here!

Disappointed? I did not say you could see Him, but He is nonetheless, here, before us, in everything and in everyone. You may not be able to see Him, but I can, always, especially at this very moment. It is one of the many perks of having a soul and no body.

Yes, human, I am well versed in your ways! We angels have introspection into the past, present, and future, and even though you have not been created yet, I can see you, and I know you are attempting to see me too. With this account, it is my intention that you become well versed in my ways as well…

…Back to my story… The insides of the great hall, in Heaven, look like a post-modern Cathedral, with the grandest cupola above.

In the middle, there is an enormous, gold, and diamond box, which we call, *"Tabernacle,"* which is adorned with many, angel-trumpet, flowers. It is as big as a building, divided into three equal parts. This puts the magnitude of the palace into perspective. The hall is quiet, bright and colorful, stunning in its elegance and simplicity.

Gods' Essence and Substance, if you will, is present in the gold, and diamond, tabernacle. The beautiful box is again simple, but decorated by the sign of God's Essence, which are three indelible, parallel, lines (III).

The tabernacle is accompanied by a red-lit candlelight. The candle is lit, which means God is present in the palace. If the candle were turned off, it would mean that God's Essence is not directly present in the box. I know, confusing, right? Not for me, though!

It is appropriate that God's Essence is attached to the tabernacle. Usually, His Essence likes to become attached to living beings, to share with them His love. The truth is, I wish the majesty of God could simply be described as a, simple, tabernacle and an Essence, but for now, this is the only way you can understand the awesomeness of the Lord. For now! I like to call this presence, Divine Radiation!

The Gallants now stand in a straight line, humbly, before the tabernacle. More importantly, they are now in the, awesome, presence of God. They raise their eyes to His splendor. I am a few steps behind them, keeping my head reclined so as to revel in this reverent instant.

Their faces, clearly, face the Lord, and the detail of their complexion is more visible with the brilliant radiances of the palace. Their black, elegant, uniforms are a metal and latex hybrid, very tightly pressed to their skins. The covering of the Gallants' armors, even on their wings, is an unusual texture, a combination of feathers and metal. Their wings shine with the glimmer of the bright lights.

So you can better understand, the Archangels are very handsome males; tall, muscular, very innocent looking, impeccable, but thick-combed hair. Their eyes match the colors of their weapons. I somewhat resemble them; except they are black and I am gray. My wings are short and their wings are much longer, and they are quite a bit taller. I have always thought this was appropriate because gray is a lesser shade of black. Just as I, a Cherub, am a much lesser angel than they, and the same can be said about our wings and height.

As all four Archangels stand, side-by-side, facing God, the first of the Gallants kneels, and his enormous, black wings expand. Now, it is the time where they can properly break the silence and pay their respects to the astounding Lord.

The first one to kneel is Satan, who had earlier landed with Raphael. I am ashamed not having given him his proper veneration as we walked. I was so distracted by Raphael and the, incredible, staff of souls, that it completely slipped my mind. I can now make up for my distraction and praise the Gallant of persuasion with the reverence that he is deserved.

Satan, with his thick eyebrows, says the word, "Serviam!" accompanied by the most reverent and pious genuflection.

Satan is distinctly recognizable by his beauty, but more for the stamp of a red trident on his chest. In his appearance, God got it right, the first time, with him! He is the lord of all things red. The red trident emblem on his chest resembles the light burning beside God's tabernacle. This is the light, which he meekly stares at as he kneels in front of God.

I am thankful to Satan for many things… above all, for the attention to detail in my creation, which he assisted in the planning of. As the first Archangel, he also had the privilege of aiding God in His future plans to create his Gallant brothers. He even taught his Gallant brothers how to fly, patiently transmitting this trait on how to use their wings. He spared no secret and even allowed his siblings to be as good as him in their flying capabilities. It is said that he is the only one who can teach and convey this great gift, and perhaps he only grants his knowledge to the worthy ones. I am very happy the way I turned out, and what would Heaven be without its soaring

Gallants? So many believe that they owe him a debt of gratitude, but really all debts of gratitude are owed to God.

Since he was the first to be created, for a long time, he had the pleasure of serving the Almighty all by himself, bearing great responsibility. Imagine having God, in His Trinity, all to yourself? I thought I was lucky right now, having God and the Gallants to myself, but my lesser honor cannot even compare to his privilege.

As God's most beautiful Archangel, he is the one who attracted all of us to our vocations as servants of God, making our duties very enticing, and for this I am even more thankful because what would an angel be without the privilege of servitude? In serving, we become free.

Indeed, Satan's powerful trident was pivotal in the construction of Heaven, giving all angels wonderful incentives for our service to God, and all the incentives he gave us were always well backed and fulfilled. He encouraged us, daily, to go above and beyond in our service, not just to the Almighty, but to himself too. In return, he promised us happiness, security, companionship, and brotherhood. For the most part, I think we are all pretty docile and not needing much persuasion, but his weapon, ***"The Trident of Persuasion,"*** is still a wondrous asset in God's plans. Even though it was persuasion he instilled, I always saw it more as a privileged duty.

After my creation and after the heart-warming welcome into Heaven, by Raphael, I then had the pleasure of meeting him, my Gallant, Satan. It seems like yesterday that he used his extraordinary gold, silver, and red ruby trident, persuading me to live peacefully in God's kingdom. I remember being disoriented and recall him helping give purpose to my existence. He promised me peace and blessings. So far, as you can tell, all his promises have been more than realized. He even persuaded us, the first angels, to construct and protect the city of Heaven, and we did it, following the Lord's specific plans.

As you can see by now, I have been given the best four-way training anyone could ever hope for. No complaints from this Cherub! Every moment spent in my God's and Gallants' presence is like sweet nectar to a hummingbird.

To this point, God has always been well served by all His Gallants, yes, even Satan, I think? (He might have been putting up a front from the beginning). This is the image I have tried to portray... I hope you understand that I love all my superiors, very much, and I would do anything for them, especially my buddy, Michael, and of course, primarily, God.

One by one, the Archangels continue to genuflect in front of the golden tabernacle box.

The next Archangel, kneels, right next to Satan and professes the usual greeting, "Serviam." It is my master, Michael, with his bright blue eyes.

Then, the subsequent Archangel, Gabriel, kneels next to Michael, hailing, "Serviam!" Bowing his head as he breathes passionately, his green eyes wide open.

The final, and youngest, Gallant, the purple eyed, Raphael, kneels next to Gabriel. He proclaims, "Serviam!"

The Gallants' weapons are on their backs stored in sheaths, but after they all kneel, bowing their heads, with their hands extended, they present the weapons in front of them. They do this as an offering. It is a sign of fortitude and humility. With the slightest touch of their astonishing weapons, they become activated, intensely dazzling, exuding immeasurable power.

At the same time, they join in singing the most epic *Alleluia* and *Amen* hymn ever heard. They do this to praise and adore the M*ost Highest* of beings, the *One, True, Almighty, ever-living, God.*

Their heads remain bowed. They know that the weapons they bear are theirs, but they also acknowledge that they are not worthy of ownership, they are just entrusted guardians and that God can take them away if He should choose to do so. They also know that they really have no power of their own because it is God's power that is present in the weapons. Even though their weaponries are a big part of who the Gallants are, they are not materially attached, well… at least three of them are not attached…

The detail and precision in their weapons is now clearer to my gaze than ever. Seeing them now is as exciting as the first time I laid my gaze on them, as is the notion that I am that much closer to finding out the answer to why I have been summoned to this meeting. The anticipation grows with every instant…

Together, Satan's three-tipped ***Trident of Persuasion,*** Michael's crooked, ***Sword of Justice and Mercy,*** Gabriel's double-angel, ***Shield of Good News,*** and Raphael's twisted, ***Staff of Souls,*** are weapons of immense power, yielded by God to enforce His will. The Archangels are powerless without them. These four weapons are known as ***The Essences.***

In one of the stories depicted on the walls of the palace, there is an unspeakable prophecy, which has also circulated among the choirs of angels… it involves the Essences… A prophecy of a dark time to come…

An unbelievable time of great strife and choosing… A fall and a falling out… The Essences will play a major role in this black foretelling. But above all, to stop this prediction from coming true, the Essences must never be separated from the Gallants. The Archangels must always remain united. He who possesses the Essences shall have the power of God, unite the angels and end this time of obscurity.

And even though there is a dark prophecy, we do not let it worry us or dictate our lives, although in retrospect, we probably should have!

Chapter 3

Watchful in the Garden of Eden

Now that the Gallants have gathered and are properly disposed, the meeting with the Lord, God, begins… I stay in the meeting as a special guest of lesser honor, but not before I too salute, as I kneel and profess, "Serviam!" The suspense in me continues to accrue because I still do not know why I have been summoned with the Archangels.

God's voice is now heard coming from the tabernacle; He is a calming fatherly figure. When He speaks to the Archangels, He does so individually. Nothing is hidden from them, speaking to each one of their hearts openly.

God always tells us what we need to hear. He is both timely

and considerate. This time I cannot hear the entire conversation. I can only get a glimpse of their faces, their expressions. Each Archangel smiles… They seem inspired, as they have a few laughs, but also acknowledging the seriousness of God's words.

I am pretty sure they are rightfully celebrating the creation of the universe, Essences in hand. I can see the beauty of the universe so vividly represented inside the Essences' luminous detail. This celebration is well warranted for them all because it is the culmination and fulfillment of their hard work. I know in my heart, that the Lord probably shows them, first, why and how light was created, and how, in the same light, all this will be seen millions of years from now. He likely shares with them a glimpse of the goodness and transcendentalism in His plans.

More importantly, I would think God is explaining to them how human life is to be created in the near future. God always talks very highly of these humans. He only has exultation and positive things to say about them. Nothing but praises are extended their way… Of course this speculation of what the Lord is saying to them, is just an educated guess. Still I have a feeling that their conversations are muted from my ears for a reason. Not for a bad reason! Like I said, God tells us what we need to hear...

I do admit my curiosity gets the best of me, and I too

desperately long to be in on the conversation. At that very moment, when my sentiment was yearning to be included, my Lord speaks to my heart… He specifically tells me, ***"Uriel, I want you to be present at all times in what is to come… Stay close to the Gallants, whenever possible, and be a witness to the paramount events that are about to unfold…***

"Truly I say to you, if there are any details, that are hidden from you, that you wish to know, as always, I will fill in the gaps. Ask and you shall receive!

"I will always take you where you need to be... Do not intervene in what you see, just document!

"This is not about you, do not make it about you; it is about Life."

I ask, "Why have you chosen me, Lord? I get a hunch, wondering, are these the prophetic dark times that are about to come? Light has just been created, darkness cannot come so soon!" Reaching my hasty conclusions…

I receive no answer… I know this is just the answer I need to hear... I am not worried in the least, just optimistic and courageous, in my new task, grinning and positive to the realization that light is here to stay, that the Essences are in good hands and shall never be separated… See? I told you, God brought me here for a reason!

My new task, of supreme honor, leads me to believe that what is about to come, whatever it is, is still of great importance. I shall do my best to be an informed journalist in this matter, and to document the facts as I see them. I see it as God making me the official documenter of reality: ***"A Documentary of Creation, by Uriel."*** I like the sound of that! Not just that, but in my head, God has just granted me wings (figuratively speaking) to continue to be, me, as nosey as possible! I repeat the words over and over, "Lord, that I may see! Lord, that I may be docile!" Giving many thanks for this task.

The meeting does not last long, it is a refined and timely celebration, but the Archangels are no less energized and inspired to continue their integral work, and so am I. What better than divine inspiration to quench our souls? Nothing! I know this first hand.

As the Gallants exit the main hall, they again bow and profess the word, "Serviam," never turning their backs to God. I do the same, piously mimicking my masters in all that they do.

They exit the main hall and begin walking to a different chamber in the Palace; Essences still in hand, used as walking sticks... Their footsteps are echoed through a new hall. Their eminence is felt everywhere. This hall contains statues of the most important angelic figures, including my Gallants… I like to call this hall, *the hall of fame.*

Now they walk up to a round, golden door in one of the gigantic halls. The archangels reveal the entirety of the door by lifting the blue, star covered, sheet that is concealing most of it. The door is an enormous portal, and its purpose is to transport angels, swiftly, anywhere we would like to go. As soon as the cover is vanished, the portal is activated. The material outer space is visible and the Archangels step onto the portal path. The conduit where they stand to be transported is translucent and rainbow colored. This is no coincidence...

One by one, the Archangels step onto the rainbow path, stabbing their weapons into the color of the rainbow that best represents them. I rub my hand through the blue pixels since I am of the lineage of Michael and his sword… Immediately sucked in, we are taken on a journey… Their wings extend as they are propelled into space by the swiftness of the rainbow path.

They pass through the stars and several planets; Constellations, galaxies, supernovas, and meteors are vivid… Asteroids mimic their paths. They rush quickly, but timelessly, through suns, black holes, Saturn, the Milky Way, even by the earth's moon, which has no craters on it and is whiter than ever. Countless other universal and galactic landmarks are visible for us to marvel in.

Finally, the rainbow path begins to decelerate, as they come upon a blue, green, white, and brown, planet that is still under construction... It is interesting that this planet is one major continent, also known as *Earth* or *The World…* All creatures, which God has created here, are united by one piece of land.

The rainbow we ride descends into the earth's ozone. As Satan enters this kingdom's atmosphere, he resembles a ball of fire that grows with the combustion of earth's oxygen. Michael looks as though he is covered in a barrier of blue water that begins to drip, melting with the speed in which he travels. Gabriel resembles a piece of earth, covered in minerals, soil, and mostly, green, plants that crack as if he were quick erosion. Raphael floats almost invisibly purple, as the air does, like a powerful gust of wind. I look at myself to see if I too had transformed to resemble anything extraordinary, unfortunately, I do not. As far as I can see, I am still myself! Maybe if I had been holding onto Michael's back, like I usually do, I would have converted into something amazing.

The Archangels' land gently on earth's firm ground and the rainbow continues to be seen, emanating its radiant colors. Soon after their landing, they look around to see a massive gate, very similar to the door they just uncovered in Heaven's rainbow room. This gate has been constructed to emulate these doors; they are made of beautiful redwood. Above the entryway there is an arch with big letters carved that simply say, *"EDEN."*

The doors of this gate are wide open. The Gallants take the fresh breeze in, astonished at every detail, and they are excited to go into this earthly Paradise. It is the first time they get to experience the world. They are like tourists but they are also on a business trip. All expenses are paid; yet, they have the pleasure of experiencing something new and unforgettable. Even so they are there strictly for business and this is the main thing on their minds.

From now on, I will try and limit what I have on my mind because I do not wish to detract from the true protagonists, the Archangels, just as the Creator has commanded… to not make this about me. If at any point, in time, you wish to know my reaction, especially now, just imagine me surprised, excited, cheerful, and optimistic. This is how I try to be! It is now my time to stay grounded, to step aside and simply bear witness to the events. Do not worry! I will chip-in when necessary and ask the Lord to show me what I cannot see. I long to be a humble servant. Lord, that I may see! Lord, that I may be docile! Know now that this is also the first time I have stepped in what will become the kingdom of the human, but many fortunate angels have been here before.

After our landing on earth, I can see from far away that there are many legions of Cherubim angels, in ranks, guarding the doors of Eden.

Although we do not have gender, the best way to explain, us, Cherubim is to say:

Cherubim or Cherubs, as we like to be called, are male angels and we are double-winged. I look at my wings and they are much shorter than the Gallants'. Then I do some wishful thinking as I say to myself, "If only we could use them to fly!" We Cherubs always wear our gray armor, which is a part of us, like our skin. The guards that were standing outside, the wide-open doors, of our Lord's palace with the long spears, were also Cherubs. I am not ashamed to say that we are the lowest ranking choir of the angelic hierarchy.

Long ago, Gallant, Satan, had helped encourage the Lord in the plans to create two new choirs of angels. These choirs were to be inferior in rank to the Archangels. Satan's reasoning behind the matter was simple. Since the Archangels were all equal in power, he wanted to command subjects beneath him. He wanted to be in control, and at the center of a certain force to improve productivity. He claimed that these lower choirs would increase the Lord's glory. Really he presented it as a win-win situation for everyone.

Deeply valuing his General's opinions, the Lord created the two new choirs, one of them being the Cherubs. This is why I previously stated that I am very grateful to Satan for facilitating my creation, and that of my kin. The creation of these choirs was always in the Lord's plans; Satan merely expedited the process by expressing his enthusiasm and helpfulness.

I am not complaining at all. It really did make more sense to create us to be inferior in rank to the Archangels. If not, there could arise a conflict of decentralized power. There would be too many angels with too much power. Instead I am sure that I am an extension of Gods immense power, but not a power source myself. Like all of God's angels, we are His tools, like His hands, tools that gladly do His bidding and are fulfilled in serving alone. And now you know a little more about the choir I belong to!

Satan's most loyal friend and advisor, Beelzebub, is in command of guarding the gates of Eden and these impeccable troops. Beelzebub is a Cherub, a very handsome one, just like me. His piercing, red eyes show that he is of the understudy lineage of Satan, having learned and closely mimicked his Gallant friend in all he does. Angels who have any shade of red eyes belong to Satan's lineage and the same goes for the other Gallants and their colors... It is just as I have explained about my blue eyes and my relationship with Michael.

The troops that Beelzebub commands are a fearsome group of Cherubs called, *The Watchers*. All of them stand erect in perfect lines outside Eden's portico. They have a solid gray, granite, complexion. There is a certain smoothness and sophistication to their appearance. These are my brethren! I am proud to be one of them, although not specifically a Watcher. We are still so much alike in both spirit and appearance. I can see myself reflected in their mirror-like weapons, and even though I do not belong with them, I can see myself fitting in their ranks quite nicely.

Satan and his good friend greet with a warm embrace. I can tell that the hug starts out a little awkward from Beelzy's side. Satan sees this awkwardness, but quickly brings his friend into his arms for a strong hug, taking control of the situation, and neutralizing the discomfiture. Beelzy looks embarrassed, but they both end up laughing.

He says, "Whoops."

"Beelzy, good to see you, my friend," says the soft-spoken, Satan.

His friend answers, "The pleasure is all mine, my Gallant

and my friend."

As the greetings continue, Gabriel and Beelzy share a momentary stare. A split second later, Beelzy looks to the ground as if his eyes are not worthy of Gabriel's. He avoids conflict, even though there is no conflict to be had. In my interactions with them both, I have always noticed that the relationship between Beelzebub and Gabriel has always been civil, but there has also always been a sort of tension between them.

Beelzebub's personality is calm like mine, but he is also a little unsure of himself, and this is completely unlike me. He told me once that he likes his words to always be tactful and well thought out; this is on purpose, so that he does not make a fool of himself. The more spontaneous he is, the more he tends to ramble and say the incorrect thing out of nervousness. I have heard him say the deepest things, but also the dumbest… I have also noticed that this Cherub's character peaks and troughs are higher and lower than most. His soft-spoken personality has been learned from Satan. For instance; currently, he says his greetings to the Archangels with a small, timid bow, and then, the contrast of his character is apparent as he addresses the legions in a commanding voice…

"WATCHERS," he yells. "LET US GIVE OUR GALLANTS A

PROPER GREETING, SHALL WE?"

The troop of decorated Cherubs stand in attention ready position, all still in perfect lines and ranks. They are excited to see their Gallants. Many of them have been on earth for a long time now and have not seen their Gallants since they were young Cherubs.

The Watchers firmly hit their chests, followed by the lifting of their mirror-swords and all sorts of different, interesting, looking weapons into the air. They do so as if pointing them towards the Gallants.

In one loud cry, they say, "ALTISSIMO FAMULANTUR," which in angel-talk, means, "SERVE THE MOST HIGHEST," then they say, "AVE SANCTIS AMATORIBUS," meaning, "Hail Holy Gallants." See? Just then I had to jump in and translate, otherwise you would be lost! I will have to translate a little more than usual for my Gallant, Raphael. Since he is the youngest of the Archangels, he still uses the ancient angelic language and continues to improve in his modern dialects. Be patient with me because just as his modern dialects are rusty, so is my angel-talk!

The Archangels are honored to be greeted with such respect, especially by such a decorated platoon, and they lift their Essences in unison to return the veneration shown. The Watchers are mesmerized by the Essences, just as I am.

CHAPTER 3

Beelzebub invites the Gallants to enter Eden. Before they enter, the Archangels thoroughly inspect their legions, and the platoons reciprocate their Gallants, like a sincere system of checks and balances. I can tell this army of Watchers has been well trained, by Beelzy, in true Heavenly spirit. Their demeanor and composure unmistakably reveal this.

Raphael does his usual, kindly winking one of his eyes, smiling, and saying hoarsely, "Sententia, Vigilum! Watchers, at ease!"

The troops break their formations and begin to talk among themselves. Most of the conversations are about the Gallants and their Essences. It is chatter and gossip. Some of them approach their commanders, surrounding to reacquaint and greet them personally, to receive graces, blessings, and to get a closer look of their weapons. The Archangels gladly give them a better look and insight into the Essences performing several astounding miracles for their amazement.

Just as the Watchers know their superiors names, their chiefs also know their individual names and what is hidden in the depths of their souls. All this they can see with a quick swipe, by scanning them with their Essences… They are all greeted and thanked personally with names such as: Jehoel, Jerahmeel, Poyel, and Qaphsiel, each of them with their own special gifts and powers. It is an impressive, yet minuscule representation of the Gallants inestimable knowledge. I can tell that no one leaves disappointed. All Watchers are left with an encouraging, everlasting, impression and a renewed sense of purpose. I do too, constantly!

Beelzebub, who now accompanies the Gallants, again showing the volatility of his personality when he commandingly says to his troops, "THAT IS ENOUGH! RETURN TO YOUR POSTS!" They mobilize faster than fast.

To the Archangels, he humbly says, "Please enter… You will be happy to see our arrangements… The progress in Eden will undoubtedly please you…"

The Archangels walk through the Watchers ranks, and then passed the redwood gate. This gate gives access to a long, dirt canyon. The canyon is dark, and so the Gallants use their Essences to illuminate their walking path inside the cave-like structure with the brightness of their unique colors. The humidity of their surroundings and especially inside the cave is something they are not accustomed to.

As they continue to walk in the darkness, they see a light at the end of the tunnel. Then, with profound amazement, they slowly exit the ravine…

Therein lies a view of a beautiful, lush jungle, resembling

a rain forest. Enormous snow covered mountains surround the scene. We see turquoise water with beautiful, white-sand, beaches. We see waterfalls and other striking, picturesque, vegetation. Palm trees, flowers, and many other, exotic, types of trees. There are landscapes and vegetation that have never been seen before, plants that have not yet evolved, rivers that zigzag and intertwine like very long snakes.

The rainbow continues to be seen in the background. It is not an arch, but it is a single, straight beam from Heaven down to earth. Many more rainbow portals come and go, flashing in and out, but their massive one stays put.

Gabriel, referring to the jungle, comments, "Beautiful!"

Michael exclaims, "Remarkable, is it not?"

Their expressions say it all... The wind blowing in their faces, the sun shining down on their armor and Essences.

Flocks of exotic birds are flying; the sounds of organisms, small and large are everywhere. Dinosaur looking creatures like the Plesiosaurus are in the horizon. There are crops of fruits and vegetables, more flowers, and towering conifers. I can see ostrich-like birds that are able to fly, and so many miscellaneous animals running freely. It is interesting that predator and prey are running wild and closely, but peacefully. This is biodiversity at its peak!

These creatures have no enemies, no worries, no hierarchical food chain, and no need for carnal sustenance. Their only need is for water and what grows from the earth.

In the background, majestic, prehistoric whales, and dolphins swim freely thrusting up to the surface. No contamination is visible. No millions of years of destruction and decay… Intact beauty is the name of the game.

The very serene, Satan, says, "How great are these deeds! I could get very comfortable here. I can see myself persuading some angels to build me a palace and join me too… Together, we could protect our Lord's creations."

Gabriel responds calmly, saying, "That is not God's plan. The Creator does not want us to stay long… We have our own kingdom in Heaven, and these creatures have their own kingdom on earth…

"We are very lucky to set foot on this planet and witness such beauty. Many angels will not have the opportunity to do the same."

Satan humbly agrees, but does not continue without voicing his opinion, stating, "But the Holy Spirit of God lives here and shall remain on earth! The Holy Spirit could not do without His servant, Raphael! If He could stay and make this His kingdom, then so could we."

CHAPTER 3

Gabriel has made an optimist out of Satan. They both smile and continue to traverse through the scenery, soaking it all in. I can tell that all four Archangels are infatuated with earth. Raphael likes the idea of remaining in the world just as much as Satan does.

They take a further look around, realizing most creatures have already been created. There are beautiful, many colored, prehistoric birds, flying about. Let me remind that humans have not been created yet. You are among the few creatures absent in the scene.

Around the Gallants are also many, Cherub angels, working on maintaining and up-keeping trees, fruits, bushes, etc. It seems like they have golden paintbrushes and tools. With great joy, they are helping in the painting of a wonderful masterpiece. I approach one of my brothers to inspect his work, deeply longing to join him, but I too have my specific orders…

They are not creating anything because God is the only Creator who makes things out of nothing. From design, the Cherubs are only putting the final touches on everything. They are sowing, special seeds, that shall grow minerals, plants, and a rich diversity of flora. Some of the seeds planted, instantaneously turn into mountains and hills of all sorts. These seeds only need minimal water, soil and light to grow, which are easily summoned by the angels' powerful tools.

Most of the Cherubim are holding blue prints in golden parchments. They analyze design schematics and are following the scroll instructions very closely. Many things appear out of the blue and many more intricate objects are transported via rainbows, from Heaven to Eden's archway, in big transportation arks.

Some of the Cherubs unleash some hyena-lion looking animals from a cage. The Archangels walk by another, saber tooth tiger, cage, where the beasts are in pairs, both male and female. They see the animals' eyes staring back at them, hearing a few tamed growls as the other tiger loudly yawns.

As soon as the cage is opened, the saber tooth tigers run out... Luxiel, one of the angels tasked with releasing the saber tooth from its cage, is scared because the tiger growled menacingly and almost claws him. He giggles, but looks embarrassed when the Gallants walk by, pretending as though he has everything under control... I was about to go ask, Luxiel, if he needed help. Good thing I did not, because I would have probably suffered his same fate, and then I would have been the embarrassed one…

The freed tigers are playful with one another and run into the horizon. Then they reach a river and tenderly lower their heads to drink the crystalline water.

All around we see Cherubs releasing birds from other cages… Fish and other animals are also liberated, into the wild, in many shapes, colors, and sizes.

Raphael says that they must supervise evolution as commanded, and that they must also assure that God's creations are properly distributed and taken care of. I am translating for him…

They continue to walk into an even more beautiful looking garden. Michael looks at a piece of scroll, unrolls it, and says, "Thither is a section of earth that will be f'rbidden to all because 'tis said to be a sacr'd place. The resting place of a sacr'd artifact, but I cann't seem to remembereth whence 'tis!"

Raphael says that Satan should know where the object is because he is the only one that has seen the artifact. He is the only one who even knows what the sacred relic is. I also translated this from the angelic language in which he usually speaks, but I do not know if I was supposed to... I get the sense that he said this in angel-talk, for me not to understand what they are saying about the sacred relic. Maybe they think I do not speak the ancient language, but I know Michael knows my knowledge and rustiness.

Raphael further says, "Artificium quin hic! Quod obiectum

fabulam ostendisset nobis Dominus noster… I doubt that the artifact is here! That object is a legend, and our Lord would have showed us."

Satan smiles… Something tells me that his smile is because he knows how fortunate he is to have seen the artifact. Yet he remains quiet, neither confirming nor denying my suspicions.

Raphael, now realizing that I understood everything and that I must be informed, with his croaky voice, says, "Yes, such a relic would be well occultum, concealed, and, protexisti, protected. Whether the artificium, artifact, lies there or not, it is still a vetitum area, forbidden area, and we must strive to avoid its locus, location..."

I can tell that this prohibited area along with the promise of a sacred and unknown object have peaked Satan's attention. Instead of avoiding it, he is charmed to this notion.

As the Archangels look around and try to figure out each of God's specific orders, in their parchment, Satan uses this distraction to wonder off through some trees, and he should not do that! As a part of the quartet of Gallants, this is where he should remain. The Lord has sent the four of them, together, for a reason!

My curious mind tells me to follow him, but at a distance,

and so, I must try my hardest not to be seen and remain hidden in the background as if I were not even there. If he sees me I could become a distraction to him, one, which I do not wish to be.

Chapter 4

The Golden Tree of Knowledge

Satan begins to walk in the thick jungle, as many plants brush on his being. There is not much room for walking, but he manages to veer his way through the vines and branches. His footprints are marked on the muddy ground, which helps me follow his long strides and fast steps. He makes his way through puddles, stepping over large tree roots, and jumping from rock to rock on minerals of all sorts.

Now there is an opening of the jungle canopy, where he is able to more easily walk without having to dodge too much nature. He now picks up his pace, trotting… This plain of land is short, but I can tell it is a much-needed rest from the thick enclosure, which we were both beginning to experience.

CHAPTER 4

All around, swamps are filled with ominous, but peaceful, alligator-like species. He traverses through the darkest parts of the forest accompanied by the luminosity of fireflies and other bioluminescent creatures, which clear a path for him.

He no longer moves very quickly, sinking into mud pits that submerge him up to his knees. He seems uncompromising in his resolve to advance; yet he has all the time in the world and is in no rush to continue exploring…

Suddenly, while submerged inside a sludge pit, above, he sees a curious animal moving from tree to tree, which catches his attention. All the fauna present in the trees begin to make way for this creature. They jump and fly off, so as to not cross paths with this stampede of one. The lord of persuasion does not manage to see what animal it is. Even as it passes over his head, the thick leafs, in the surrounding canopy, fall and are further concealing it. Whatever it is, it seems to command the respect of all creation, as if making a triumphant entrance into the area. The animal swings from branch to branch as if it had monkey's arms, yet he eventually realizes, the animal is not a monkey, it is a snake...

The snake, now clearly, bounces from tree to tree, occasionally hitting the land. When it hits the ground, it bounces up like a coil. It then elevates itself, flying, with retractable appendages, and it seems to draw the gawk and respect of many more creatures of the earth, water, and sky. It definitely draws the attention of my Gallant.

Satan extends his wings, exiting the mud pit with ease, and begins to follow the snake as if racing it below and above the canopy. I try my hardest to keep up, running as fast as I can.

Displeased, the snake notices that Satan is following it, so it accelerates. Its speed is incredible and almost matches Satan's velocity. Of course it is not as fast, so the Gallant shows off a little. Looping and flipping, he follows the snake as it soars through the air.

The snake enters a crystalline river, splashing into the water, and Satan follows it in. They continue to race upstream... He again loops around the snake, jumping in and out of the water like a dolphin. He smiles and sees it as nothing more than a game just like when we saw Satan and Raphael approaching us in the sky before the meeting in Heaven, but I can tell the snake is not as amused as he is. As they race on land, water, and through the air, there is a pleasant vibe from Satan and an unfazed one from the snake, who shows no emotion or competitiveness whatsoever.

During this game, the snake reaches a dense tree, loops around it, losing its tracker for a slight second…

CHAPTER 4

When the creature turns around, Satan decelerates by sliding feet first into the ground. A cloud of dirt flies into the air and forms a barrier between Satan and the snake.

Then, concealed behind the tree-trunk, the snake hooks around and abruptly snaps its fangs at its pursuer... It is just a warning…

When some of the dust cloud fades away, the serpent again snappishly lunges at Satan, who is still on the ground. The animal tried to use the cloud of debris to conceal his attack.

Right before it reaches to attack his face, the Gallant easily snatches and chokes the snake with his hand, preventing it from biting him.

The fangs and tongue are visible in his open mouth as he struggles to get free from the clutches of Satan's, firm, grip…

The dust cloud has completely settled… Now Satan looks all around. In the surrounding trees and on the ground, there are hundreds of snakes menacingly sticking out their pronged tongues at him. They approach slowly, ominous but grandiose, irritated to see their comrade captive in the hands of a strange enemy. Their tongues are three-pronged and not two-pronged. In fact, their tongues look almost identical to Satan's trident of persuasion.

I can tell that Satan is not afraid of the great numbers in his midst, he welcomes them, but becomes more alert, scoping his surroundings, as he is now outnumbered, and standing tall on his feet.

The snakes converge slowly, jumping off the trees, cornering him against a big, granite, slab. He takes a few steps backward... The sneaky animals hiss and slither as if they are all going to attack at once...

The Gallant asserts his dominance, taking control, by pummeling the ground with his trident, which is now unsheathed. The strike of his trident leaves an incredible crater on the ground.

Many of the snakes escape and are now afraid of his might. The great majority, however, are not afraid. Most, stand their ground, as he performs some fancy trident, spinning, tricks, and points his weapon's red energy in all directions. I love bearing witness to this!

When tensions have settled, Satan says, "I like your persistence and your cornering tactics! You baited me well!" His calm demeanor is still apparent.

The snake that Satan grabbed in his hands is now slowly released from grasp, and allowed to speak. Its name is, *Ophis.*

In a slithery and wise voice, it asks, "Why do you follow me?"

Satan, now more energetic, unlike himself, says, "You can

speak? Incredible! I did not know you would be able to speak! Bonus! This shall be useful…

"Was I bothering you?"

"Yessss," the snake responds annoyed… "Can you not tell? How did you know we were baiting you? How did you know that thisss wasss a trap? Who are you?"

Satan says, "Those are a lot of questions, skinny fellow. If you wish to know, I am the first Gallant and therefore your Gallant. They call me, SSSSatan, from Heaven…

"I helped in your design. I know your tactics, your instincts, your thoughts and your hunger for knowledge. That is why your tongues mimic my trident… Can you see?"

The snakes listen, looking at each other's tongues and at the trident as they hiss. In doing so, they have a moment of realization.

"You disappoint me, though," says Satan. "I remember training your instincts much better than what you just displayed! No need to thank me!"

The snakes bow, saying, "Sssorry to disssappoint you, Gallant, and sssorry for attacking you! Thank you! Thank you!"

Various of the serpents that had fled from the trident's burst of energy, now return, intrigued to hear what he has to say. They now have a certain reverence towards him, as if they were attracted to the brilliance of his trident. For them it seems to be a sacred object, a beacon or a relic, that helps explain their existence. They move wherever the Essence moves, they bow whenever it dips a little and they rise when it is raised. They seem to venerate him.

Now with a broader audience, he says, "It is ok! I like you snakes! You are wise! I distinctly like how everything about you attracts other animals. There is a certain charisma and appeal, but then you work together, putting your talents to good use, and can be deadly… and you never back down... All you need is that extra push to become venomous assassins, killers, and murderers, which is the true purpose of your existence, poison. Power is in the numbers, in the will, and in the strategy! You definitely have all of these traits. Wonderful!"

The cunning snakes, humbly say, "Thank you," as they bow in unison.

Satan, arrogantly, says, "I like when you bow to me too, and you bow without much persuasion!"

The serpents continue saying, "If we can ever do anything for you, pleassse let ussss know. We are forever at your sssservissss."

Satan answers, "I know you will, when the time comes! I might need you to become my own personal Watchers… Right now I have business to attend to, but I will call on you shortly… Stand bye! But in the meantime, prepare yourselves for my second coming, to be worthy of your Gallant!"

Then Satan flies away. The snakes look at each other, ominously, and then disperse into the thick grove, eyes no longer fixated on the trident, but their spirits are very much in tune; they still long to be in its presence. They wonder eagerly, when will he return?

Ophis, the one who was captured is now the celebrity among the snakes, having been touched by who they think is their creator. This is how he, so easily, won them over... This is how he so easily wins everyone over!

This whole time it is a miracle that they have not seen me hiding behind a thick vine. I have been pushing my luck to its extremes. But now, since the snakes were everywhere, they had begun sensing my presence, and so I think it is a prudent time to make my timely exit, and continue the pursuit of my unpredictable Gallant.

Just as he saw his pursuing of the serpents as a game, so do I see the stealth pursuing of my Gallant. It is a marvelous game, which I must not lose; the only way I can do this is if I am discovered.

After leaving the serpents, Satan lands close by to his previous location, right in the middle of the jungle, still not re-joining with his brothers. I was able to track him by following the faint, red, smoke that his fiery ambiance emits, although the trail has begun to fade quicker than usual. It seems like this fast dwindling of his red Essence is done purposefully to make sure that he leaves no trace.

All around him, there are ants, multiple colored, spiders, and bright bugs. The insects are not fearful of each other or of Satan. There are also hundreds of big, pesky, mosquitoes flying all about. They continually harass me with an annoying, invasive buzzing close to my ear, and there is nothing I can do about it. They fly in and out of my personal space, zipping by, playfully attempting to enter my nose and ear, but it is ok. I don't mind as much as Satan does. I can see they are also annoying the one I follow, as he continually endeavors to swat the ones around him. I am a first hand witness to the harshness and dampness of this environment.

The Gallant seems to be tracking, and fervently looking for something, just as I am with him. He looks at his surroundings to see if he is alone. When he is in the clear, he then removes a roll of black parchments, which were stashed in his back. The scrolls are written with red ink. They seem to be maps and diagrams of some sorts. Turning in all directions, and looking at the primitive sketches and writing, he has finally found his bearings and path. I duck when his gaze is directed towards my general vicinity. I think it is safe to say he has not seen me.

Using his remarkable gift of sight, in the distance, Satan sees a faint, golden, glimmer… Placing the black parchments back in his armor, he continues to walk through the jungle's thick vegetation to see what the gold glistening is.

As he approaches, he first dodges many of the frogs and many of the other arthropods around him. Once he inadvertently steps on one, injuring it, he realizes these puny creatures are woundable, and in his way, but more so, they are defenseless. I can tell by his boldness towards them that this is the case. This earth seems to be enhancing my gifts of insight or maybe it is God who is helping me as promised. Now, he gladly steps on them with apparent hate as he targets and persecutes many of the scurrying creatures.

To make things worse, out of curiosity, the Gallant spots and grabs a poisonous, orange, frog, in his bare hand, which has just developed these poisonous defenses as an evolution, in response to his attacks on the other creatures. Stripping it from it's niche, the frog's venom affects him, burning his fingers, so he moans and throws it into the air to get rid of the pain. It lands lifeless, flattened, against a tree. He now stares at his trident tips, and by this simple gesture, I can tell he wishes that he could somehow pass this lethal venom to his, new, serpent, friends.

On command, a black vulture, bird, descends from the sky and snatches the frog. It too dies of poisoning, falling and hitting the damp soil. Satan creates prey and predator where there should be none. These are the first creatures to ever perish in the history of the universe; I only hope they are the last! I sadly see death where there should not be death because I know God created all of His creatures to coexist.

A moral dilemma now grows within me… Should I report to Michael what I have just seen? But I do not know! Those were not God's orders, for me or for Satan, and I do not wish to be a tattletale against my General. Maybe it was I who did wrong in following him. Satan has to be doing God's work, right? I make up my mind then and there not to speak of what I have just witnessed. If my superiors ask me, then I will loosen my tongue, but not before it becomes my duty.

He continues to walk trough the vines... Since the vines are in his way of reaching the golden glistening, he shoots them open with his trident, destroying and exploding everything in his path. I can now clearly see the golden glimmer…

It is the most beautiful, golden, tree, I have ever seen. The tree looks like a live oak tree, but with golden bark, branches and leafs. On the front bark, I can lucidly see God's three parallel markings (III). The tree looks exactly like that wondrous tree, depicted in my favorite mural, inside Paradise Palace, that unfinished artwork containing Satan, which I often find myself appreciating and contemplating. What a treat to finally see the source of my admiration in person!

All around the jungle, the thick vines had been protecting the area, as if creating a wall of nature to conceal the secluded tree. I find a place that appears to be safe, simply concealing myself, lying behind a very tall bush and remaining silent.

When the Gallant approaches the tree, birds and insects fly off of it, making way for him as if they had just seen how he hatefully treated some of the previous creatures that were in his path.

He touches the texture of the (III) bark markings with his hand. Looking up, he sees the brightest red apples hanging from the tree, sunrays penetrating the canopy.

There is definitely something special about this tree because red is not a very common color. Satan is the lord of all things red; therefore, I am astonished to see it, lucidly, in the apples on earth. I thought that he was the only one allowed to bear and pass the color along. Could this also have any significance? God's creations and actions always have to them more than meets the eye.

The Archangel wastes no time, stabbing an apple with his trident, and then placing it in his hand. He looks at the fruit closely; the stem and the skin and then he looks at the tree, perusing the trunk, branches and leafs, top to bottom.

Then, he takes a bite out of the apple. By the expression on his face, it seems to be the best thing he has ever tasted, juicy and sweet, and then he swallows.

Satan has no business eating this apple! He has no need for food or nutrition because he has no body. Nonetheless he savors the taste, and then looks at the tree, looking surprised, almost as if he were expecting something incredible to happen after the bight.

Nothing out of the ordinary occurs, so he begins to climb the tree. Branch by branch, he scales as leafs begin to fall. He searches, lifting up roots and branches, killing more creatures that live even remotely near the tree, and leaving no crack or crevice uninspected. One by one, he systematically bites, nibbles, and feasts on every single fruit, sometimes consuming them to their core as if he were desperately starving. When he is done tasting each one of them, the fruits grow back, intact and beautiful... When he sees this, and does not find what he is looking for, tremendously frustrated, he despairs... He pulls an egotistical tantrum, of sorts, trying to burn the tree to the ground, torching it with his trident, but despite many attempts, the tree will not catch on fire.

As I approach to get a better view, I accidentally step on a mangled tree branch, which makes a loud, crunching noise. I also did not know how to deal with some red, fire, ants that had crawled on top of me as if trying to build a mound on my back. They tickle, but they also burn pretty painfully.

If this were not enough, a nosey group of apes, in the surrounding trees, rat me out disclosing my position. They point their index fingers at me, jump up and down, and holler like annoying alarms. Tattletales!

Having heard the commotion, Satan stares in my direction and immediately stops what he is doing.

Now, with no fear, he quickly and violently approaches my area. Without any hesitation, using his trident, he annihilates the bush where I was hiding. Once the apes gave away my location, I made sure to, hastily, move my spot. The red ants crawling on me, and their growing mound immediately slid off my back. I hope the insects are ok!

I am barely ok, myself! Good thing I moved! If he had found me there, apparently, his trident would have shown no mercy!

And I did not have my weapon to block his attack. Now, I know to think twice before following him…

As he continues to, thoroughly, search the tree, I leave, running quietly through the fields, scared that he should find my new hiding spot, and this time blow me into oblivion, with his weapon. I am terrified of what I just witnessed and eager to return to my other, more stable, commanders' sides. I leave, victorious in this game of cloak, but by no means is it on a high note.

You have never seen me run as fast as I do now, and I am pretty fast... Good thing I did not lose my bearings, even with Satan's confusing trajectory, and am easily able to make my way back, jumping, swinging and swerving through the trees, much like the snakes did before me.

After some extensive running, at a distance, I can now hear a familiar voice, Michael's voice, oh how sweet it is! This whole time, they did not even realize I was gone because they had been busy attending their duties.

They are still trying to figure out where this unfinished, forbidden area is. They point their fingers to different areas in the scroll.

Michael says, "Hither is the valley and so the f'rbidden area shouldst be closeth to the valley."

Gabriel and Raphael elevate themselves to the sky to search for a special, landmark, a majestic, golden, tree. According to their directives, this tree is supposed to be at the center of the forbidden area. And now I realize that this is the same golden tree Satan was tampering with. I was just there too! Oops! But I didn't know! I am sure Satan did not know either!

Michael grabs a hold of me and lifts me up to the sky to join them. It is a marvelous view, here, at the top of the world. I am still shaking from what I had seen Satan doing, also realizing that I had been at the center of the forbidden zone. Michael notices my shivering and assuming that I was cold, he elevates me closer to the sun. It is not the sun that comforts me, but the arms of my fatherly friend. He also notices the small ant welts on my back, which those red creatures had left on me, when I was concealed on the ground. I did not know they were that noticeable, and that they had even penetrated my natural armor. They are red bumps and a little inflamed. Michael does not worry, he assumes I am ok, or else I would have told him something.

As they rotate in circles, searching for the tree, they find nothing. Even with the shield of good news in his hands, Gabriel is not able to locate the tree. In his mind, he suspects that the area must be so secret and forbidden for a reason. God must have not wanted it to be disrupted by anyone, under any circumstances, not even His Gallants, yet He allowed Satan?

Then they return to the ground, placing me on my feet. Suddenly, Michael cries out, "Aha, Behold! The f'rbidden area, 'Tis hither!"

To show in which direction the forbidden area lies. He is right, the tree was in that direction! Michael holds up his scroll, at eye level, near his face, and points to the area of the jungle where Satan is now reemerging from.

Satan walks out of the vines and trees, as if nothing had happened, rejoining his brothers. He has been gone for many hours after I last left him, yet for his kin, it only seems like a few minutes.

To avoid any questions, Satan launches Gabriel a bright, red, apple, saying, "Catch, oh green one!" Giving a humble bow, adding, "Taste and see! Taste and see!"

Gabriel catches the apple, and strongly refuses to eat it. He knows better than to eat anything and that it would be extremely wrong to receive nourishment that does not come straight from God. His soul is already full, just like our Lord always says, ***"One does not live of bread alone, but of every word that comes from my mouth."*** This is all the sustenance that we require.

Satan insists, saying, "It is delicious! Come on! Eat it! I have already eaten one, and I feel better than ever... Just one bite will not harm you!"

I am sure this attempt to convince is good practice for the Archangel of persuasion…

Gabriel finally caves in. He takes a bite out of it, and says, "Delicious!" He does not swallow so as to not break the rules. Then, he says, "But the apple would be much better in green!" He chuckles.

He says this because he notices the apple's redness is the same color as Satan's red. Since Gabriel's color is green, he turns the apple green with his shield and tosses it back to Satan, to test his theories of whether it is better tasting in green. The same apple has no bite marks and is intact.

Gabriel asks the same question I just asked myself, "How is it that the apple is red if only Satan is allowed to bear the color?"

Michael tells me his conclusion, saying, "Perchance Satan turn'd it red with his Essence," but my friend is not completely sure…

As if to appease the minds of the Archangels and so that they do not bother God with the feeble questions, which they were about to ask Him, Satan says, "Well, I suppose that since the Creator allowed there to be so much of your green on earth," as he points to Gabriel, "Maybe he gave me a little red as a gift too… just a smidge."

Then he says, "You do realize there is a lot of green, do you not?"

The Archangels look around and see the green everywhere in the luscious jungle. They share a laugh.

Adding to his theory, Satan looks to Michael and says, "Why are you laughing? There is a lot of your blue in the water of this world as well... Even more than Gabriel's green! It seems like Raphael's purple and my red got the short end of the stick on this deal."

Michael chuckles but Satan is serious as if truly bothered by this.

Satan continues to hold the green apple in his hand; he tosses it to himself and catches it a few times. In just a few seconds, he goes from stern to teasing…

Finally, taking a bite, he says, "Better in green? No, no, no, it is too sour!" He spits out the green apple to probably put up a front or because he has already had his fill of the fruit. I can't imagine how many he ate after the fruits regrew and in the hours since I left.

All the Archangels continue to laugh at Satan's face and

remarks of bitterness after eating the green, sour, apple.

Their laughter is temporarily halted; Raphael notices something on the back of Satan's neck and head… He seems to be hurt...

Pointing to his wound, Raphael says, "Quod factum vobis, Satan? What happened to you, Satan? Bene es? Are you ok?"

Satan, not giving much importance to the question, answers, "I am fine, just scraped myself. No need to worry! It is just a scratch!"

He holds the back of his head to add pressure to the wound. What a mistake! He forgot that his hands still had traces of the orange frog's venom as well as the toxicity of crushed apple seeds. Now his wound is even more aggravated, stinging and pulsating, with immense amounts of pain, but I know he will not complain about it; this is simply not what a Gallant does… At the same time, I can feel his pain in the ant nibble marks on my back. We share it but he is much better at hiding it than me.

Raphael, concerned, replies with his raspy voice, "Si sanatione indigent baculo facies ut sciam! If you need some healing, from my staff, please let me know!"

Then he smirks and winks his eye twice, once at him, and once at me. He too has attentively noticed the small stings on my back.

Aside from the wound on his head, Satan also seems to have many small stings and bite marks on his chest, which are being camouflaged by his red trident emblem. It seems like the ants bit us both or maybe something else bit him.

"No need for healing, just a graze!" Satan forcefully says.

Chapter 5

Following What Was Promised

The first choir that was created partly due to Satan's suggestion was the Seraphim or Seraphs, as they like to be called. We Cherubs, their subordinates, were created quite some time later to compliment them… To be their companions and allies…

Beelzebub, who you previously met, and the lovely Seraph, Seraphina, show up inside Eden to rendezvous with the Archangels.

Seraphina is so beautiful! Clad in a spectacular, tightly pressed, white armor. Six small wings are prominent along her gorgeous back. The highest wings serve as a veil that slowly unwind, revealing her precious face. The remaining four wings function as appendages and body armor. Seraphina's thin wings give a delicate impression, but this could not be further from the truth. Her additional wings make her abilities much stronger, as if extending her many capabilities. It is obvious that she is of both Gabriel and Satan's lineage, proudly showcasing her lovely, brown eyes. You see… Red and green combine to make brown. This combination of masters, this unique feature of hers, is not very common among angels.

I would have chosen Seraphina to be my companion if she were not already taken. But it was still doubtful that she would have chosen me, anyway, because she has always been well in demand, and was quickly picked by someone much worthier than I, none other than the Gallant, Gabriel. And so I continue to look forward to the day when I pick a Seraph, and she picks me for all eternity, if that is what the Lord wills.

Seraphina and Beelzy gently bow to their Gallants and say, "SERVIAM."

The Archangels are now heading towards the gates where they first entered Eden. Seraphina approaches Gabriel, kisses his cheek, and whispers in his ear. They are all smiles.

I can tell Satan is not too happy to see them together… In fact, he seems pretty mad to see them so close. All I can say is, wow!

CHAPTER 5

I hear what Seraphina whispers to Gabriel. Seraphina greets him, tenderly, and tells him that they must attend to God's project, ***Mariam.*** Additionally, she insistently says, "Tell me a story!"

For which he responds, "What sort of story?"

"A love story!"

Gabriel replies, "All my stories are love stories…"

She cleverly says, "Then…it should be easy..."

"Later, ok?" He nervously pauses while Beelzebub and Satan gaze their way. Both Beelzebub and Satan occasionally stare at the couple and continue their conversation.

The other Archangels are looking around and talking to some Cherubs. They take advantage to discover other things hidden in this mysterious land.

After many hours of longing to help, Raphael and Michael decide to do their part and free some animals into the wild. Raphael is interested in some white birds. One of the doves, which he grabs from a cage, defecates in his hands, leaving a grotesque, smelly, white, puddle. He is still fascinated by it!

Michael laughs at this unfortunate event, but at the same time, the small monkey, looking, creature that he is paternally hugging puts his finger into Michael's ear and twists. Then he puts his finger into Michael's mouth. As this occurs, he uncomfortably lets go of the monkey, and it runs off making some chattering noises. The creature joins the rest of his clan that had been waiting for him, eagerly, hanging in the jungle vines. Now both Archangels laugh at each other's misfortune.

While cleaning his smelly, white, hands, Raphael sarcastically says, "There is nothing more gratifying than setting these creaturae liber, creatures free!"

Satan hears these words and has a twisted smile, as if Raphael had just given him an idea. I could read his lips as he obsessively repeated to himself, "Set them free, set them free, set them free… Dimiseris eos liberos …"

Michael, the wise, says, "Thither art many moo rewarding things… We hast witness'd but a few on earth. 'Tis but a taste of our L'rd's gratification."

As for me, I personally enjoy the simplest of pleasures… My eyes are ever wandering and my ears are wide open. Taking it all in… the journalistic experience! My being feels the cooling breeze and my mouth remains shut. All my senses are being stimulated. But this is not about how I feel…

Now, we have all made our way back to the rainbow…

Beelzebub says to Satan, "Goodbye, my friend… We must

now attend to project *Mariam*."

Satan calmly says, "Goodbye, Beelzy."

Satan then stares at Seraphina and grimly says, "Goodbye, Seraphina."

She pleasantly curtsies, keeps a straight but nervous face, and says, "Gallant."

They briefly stare into each other's eyes, but then Seraphina breaks eye contact, returning her attention entirely to Gabriel.

Satan again looks displeased, as he sees Gabriel, Beelzy, and Seraphina leaving together. Something tells me that I must follow them to document their duties. This time there is no need to hide like I did with Satan. Maybe I have already learned my lesson from my previous unpleasant experience. Since they know my mission, and God's orders for me, I am allowed to join the trio. At least, I think, they understand my mission… I thought I understood my assignment, but with my commander's mischief by the golden tree, my task has become somewhat gray, like me!

It begins to drizzle, but the sun is still brightly shining. I become drenched… first from the fountain at the palace, then from the jungle's humidity, and finally from the rain… What else can be thrown my way? Everyone laughs at my expense… They seem to be acclimating to this planet better than me.

Gabriel, Beelzebub, Seraphina, and I, stand on the rainbow... Gabriel hits the ground with his shield, a green lightning bolt strikes us, but it brings us no pain. We disappear with the sound of thunder and we are transported… Off to our next location…

Satan and the other Archangels stay in Eden, watching closely, as the three of us are transported…

Since we are being transported from one point to another, on the same planet, the rainbow is now in the form of an arch and not a single beam. We are taken to the Project *Mariam* headquarters, just as Eden is the project human HQ.

They begin to walk around and I realize that there are no Cherubs working here, only beautiful Seraphs. There is no need for a squadron of Watchers here because the Cherubs in Eden are more than enough, and capable, to guard both locations. With rainbows, the Watchers' response time is like no other, not to mention that Seraphs are superior in rank to the Watchers, because the Watchers are Cherubs, and so I am pretty sure they can handle themselves quite well.

These Seraphs are doing the same thing the Cherubs were in Eden, putting the final touches on everything. They are sowing seeds and placing rocks in their respective places, painting the setting with their golden brushes. Their six wings are put to good use, which help them multitask and become more productive.

The special seeds that are planted are sown deep into the earth with hole punching tools. From them, forests, water, and light, immediately emerge. Roots come to surface, canopies of thick vegetation, small cotyledons, and even the streams of the earth are formed.

Because of their seeds, there are now rivers that flow, flowers that absorb the sun, and rocks of all sorts. The land that will become Israel, which is where we are, looks drastically different than it will in the future.

Even though there are many, beautiful, Seraphs about, Gabriel only has eyes for Seraphina. I can tell that the love between Gabriel and Seraphina is a lesson to all. Those Seraphs that do not yet have their companions, like me, and wish to have them, follow the example of this love.

I, on the other hand, am having an extremely difficult time controlling my eyesight. All these beautiful Seraphs for little old me? No, who am I kidding? No doubt, many of the spectacular Seraphs already have Cherub companions. I immediately recognize a few of them who are the companions of some of my brethren Watchers. I must also guard my sight because Seraphs are my superiors in rank and in power. I would not want to overstep my boundaries.

The presence of my superiors, in this place, shows the importance of this project, *Mariam*, and the land, which we survey. It must be more important than the project human headquarters because here in the Promised Land, it is full of high-ranking officers. The Lord always assigns His highest choirs to His most important projects.

Still, superiors or not, there are no words for the beauty that the Seraphs portray. Their skins glow with the sun. They are the complete definition of the beauty in God's creation. It is a different type of attraction that I feel for them compared to my Gallants, although never lust!

The Seraphs about, work diligently without distraction. They are much different from the Watchers, more disciplined, in that; nobody stops what they are doing to admire Gabriel and his shield. It is not that they are not interested; it is simply to show dedication, poise, persistence, and love for their work.

I am embarrassed to be so frenzied in front of a multitude of my superiors. But even with their serious and apparently disinterested façade, they are truly happy to see the important trio. I would like to say they are happy to see me too, but since the importance of my companions greatly overshadows my own, the focus of their excitement is hard to read.

CHAPTER 5

Many of Seraphina's friends are working in the fields; they look up for a second, but continue planting pastures and working. You can tell that Seraphina had just left them mere minutes ago. She had only come to Eden to retrieve Gabriel and Beelzy because this Promised Land is where she is mainly stationed. So many important Seraphim work here that even Beelzy's companion, Dumah, is somewhere among the workers.

All of a sudden, interrupting my train of thought, I see the shadow of a veiled Seraph moving inconspicuously through the fields. Her white top wings ominously cover her face. She runs, unnoticeably, with the coverage of her many sisters and of the surrounding flora. I am the only one who seems to see her in glimpses, which come in and out of the crowd… Darn! I lost sight of her…

With the intensity of her jump and clasp, this discreet figure pounces on Beelzebub. They are both brought down to a soft ground of many colored flowers.

In his jittery nervousness, Beelzy pushes her off with all his might sending her into the air. The white hooded figure playfully laughs with the shove, having glided unscathed back to earth, softly landing on her two feet.

Much to our amazement, the attacker reveals herself… Beelzy did not know it was Dumah... his companion… Shame on him for not recognizing her! I must admit that nobody else recognized her, either, but she is not my companion! Apparently, she is the only Seraphim who cannot contain her happiness to see Beelzy.

This "attack" was the action that finally allows the Seraphs to postpone their labor and focus on Gabriel. After seeing the commotion, they were on the brink of intervening to protect their Gallant, thinking that the attack was meant for him. They simply unsheathe their many curious looking weapons and approach the area, surrounding quickly with their threat of might. God had told them, explicitly, to be on the lookout for hooded figures, although no one knows why…

The green-eyed, Dumah, ran towards her partner to surprise him. She had only pounced on him because she demanded a hug, but never meant to alarm anyone, and for this she is embarrassed.

When he realizes it is her, in a pleasant and nervous way, Beelzy urges, "Please, return to work, Dumah!"

Dumah replies, "You have no business bossing me around!" And then she laughs, referring to her superiority in rank. She subsequently looks at Gabriel for permission to briefly stop working, and continue hugging Beelzy and says, "Gallant?"

Gabriel says, "Nonsense! Share with her Beelzy! Please,

resume! She has not seen you in some time, since you have been stuck by the gates of Eden. Take all the time you need!"

Beelzy is grateful and so is Dumah. For a few minutes, they take advantage to catch up on their own affairs; Gabriel and Seraphina benefit in doing the same. Gabriel grabs an exotic, pink, flower from the ground to give to his beloved, and then, with a swipe of his shield, he engraves it on her weapon carrier, as a token of his undying affection.

The flower suits her well and matches her complexion. Seraphina, blissful queries, "Now will you tell me a story?"

Gabriel chuckles, saying, "No, not yet, but soon!" He builds suspense… She does not protest.

After a few moments together, Beelzy rejoins his group and so does Dumah. They will be reunited soon, waving goodbye and relaying their regard for one another.

They continue to traverse, climbing a very rocky hill, seeking a place where they can be alone, to better discuss project *Mariam,* without interruption. Not only that, but the mountain they wish to climb shall give them a better vantage point over the area they wish to survey.

As they follow the trail on top of the hillside, there begins to be an ominous feel in the air. Beelzy and I are the first to sense it...

As the three of them walk with a new set of orders in their scrolls, Beelzy feels a chill down his spine. He stops to look behind. There are many olive trees all around. He sees nothing but a heavy, black, snake rolled up on the branch of a nearby tree. The snake sticks out its three-pronged tongue, hisses, and makes eye contact with Beelzy, but Beelzy thinks nothing of it and continues to walk.

A few steps later, he once again turns around to see if the snake is following them, but it has disappeared.

Gabriel and Seraphina are oblivious to this, comparing scrolls, and talking about the plans, discussing what is left to do.

When they are in the clear, and far enough from the multitude of Seraphim, Gabriel finally explains, "It is a great honor to be in charge of project *Mariam.* Within earth, God has entrusted us with this…

"This project is only a contingency plan... This means, there are certain historic events that will have to happen, in human history, in order for this project to be put into effect. It is not a sure plan...

"Even so, we must still follow our orders in the scrolls to a tee, and make sure that everything has been done according to His will. Are you listening, Beelzy?"

CHAPTER 5

He seems to be everywhere except for here; his thoughts and imagination are very scatter brained.

Beelzy pounds his chest with his fist, and intones, "YES, GALLANT! PROJECT *MARIAM* IS A CONTINGENCY PLAN!" Repeating his statements.

Seraphina, softly, says, "So, if the contingency plan is activated, it will happen here?"

Beelzy joins in authoritatively chanting, "YES, AS-ORDERED-BY GALLANT, GABRIEL…"

He says this almost as if to show he was listening, in fact, that he heard so well that he is now able to explain details about the plan. I can tell he desires to be in Gabriel's good graces and suck up a little. He knows how to flatter because his comments are indeed pleasing to Gabriel, and so he smiles.

They are interrupted by a gust of wind, which touches them, and they immediately extend their wings while still planted on the ground. The smell of fresh air gives natural propulsion to their appendages. Even though Gabriel is the only one that can use his wings for flight, each of their feathers vibrates individually. It is almost like the Cherub and Seraph wings are longing for flight, as if that is what they are meant to do, as if all they needed were a little, loving, activation from God.

Gabriel gets an incredible panoramic view and creates an intricate hologram with his shield that covers the land, showing what additional natural phenomena must still be placed, as well as projecting what the evolution of this land will look like several millennia into the future.

Inspired, he says, "I present to you… The Promised Land!"

With a hearty smile, Seraphina asks, "God's throne will be here? It looks so simple, so meager!"

Gabriel says, "God's throne is everywhere!"

Seraphina does not even think of questioning him. Focusing on the task at hand, Gabriel then asks, "Have the stars also been aligned by our Seraphs?"

Beelzebub militarily responds for Seraphina, reciting, "YES, THEY-HAVE! THIS-IS-THE-LOCATION-HE-REQUESTED." Pointing to the sky and onto Gabriel's hologram.

Gabriel jokingly yells back at Beelzebub with his same military tone, professing, "NO-NEED-TO-BE-SO-FORMAL…" Then with a smile, he tones down, saying, "We are among kin, Beelzebub."

But still Beelzy is all business, adding, "OUR-SERAPHS-HAVE-ALIGNED- THE-STARS, PARTICULARLY-THE-IMPORTANT-ONE; THE-STAR-OF-BETHLEHEM."

With a stern look, of rebuke, from Gabriel, Beelzy then

loosens up his tense speech, timidly adding, "The star will approach from the orient. I saw the Seraphs aligning them as I took the rainbow down to Eden."

Gabriel and Seraphina are happy and somewhat honored that he has relaxed; acknowledging that he usually only relaxes with his closest loved ones, when he is with Satan and Dumah. They all see the, holographic, animation of what the star of Bethlehem will look like, as well as other natural phenomena.

Gabriel, satisfied with the simple reports, says, "So be it!"

They continue to move, slowly, to the top of the mountain. Suddenly a very big crow flies over their head and squawks with an extending echo... This time it is me who gets the shriveling chill down my spine.

After a while the crow, again, passes over our heads as if doing rounds. This time it stays put and hovers over us from quite a distance away. Since the crow circling and hovering makes a shadow close to our feet, this time it is Seraphina who notices it above.

Seraphina looks up and says, "Look!"

Beelzy, alarmed, confesses, "That crow has been following us for quite some time now..."

Coincidentally the crow looks exactly like the vulture, which snagged the poor venomous frog, thrown by Satan, in the

Garden of Eden.

"How odd," responds Gabriel. "What a magnificent creature to recognize our importance and the importance of this land. It is blessed to make its home in this area and have commonalities with project *Mariam*. How cool! I bet it is just curious and trying to get a better view of us from above..."

Seraphina, uncertain, says, "I do not think it recognizes us, or understands the importance of our actions. It is an animal! I think he is more interested in protecting his territory and providing for his next meal, which could possibly be us."

Gabriel jokes, "We are too big to become his next meal and if he is defending his territory, what I originally said must be true. The importance of this land is indeed apparent to him."

"Well, if you put it that way, true, true!" Says Seraphina smiling.

The very smooth Gabriel, then says, "If he should attack I will protect you, Magna, and it will make for a good story!"

Not that any of them need any protection. Believe me, they are more than capable of protecting themselves, especially Seraphina, whose nickname is, *"Magna"* because she is the *Magna* or *Best* warrior of all the Seraphs, and no doubt this title is well deserved.

In this setting, Beelzy and I are the odd Cherubs out, and we stay quiet. I can tell Beelzebub is almost annoyed in their flirting chatter. I am indifferent about the whole situation. It did not bother me when I was the only odd cherub out, just a while ago, when Beelzy was with Dumah and it does not bother me now. And I do not know why Beelzy is making such a fuss about it, since he was just in their position when he was with his darling.

Gabriel continues, his jokes, about the crow, saying "I do not think we would be a tasty meal for him. I doubt we are even an option in his food chain. We can offer him spiritual nourishment, but that is about it. I think he would require a little more carnal sustenance than us!"

Since we have now spotted him, the crow moves out of sight, but not without leaving a loud squawking. Beelzy continues to look puzzled and pensive as if there would be more of interest about this crow.

We reach the top of the hill, which Gabriel calls, *"Golgotha,"* or *"Locus Calvariae,"* and from one side of the summit, we can see a great view of the ocean. On the other side, at the bottom of Golgotha, I can see the thousands of Seraphim working in the territory.

Near my feet, in the muddy ground, I see a mound of black worms erupting from the dirt. Astonishingly, at a distance, there is also a volcano that is erupting, covering the ocean water with ash and magma. New land is formed as the water cools down the lava.

Both the erupting volcano and the spewing worms form a sort of superstitious déjà vu, in my mind, and I think everyone else notices it too. The duplicity of these sights triggers a phenomenon of repetition that is obvious to all. I wonder what this could possibly mean…

Suddenly the same crow that had been hovering, over our heads, dives from the sky. Beelzy pushes us to the side, and then covers himself, thinking the crow was going to attack us.

Gabriel and Seraphina fall to the ground with Beelzy's strong push. It turns out the crow was diving to feast on the mound of worms and does not harm any of us.

Gabriel stands up, smiles, and says, "See Beelzy? Nothing to be afraid of! Nonetheless, good reactions! Just a little gentler next time, please!" as he dusts off the dirt from his being.

Beelzy feels embarrassed, almost ridiculed, as Seraphina also chuckles. I can tell that Dumah's surprise hug, and everything else has put him on edge, these are the real culprits for the way he reacted. Not to mention that he takes his job, of security, very seriously, seeing himself as a security consultant that must prioritize the safety of all of us.

CHAPTER 5

There seems to be a growing connection between the crow and Beelzy. As the creature feeds on the black worms, once again, its staring eyes pierce Beelzy, and they do the same to mine, feeding off of our doubts.

Beelzy, concentrated, asks me, "Did you see that?"

Before I get a chance to reply, Seraphina responds thinking the question is directed towards her.

Seraphina, teasing, says, "Yes, I saw you scurry to the side..."

Beelzebub handles his embarrassment, rather well, laughing and saying, "This crow is up to something…"

Gabriel teases, "Yes, he is up to getting his rations for the day. Nothing to be alarmed by…" Milking the joke a little too much for Beelzebub's taste.

Beelzy, once again, feels silly... whereas I continue pondering the meaning of this in silence.

Many other crows join in on the feast. This species of crows carries their nestlings in a pouch like a kangaroo. The mother, crow, which was the first to dive, is feeding its pouched nestlings by regurgitating the worms it has eaten.

All of the sudden, the black snake that had elusively disappeared, reappears from underground to violently swallow and devour one of the crows whole. Then, noticing that it has an audience, it quickly dives back into the hole, disappearing from sight and mind. The other crows scurry off.

Seraphina seems disgusted by what she just saw. They cannot stop them from killing one another. Just like my orders, they have been advised not to interfere on the affairs of animals.

Gabriel says, "Do not be disturbed... All of God's creatures are beautiful, but unfortunately, not all their actions are beautiful… They are not as graceful as we are, neither are they meant to be. They are different…

"After all we are angels of Heaven and they are creatures of earth, with body and soul...

"We must remember that many of these creatures are new to us, but this is always optimistic. These earthly beings, especially birds, are always bearers of good news. For instance, look at their similarities to me… They have black wings and can fly." He says all this as he rotates his shield of good news on an axis.

We now walk away… Gabriel continues to talk and I hear a faint term, "They will call it, *Judea,*" as Gabriel points to a new, holographic, schematic, of the land.

Seraphina points, saying, *"Jerusalem, Galilee and Bethlehem…"*

Beelzy's relaxation does not last long, as once again he regimentally says,

"NAZARETH-AND-THE-DEAD-SEA-JUST-BEYOND-THAT…"

Distracted by the, ever ominous, air, I turn around, and

from behind a big rock, I see some black wings emerge. Some menacing red eyes, covered by a dark hood, are spying through the bushes.

Little did we know that the one following us the entire time was none other than Gallant, Satan. At first I thought it was Dumah, again, trying to surprise Beelzy with her shenanigans, but it was the wrong eye color.

Gabriel and Seraphina never suspect that they were being followed. Beelzy, on the other hand, was not completely fooled, he is the only one, other than I, that sensed something, but he thought perhaps it was just a predator on the prowl. Now I know that it was really his bond of friendship, which Beelzy was sensing. But what was I sensing? Other than my respected Gallant, Satan is not a particularly close friend of mine!

Satan looks at me from behind the rock, noticing I have spotted him. He slowly places his index finger, over his lips, and orders me to hush and remain quiet.

What is going on? First Satan's secret excursion in Eden and now it is as though Gabriel, Seraphina, and Beelzy are also sneaking around, like if everyone is following one another, testing their cloaking skills. Or is it Satan who is still sneaking around?

It is as though two of my Gallants have become separated,

from one another, and I do not understand, in the slightest, what they are up to. I do not know what Satan's mission by the tree was, nor do I know what this *Mariam,* contingency plan, is. What has the Lord gotten me into?

Puzzled, I simply walk away. Then I turn around, to look behind me, to make sure I am not imagining all of this. Satan has vanished! But I am sure that what I saw is not my, sometimes, vivid imagination playing tricks with me.

Suddenly, in my mind, I hear a potent voice, saying, "If you tell them I was here, I will tell them that you followed me in Eden. I will tell them you were in the forbidden area…"

I can recognize the voice. I know these words come from Satan. With sharp angst, my heart drops to the ground. All my concealing efforts when following him in Eden had been for nothing! I would have been better off, just, letting him find me…

Looks like I lost that game of cloaking after all! Point revoked… I do not like losing! Give me a chance to redeem myself! Let's say the score is **1-0**, Satan is winning… For now…

Wow! He is right! Nosey me, I did follow him! I was in the forbidden area, but so was he! But this favors him because if it should come down to putting his word against mine, I do not think I would be triumphant.

CHAPTER 5

The sky turns dark black as the obscurity spreads like a ripple. It is now the dewfall, followed by the hastening nighttime. Darkness fills the land. We are all surprised to see the black sky. We were not told of darkness being a part of creation. Light is supposed to be the only staple. Darkness is what God eliminated during creation.

The only logical thing that occurs to me is that perhaps these ominous circumstances have taken away from the light. I am still left with questions in my mind… Is it Satan's actions that create darkness? Is it Gabriel's? Or, is it my own?

I use my intellect to further analyze the facts. Why would Satan not want me to tell anyone of his presence, unless he was doing something wrong? And so it is logical that he now changed two things in nature.

1. He generated the predator and prey dynamic when he served the frog to the vulture.
2. He has just caused darkness to engulf the land.

What is worse is that this information becomes automatically coded in the minds of angels and earth's creatures, as if God meant things to be this way. He did not! I know it! This is why Gabriel sees the crows feeding, as a natural thing, as a part of the status quo.

They continue to walk as an even thicker darkness immerses the land. Nothing that pleases the Lord happens in the thick of night, and so, Gabriel marvelously re-lights the sky with his shield. First by bouncing the sun's light off of the moon, and then by allowing the brightest stars of the firmament to shine. Additional dark traits and secrets are added to Satan's repertoire and as much as I would like to, I cannot say anything.

Chapter 6

Humans Will Not Be Animals

Raphael and Michael are in Paradise Palace reporting on the status of earth. Only Raphael, with his staff, and Michael, with his sword, are present because Gabriel is attending to project *Mariam* and Satan stayed behind to "supervise" in Eden. But, you and I both know that he was really spying on project *Mariam*.

I have now returned to my friend Michael's side where I feel the safest. So far, he and Raphael are the only of my Gallants who seem to not be sneaking around. Not that I have been doing any better… but at least I know my commands come straight from the Almighty Himself. I can usually say the same for the rest, but not as of late…

So now it is only logical that I would want to remain with my Father, God, and my friend, Michael, as much as possible, but of course, I am still open to being sent wherever the Lord needs me…

I still cannot shake-off the disturbing sights that I witnessed on earth. Is there corruption among God's Archangels? But, again, this is not about me, about what I think, it is about them… I will let you reach your own conclusions…

Raphael begins addressing God, "Laudamus Te, benedicimus Te, adoramus Te, glorificamus Te! We praise You, we bless You, we adore You, we glorify You! We give You thanks, for Your great glory! Lord God Heavenly Rex, King, o God Omnipotens Father. Preparations are going well, our Dominus, Lord. Better than expected! There is not much need for us."

God's potent voice inspiringly replies, ***"There is always need for you, but excellent! Where is Satan?"***

Raphael responds, "Dixit se stare super terram. He said he would stay on earth a while longer to do his part and supervise Your creations."

His words are followed by his signature eyewink as if he also knew what was really going on with Satan.

God knows how things are coming along, but wants His Gallants to feel included. There is a need for community in all of us, just as He is a Trinitarian community. When we are in community, that is when we are numerous and the strongest, and so God encourages involvement. More than anything, our Lord probably wanted to hear what excuse Satan had given his brothers for wandering off into the forbidden area. Of course, I cannot read the Lord's mind, but before I know it, He explains to me what I need to know.

The Almighty continues to speak to both of them and says, ***"Since you two are the only of my chiefs here, you get to choose the name of the first human..."***

I can tell the Archangels are honored that they have been chosen to pick a name. I know, first hand, that Michael has already meditated, long and hard, on the subject... Not too long ago, he even asked me if I had any suggestions, just in case the Almighty would ask, because He would often ask for creative input on things of the sort. I cannot exactly recall what names I gave Michael...

Ah yes! Now I remember! If it would be, left, up to me, your first ancestor would be called, Moleculo, Ionio, Electronio, or something like that... I wonder if he listened to my input, maybe my suggested names will make the cut...

Raphael replies, "Lord, we are honorari to make this arbitrium, decision. After careful consideration, I think he should be called, *"Adam,"* after the minima, smallest, amount of matter, the atom! So that humana know that they need to be small in Your oculos, eyes, Dominus, and that those who are small in their own oculos, are big in Your eyes, Pater, Father."

Michael says, "And indeed they art small… Adam, I liketh it! Well said mine broth'r! I guesseth Adam is much bett'r than Proton, Electron 'r M'lecule!"

They both stare at me… With a hearty smile, Raphael winks his right eye at me, and Michael also gazes my way because these are the silly names I had suggested, and they both chuckle. I laugh along with them, showing my expression of bewilderment.

I say, "Hey! I was headed along the right path!"

Both Archangels are happy and agree on the chosen name. I enjoy repeating, "Adam," in my head. It has a good up and down sound that is easy to say, "A-dam, A, dam, Aaaaa-dam."

God, tenderly, says, ***"Very well! Amen I say to you, so he shall be called, Adam."***

Excited, Raphael asks, "Et Adam creari hodie, Domine? Will Adam be created today, Lord?"

Behind me, I hear a few faint footsteps. Satan has finally showed up, but no one else has seen him… I can tell he is eager to hear God's answer to Raphael's question, pausing in the hallway, listening closely and continuing to spy on his brothers. He knows that I have seen him… He once again places his index finger over his lips, as his red eyes pierce me.

I again hear his voice in my head that powerfully says, "Sshhhh! Do not alert them of my presence!"

How am I able to hear his voice in my head? Even more disturbing, how long has he been able to penetrate my thoughts?

God knows that he has arrived and invites him in. Thank God to relieve me from this burden of secrecy. It is not good to keep secrets or leave anything hidden! If God knew that Satan was sneaking around, so as not to be seen, He also knows that the lord of persuasion was sneaking around the world doing the same thing. He knows everything!

In my head, I quickly get a message from the Lord, that says, ***"Just document, Uriel… Worry not! Thank you!"***

This affirms me on my stance of not tattletaling. Even so, I cannot take much more of this confusion and so the Lord says to me, ***"Everything that is foul will eventually come to the surface. All will be clear in time, my son…"*** And so I do not further worry.

Michael says, "We did not heareth thou arrive, broth'r."

Satan kneels and dazed, speaks the word, "Serviam!" He seems to be love-drunk, swerving in, enthusiastically adding,

"Excuse me for barging in, my Lord, and forgive me for the lateness of the hour."

God answers, ***"No need to apologize for that... You have been busy... Putting extra efforts and details into existence."*** Implying that there are other, more serious things he should apologize for instead.

Satan, infatuated, says, "Yes, indeed! I have fallen in love with earth and made several new friendships, but none like my special, new friend... I believe the humans will call him snake or serpent. They are very wise, my favorite of all creatures!"

Michael jokes, saying, "That is good, Satan. Anon thoust two friends. Thou and Beelzy will nay long'r be lonely."

Satan sarcastically says, "You are hilarious, Michael! Same can be said about your friendship with Uriel." We both chuckle...

Because of his charisma, I smile, momentarily, forgetting about Satan's suspicious endeavors.

Michael, the master of the swords, says, "Touché!"

Raphael chimes in and says, "Ita probaverunt angues? So you liked the snakes? The slithery fellows timentes, scared me, but like Michael, I am glad that you have made a new amicum, friend. More so, I am glad to see you are beatus, happy!" Raphael jokes around and so does Satan.

CHAPTER 6

Satan says, "So far, I am pleased! But, please, do not let my intrusion take importance away from your last question... I believe you were asking if humans will be created today?"

"Oh, yes," said Raphael, looking to the Lord for a response.

"No, not today, but soon! You know the day, Satan," says the Lord, and then continues saying to Satan, ***"It is our conversation that stopped you from expressing your joy of earth, please continue, my son… Tell us about the crow and the worms… Did you like those as well?"***

Satan looks surprised that God would mention this, calling him out on his mischief.

Before he can say anything, Michael, the wise, inadvertently bails him out, responding, "Predat'r and prey from all p'rspectives, art they not?"

Raphael looks confused...

Michael says, "Alloweth me to explain: The snake at the top of the food chain, eats the crow… and the crow, one level below, eats the w'rm…

"From anoth'r p'rspective, the crow is at the top of the food chain, which can eateth the snake, and the snake can eateth the w'rm.

"But it dost not endeth hither; the w'rm is anon at the top, and can eateth at the stomach and flesh of both animals, when they art alive, and as they roteth when they art dead.

"Ominous and int'resting creatures they all are… That dost not happen in nature v'ry oft. That is so like Satan to enjoyeth the out of n'rm. This is pr'bably wherefore he likes them so much."

Satan agrees and says, "You know me, too well, brother! That is exactly my fascination!"

God, concerned, interjects, ***"Predator and prey? No such interaction should exist! Something out of the ordinary has occurred. Please devote your efforts on finding the source and focus more closely so that nothing of this sort ever happens again."***

The Gallants all agree to do better and apologize if they have not served to the Lord's liking. Although no apology is necessary, Michael and Raphael have done extremely well. I can feel that God had expected Satan to take the blame for this phenomenon and yet, does not. He remains silent and guilty.

They all digress, continuing to discuss their favorite animals.

Satan, in his distractions, asks Raphael, "What is your favorite creature?"

"My favorite creature is the scrutantem delphina uident, also known as, dolphin."

Everyone laughs in mockery, the way he said it was funny, as if announcing an edict and they laugh because they believe the dolphin is a wimpy being.

Raphael gives them a serious look for interrupting and continues very passionate about his choice, explaining, "Scrutantem delphina uident will evolve to be second in intelligence to the humana. They are agile and even the fiercest of predators fear them... They can communicate through long distances, and they sanabit cito, heal quickly. My virgam, staff of souls, sensed a strong animal soul in them, second only to the humana...

"They are kind and donantes vobismetipsis, forgiving. Even though they fend for themselves, when they are threatened, they show misericordia, mercy, and do not end the life of their aggressors. The humana would do well to use them as moral ducibus, guides. I would say they are even smarter than your serpents, Satan."

Both Michael and Satan stand corrected and remain silent after Raphael's passionate, and well thought-out, spiel about the dolphins. Raphael thinks he has won them over, but he has not! They cannot contain their laughter any longer…

Teasing him, Satan says, "Look at me, pretty little Raphael, with my pretty little dolphins, or should I say, scrutantem delphina uident."

Then he winks his eye also in mockery of Raphael's signature facial expression. I can tell this somewhat strikes a chord with Raphael.

My silly friend, Michael, imitates the sound of a silly dolphin. Everyone joins in, making fun of poor Raphael. Bursting into tears of happiness, even I cannot contain my laughter.

Satan then stops cackling, noticing Raphael's unfazed face of seriousness, and turns to Michael, saying, "If I know you, Michael, you liked the biggest, meanest, most brutal, creature… Let me guess…the T-Rex?!"

Michael laughs at his brother's spot-on assertion.

Satan continues saying, "Come on! The brutish nature of the T-Rex cannot even compare to the intelligence of our well rounded, sophisticated, animals."

It is now Satan who imitates the sounds of a playful dolphin. All laugh again at Raphael's expense.

In response, Raphael now imitates a snake, hissing, rattling its tail, and he even sticks out his tongue, making it forked. This does not have the desired effect. Raphael wanted to show the silliness of the serpent, but instead he ended up emphasizing its menacing nature. All stop laughing. Raphael looks embarrassed yet again.

Referring back to the T-Rex, Michael says, "'Tis thou that

knows me too well, broth'r. I wilt starteth to become moo unpredictable and changeth mine methods."

"Yes, that would be good," says Satan encouraging him to be more impulsive and then asking, "But tell us, why did you like the T-Rex?"

Michael responds, "I lik'd it f'r all the reasons thou stated, but also because I seeth a sense of justice and m'rcy in them, just liketh mine sword!" Proudly displaying his weapon.

Satan, livening up the mood, says, "Justice and mercy? Really? I did not get that at all!"

"Yes, justice and mercy… Is it not justice that the biggest, fiercest, animal reap all the benefits?" Said Michael.

"Amen," says Satan in agreement and getting ideas from this extremist assertion.

Michael continues giving reason to his fascination, "As f'r the m'rcy part… I am still w'rking on a justifiable attribute that makes the T-Rex o'er the top and m'rciful. But, I am sure it hath at least one trait…

"Maybe it spares animals that art too small, pr'tecting the small and defenseless from their predat'rs… If they ev'r coincide in dwelling togeth'r, perchance it will spareth the humans from thy humor, Satan!"

All laugh, and then he resumes serious, "I am sure the T-rex will be m'rciful some way 'r anoth'r. The humans will hast to calleth him, *"Rex"* 'r *"King"* f'r some reas'n. Kings and rul'rs wilt always be just and m'rciful. Nay exceptions!

"Thither art two sides to all these animals, and humans will be this way too. That is one of the things I enjoyeth the most about these creatures. They art all unpredictable, which I apparently am not, acc'rding to thou, Satan."

Satan adds, "But the *"T"* in T-Rex stands for *"Tyrant,"* is this also how a King should be?"

They all stay quiet, turning to their Lord for an answer. The Almighty says nothing, probably expecting them to know the obvious answer to that question, which is, "No! A king should never be a tyrant!"

I love to hear these debates!

God chips in to the conversation, saying, ***"Speaking of becoming more unpredictable, how is your head, Satan? Hope that tree did not hurt you too much. You had quite a series of tumbles..."***

I told you, God knows everything, and so He knows about Satan seeing His golden tree in the forbidden area, which he should not have even come close to.

He is very surprised, and even proud, that God would mention the tree. I can tell that even more disturbing feelings run through his mind, exhilaration, fear. At this moment, I too become nervous, maybe I will also be questioned about my expedition. But I know that the Lord has graciously absolved me of any fault because I was doing what I was told, and even so, I am still sorry and contrite for unknowingly having stepped foot in the forbidden area. But somehow, I can tell Satan does not share my same sentiment.

I have a flash back of my encounter with the tree. I see the (III) markings on the tree and compare them with the markings on the Lord's tabernacle right in front of me. They are the same…

"Qua arbore videris? Quid ruere? What tree? What tumble?" asks Raphael who is not informed on his brother's exploits, not even with their extremely potent, Gallant, connection.

Satan answers, "If you must know… I fell off a tree and then got hit by one of the branches after playing with the serpents. That is where my injury came from… You didn't see it?" He says with a deviant smile as he grabs his head, and redirects his gaze towards me to see my face, wondering if it was I who ratted him out… It was not I! I would never do that to my Gallant, but I simply look down to avoid conflict.

I have another flashback of Satan's face when shushing me, reminding me to remain quiet. The ant bites on my back begin to flare up with a burning and tingling sensation.

Raphael says, "Oh yeah, your vulnere, wound! Vae! How horrible! Iam te esse sperabam sentiens melius! Hope you are feeling better by now! My offer to cure still stands if you should require curationum, healing."

Satan, non-chalantly, says, "A few minor scratches, but I shall thrive. Nothing I have not experienced in combat training before…"

Satan brushes it off and says to them, "There is one additional thing I wish to propose… While I was on earth, I came up with a project idea. It is called, "*Possession…*"

"Possession gives us Gallants the power to possess these creatures if we should choose to. Our Essences shall engulf their beings; my Trident can easily do this if these animals are willing, but the Lord could give us the power to possess them, even, if they are not willing…

"No doubt there will be times when they get out of hand, and we will need to remind them that what they are doing is wrong or can be done differently, in a better way. This will allow us to have more control over these beings."

Without hesitation, God immediately says, ***"No, Satan! Gabriel is not present to hear your ideas. You know that all Gallants must be present to hear project suggestions."***

CHAPTER 6

Satan, autocratically, says, "I was not here when my brothers chose the name for the first human. How is this different? What if I don't like, *Adam*."

His brothers are shocked at his comments. The naming of Adam was not a project proposition, it was just creative input.

He continues grumbling, "At first, it used to be only you and I, Lord…" Counting out his brothers present.

God, correcting, says, ***"It has not been this way for a long time. You know that my sights were always set on the unity of my four Archangels."***

Raphael and Michael notice something odd about Satan, but they give him space for God to explain.

God says, ***"You know the rules…"***

"Then, I shall present my ideas when Gabriel arrives."

God says, ***"No, my son, this is one project I cannot accept! These creatures, and humans especially, are to have free will at all times, and have no spiritual intervention, unless in grave danger, and still we cannot do anything for them that they do not will for themselves."***

Satan says, "It is for this reason that possession shall be useful. When they are in grave danger, we will possess them and defend them. As I said, if Adam is willing, I can possess him!"

God, again, says, ***"Get behind me, Satan! You are a stumbling block to me; for you are not setting your mind on my interests, but your own. There is no need for that... How would you like if a human could possess you if he chose to? This power should not be given to anyone.***

"If my Holy Spirit lives inside them, this shall be the strongest defense for their souls; this, and another project I have in mind. Only my soul and graces must possess them and no one else's!

"Let me be clear in saying that humans will not be animals. As my children, they will have the highest of dignities and will have control over all nature."

These words hit hard, shaking Satan to his core. He is confused that his idea did not work and about the importance of humans. Not even the lord of persuasion could persuade God on this endeavor. It is one of the first times that God does not heed Satan's plans. That being said, usually his plans are not so extreme and quite sensible. All of his ideas, his inspiration, come from God. He does not have an original bone in his body. All he knows is God and His ideas, yet it is curious that this idea of possession does not stem from Godly inspiration, otherwise, the Lord would have approved it.

They are now free to go, and begin to leave the gathering.

They all kneel and speak the words, "Serviam!"

The Lord says, ***"Satan, stay a while longer... I wish to speak with you."***

He stays and has a surprised look on his face. Remaining a little nervous because he thinks God is going to talk to him, more, about his encounter with the golden tree. All the questions that God had asked him earlier, were all leading towards Satan's mischief on earth; the crows, the worms, the snake, the tree, his wound on the back of his head... Sensing that I must be present, I also stay to recount.

Chapter 7

A Conscientious Gift

God starts out saying, ***"Amen I say to you, it is ok to be curious, Satan. In being inquisitive, you have done nothing wrong. If you wish to know anything, you know that all you have to do is ask…"***

But Satan's track record shows that he does not like to ask God. He feels as though he is inconveniencing Him. Satan likes to find out for himself. It is more of a challenge for him. I once heard him saying this in Michael's presence.

The Almighty says, ***"I know you wish to find out more about the projects your brothers are carrying out, but understand that they are all busy and that each of you have a crucial part in creation. Each one of you makes me proud with your endeavors. But, still, I know that something is wrong. Are***

you displeased with my plans?"

Satan humbly says, "No, my Lord and Father... I only seek clarity on what my role is in these plans. All the Gallants seem to have definite tasks except for me. Yes, I am curious because I still do not fully understand what we are doing on earth. I thought Heaven was your ultimate kingdom."

God encouragingly responds, ***"Amen, amen I say to you, Heaven is my kingdom and so is Earth. The entire universe is my kingdom. Even places that are not places are my kingdom. Rest assured that the earthly dominion will not always exist, but Heaven shall always remain. Everything that is mine, I share with my Gallants and with my angels. You know this! These humans will be different from you, but different is not always bad, different can be good...***

"Please do not be troubled, my commander. I know you are a curious mind who likes to find out things for yourself. That is fine! Everything will soon make sense... Stay on course and do not be discouraged. I am with you the entire way. Are you displeased? Are you ok?"

"I am ok, Lord," says Satan calmly. "Thank you for clarifying. As always, I am humbled by your infinite knowledge and divine providence. I am sure your actions will be transcendental, as they always are."

Even though Satan says he is not displeased or troubled, he indeed is, and even I can still sense it. God cannot help those who do not want to be helped. He tries to mask how displeased he truly is, but I know he does not fool the Almighty.

In an attempt to appease Satan, with a lot of affection, God says, ***"Since you have been so patient, I guess I can now reveal to you, your project. I was going to tell you later, but there is no time like the present...***

"Your task, although perhaps you may think is small and feeble, will be the most important one. I know you are very fond of the material, but your task is not a material project. It is a spiritual project that will translate to the material."

Satan, ambitiously, excited, asks, "Will I be given the power of creation?"

God clearly responds, ***"No, my son..."***

"But, what you just described, is that not what creation is? Making the spiritual into matter?"

God answers, ***"Creation is much more than that, but your task is also much more than that. It is a great responsibility that no one but you can manage... It is something that only you can convey to humans."***

Satan's excitement builds with God's every word. The anticipation of this revelation reaches an all time high, and it is always bliss when revealed, bliss that he has grown very fond of, almost like an addiction.

"Yes, Lord, thank You. What does my project consist of?"

The Lord proclaims, ***"You will be in charge of project, Conscience, guiding humans on what is right and what is wrong, this is how you will turn thoughts, and the spiritual, into material deeds. What you encourage them to do spiritually will be turned into material actions, and they shall be judged on these deeds.***

"I trust you will be a great leader to them. With your trident's power of persuasion, show them only good! Truly I tell you... Whatever you bind on earth will be bound in Heaven, and whatever you loosen on earth will be loosed in Heaven."

Satan is supposed to be God's first, and only, solid, rock... I know he has already foreseen and taken his task too literally, secretly binding and loosening natural phenomena and the wills of angels in the two kingdoms.

Satan looks at his trident and spins it a few times as it shines in the light. He is surprisingly unfulfilled with his new task. God's revelation has not filled him with pride and joy as it usually does.

He quickly realizes this and thinks to himself, "I think it is not fulfilling because I still do not understand what conscience is." He asks, "Conscience? What is this, Lord?"

God answers, ***"There is no quenching you, Morning Star."***

"No, Lord, I am just wondering… What is conscience? Do I possess this conscience?"

A beam of light shines from the golden box and touches him. He looks like he has just been trespassed by a great force that makes him levitate off the ground in a trance. He is pierced and conveyed with the power of conscience.

"Now you know! You must never interfere with free will! In fact, no power that I will ever give you, can impede with free will, but that will not stop angels from trying… You must only persuade and teach…

"Conscience is a direct connection between Heaven and earth, much like rainbows, but much quicker. All humans will have this conscience and it will be you and I connected to them…

"As you will learn with conscience, it must be formed everyday. The good deeds you execute will make it stronger. The bad ones will make it weaker… A bad deed, done for the right reason, will make it even weaker…

"I cannot emphasize enough; you too must have a well-formed conscience to pick between good and evil! Pick only

good and help the humans only pick good, and you will experience the marvels of this gift...

"If you use this power as it is meant to be used, the angelic prophecy of the dark times will always be tamed. Conscience shall help you remain united with your, brother, Gallants. It will keep your Essences together...

"Let us not kid anymore, Morning Star, you know that the prophecy is in your hands; it has always been."

I am surprised because in a way, God has given Satan his power of possession, which he so desperately desired at the beginning of this meeting, and named it something else, almost as if the spoiled child had gotten his way after all. After pondering things, I realize He has also made this aptitude less powerful. Here lies the very important distinction: Conscience will allow Satan to be in the minds of humans, but not to control them. He will be able to control and play with their imaginations and help them with their strengths and weaknesses. The ultimate choice, to do good or evil, is up to them.

Even though conscience is not exactly what he wanted, the Gallant still welcomes this gift. The power of conscience has now quenched his need for grace and he has become excited to get started.

"So, now I can choose?" Asked Satan.

"Yes, you can choose," replies God.

"And these humans will also have this conscience and be able to choose as well?"

"Yes, the only difference between humans and you, Satan, is that the material will blind them, but you know that I EXIST, that I AM the ALPHA and the ΩMEGA. You know I AM THE CREATOR, but they will not always know this unless it is revealed by conscience...

"Conscience encompasses morality and without morality there is nothing. Without morality these creatures will never be happy! You will be their eyes and ears, which guide them to me."

Curious to see if he can use his power on his subjects, the snakes, Satan then asks, "Do the lesser animals have a conscience?"

"They will have a conscience to a lesser extent. Their conscience is more driven by instinct, and an animal soul, than by what is right. If you find it easy to influence humans, animals will be much easier! But you already know this, how easy it was to win over the serpents...

"An animal's conscience is all but perfect, but a human's conscience, if well formed, is always perfect. If well formed, it shall have a direct connection, with me, here in Paradise

Palace. A direct connection with my tabernacle."

"Humans will have a direct connection with you?" Satan asks, deferring the comments about the serpents, and troubled about the dignity that humans will potentially have.

The Lord says, ***"Yes, just as you Gallants do. They will need this connection, more than you, to live their lives."***

Satan has asked all he could have about his new power, now it is up to him to form his gift and train to perfect the art.

He then facetiously says, "Thank you, Lord! Conscience is sooooo much better than my idea of possession. Only You know how to fill my Essence; only You know how to fill my soul!"
I can tell he tried so hard to make this sound genuine, but he failed.

As Satan leaves the room, realizing he has this new gift, he begins to look around the room as if scared, paranoid, and worried. Countless questions, and choices, have now taken over his mind, flooding his intellect… More tools and options have been given to him.

Confused and startled, he quickly kneels in front of God and says, "Serviam!"

It is as if his new power of conscience overwhelms him. If he was ever confused, now he is in despair and more confused than ever...

"Do not worry, it will all be clear soon," says God. ***"Hone your new senses, for your conscience will give you options like never before. Pick good as you have always picked. Maintain to your duties and when the time comes of creating this human, we shall both show them the gift of conscience...***

"Stay united with your brothers and the prophecy of darkness need not take place. Keep the Essences together with your powers, just as I have, bringing my Gallants together as equals...

"Do this in memory of me, so that you may never be split of your brothers and the unity of your four Essences. This way the foretelling is void and shall always be fulfilled in your unanimity, with no need for obscurity! You know that it has always been your choice, Satan, that will decide everything!"

Wow! How interesting!

Satan stares at me... The volatility of his soul accidentally passes his inner thoughts to me. I can hear the struggle within. He has some wicked thoughts! He has just proved, to himself, that God is not necessary. The Lord has granted him the power of conscience, which Satan could have easily conjured with his Trident, but he forgets that the power of his trident stems from God. In his eyes, the Lord has just stolen his idea for possession and called it something else. These were my exact thoughts earlier… Hopefully it was not my reflections that lead him down this path of thinking. He could have easily invaded my intellect, as he has been doing, and even easier now with his new gift.

Even more disturbing is the thought that we have just telepathically traded one ideology for another. Almost as if every idea I hear from him, I have had to trade him one of my own in return.

God says one more thing to him, ***"Please, next time you are in a bad mood, do not fill the earth with darkness, for obscurity could want to stay… and… NEVER possess a snake, crow, worm, or any other creature again!"***

Now I know that my theories about darkness and predator/prey interactions were right. They have both stemmed from Satan. I may have lost my game of spying, but not this one… The score is tied: **1-1**, for I have figured something out that he wants to be kept secret, yet I am obligated to include it in what has now become my exposé of him. I wonder who will score next?

He continues to leave the room in a hurry, not giving the Lord's last words much importance. Even though they were probably the most important. As he exits the main hall, his new powers fill him even more. He now understands what has been given to him. The bliss of God's revelation hits him harder than ever. Smiling, as he feels true joy. He feels free, revived, God-like, anew!

What is more interesting is that when I exit, I gaze upon the mural of Satan below the golden tree. That work of art that I have always admired now makes a little more sense to me… The incomplete masterpiece is now one step closer to being complete. In the picture, there is a small puddle of blood, at the base of the golden tree, by the roots, and Satan is no longer in the scene. Now a black snake is looking up at the tree, the snake sort of looks like me.

As for the prophecy of darkness, what great responsibility does the Lord put in Satan's hands! It seems that with this mandate, all of Heaven's future is dependent on him, but this is no different than in the past because he has always been given the most important of tasks.

I cannot help but protest this, in my mind, because it seems as though Satan has, single-handedly, been starting the dark times, not trying to prevent them! But maybe conscience is meant to halt what he has already started; these disturbing chains of events. Yet, in assigning this paramount responsibility to him, I am confident that the Lord knows what He is doing. I trust in thee O' Lord!

Chapter 8

The Game of Dice in Paradise

After their meeting with God, Raphael and Michael are walking, together, down a golden road, just outside of Paradise Palace, still within the city of Heaven. Gabriel descends from the sky with a green flash and joins his brothers, having now returned from the land of Israel. The only Gallant missing is Satan, which seems to be a trend, as of late.

The Archangels are walking away from Paradise Palace, and so it is seen in the background. On the side of the road, there are many angels looking at the three. Some are working, some combat training, some playing lively music with great violin-trumpets and piano-harps. Others are doing their daily duties as citizens of Heaven; carrying objects, loading equipment, and preparing for their visits to earth.

There are enormous transport vessels that are being loaded with animals. The vessels look similar to big, boat, arks. The design of these vessels is simple and elegant, rectangular and enormous.

The same types of vessels are also used for transporting rocks, vegetation, marine animals, birds, and plants. They are specialized to load, contain, and unload, whatever it is that they are transporting, to and from the creation centers.

The arks levitate in the air as angels push them along the golden path. The container-like vessels are heading towards Paradise Palace so that they can be transported, down to earth, through the rainbow path. The containers being pushed resemble an assembly line in a factory, all working together, like gears. Thousands of angels are lined up pushing them every step of the way. Each task is integral like a well-oiled machine...

As the Archangels walk by, all the angels, both Cherubs and Seraphs, give a small bow. They stop what they are doing and salute.

More angels on the street greet and say, "Gallants," as they bow and fist their chest.

The Archangels bow their heads in response to this greeting.

With humility, they salute everyone with the same respect they are shown.

"Quaeso, please continue what you are doing," says Raphael.

Their Essences are stored on their backs in sheaths. Many of the Cherubs and Seraphs also have specialized weapons and tools on their backs. They occasionally unsheathe them to use in the tasks they are working on.

The Archangels walk with finesse and poise, but are still very manly and smooth, as if their steps levitate a few inches off the ground. Walking towards the bright sun, the jokester Archangels fool around with each other making apparent the bond that unites them.

Gabriel asks, "Where is Satan?"

Michael says, "I doeth not know, he wilt still be in Paradise Palace with our L'rd. He arriv'd late to our meeting earli'r today, and our L'rd want'd to speaketh with him a while long'r."

Gabriel asks, "Why was he late?"

Michael answers, "He stay'd in Eden to micro-manage, pr'bably…"

They all laugh and share with Gabriel how Satan had come up with the plan for possession and how the Lord rejected his plans. Still, Gabriel does not think much of this proposition…

Michael says, "I nev'r realiz'd until anon, but Satan almost broke the curfew!"

Raphael says, "Iustos vos esse iudicem! You are right! I had not realized either..."

What they are referring to is the establishment of the new curfew. All angels, Gallants included, must not stay on earth or outside of Heaven for more than a day. The only exception is if they have special permission to stay, or if they are in charge of guarding Eden. This means that, for now, the only angels, with special permission, are Beelzy and the Watchers, which he commands outside of Eden. This is why many of those shielding Eden had not been back to Heaven in a very long time.

"All angels must return on a daily basis, based on the earthly day." Also the rules are that they can return back to earth after one, whole, day spent in Heaven.

The simple reasoning behind the curfew is simple because many of the younger angels were staying on earth for several days and even weeks, neglecting some of their duties and lives in Heaven. Much like what has happened to Satan, angels are falling in love with God's material creation. They have become "Earthified" or "worldly" and lost sight of why they are truly there. I think "worldly" sounds better. Yes, let us use "worldly," that is a much catchier term, which could possibly be used in the future.

CHAPTER 8

All angels must understand that the material kingdom is not theirs; their dwelling place is in Heaven. This mandate is also to avoid angels from getting lost in the vastness of the universe. So for these reasons we must return everyday, at least this is the reasoning Gabriel gave us when announcing this Godly decree.

The Gallants come up on a substantial crowd. Many of them are playing with some beautiful, transparent dice, which shine almost like diamonds. The dice in Heaven work the same way as normal dice do. There are six numbers on each dice, six sides and all numbered 1 through 6.

In the middle of the mob there is an old, shriveled, very charismatic, Cherub who is working as the Bookkeeper, taking bets and regulating the sport. The Bookkeeper walks around yelling in a strange accent, and with a silver helmet in his hand, saying, "Make your bets, place your bets! Hopefully some of you will pay your debts… Come on… Let's play today… I accept coins in all sets, no threats! Hey, what do you say? Let's…. PLAAAAY!"

All the angels cheer, as he puts on a spectacle…

"If you snooze you lose gentleangels. You have nothing to lose! If you choose to refuse, crews and sloughs of angels shall call you fools... My rules are tools. Do not be fools!"

He says most phrases so as to rhyme and cause humor, very catchy indeed! Everyone silences to hear what he has to say…

"The game of dice where you can pick thrice or twice these cubes of ice. If you lose you pay a small price. So… how can you go wrong with a proud tradition so strong, and long? Do not let my song prolong you from playing along!

"Now with ease, pay the fees, please! Money does not grow on trees, well at least none that I have met yet…

"Geese, bleed me dry, you could try! If not you can shoo fly! This may apply to a certain cheer, that may reach your ear, and hit your soul like a spear, oh dear blah blah blah blah blah. Hahaha," he sarcastically says, and all cheer and laugh.

He now begins to talk to the Archangels who are watching, "Will you be playing, today, your Gallants?"

Then, he passes his helmet around to collect everyone's bets, hopefully including theirs. At this moment, Michael and the Bookkeeper stare into each other's eyes. Michael sees something familiar in the Bookkeeper's, now visible, hot-pink eyes.

Michael asks, "Doeth I know thou?" No Essence seems to help determine the Bookkeeper's name.

The Bookkeeper responds, "We are all brothers in Heaven… Are the deadly sins not seven? Does a baker's bread not leaven? Well… that depends if he uses yeast and gluten, or not... Here is a thought, if it does, it hits the spot."

All this he says to dismiss Michael's question, to continue conducting business, but in a funny way. His rhymes actually make some sense, speaking in twists and riddles, but understandable twists and riddles.

Michael says, "Thy rhymes art quite funny, but ridiculous. What is thy name, Bookkeepp'r? I cannot det'rmine it with mine sw'rd of justice and m'rcy."

The Bookkeeper yells and quickly says, "You dareth telleth me'eth that my rhymeth areth ridicululeth?!"

Everyone laughs at the top of their lungs at this almost perfect imitation of their Gallant. The bookkeeper sounded just like Michael.

Then the bookkeeper continues his antics, announcing to the mob, "So that I am not in danger of becoming a stranger in this manger, my name can be arranged here... Angels, please, appease the Gallants with ease, and tell and spell what my name is…"

They all yell in a big cheer, "BOOUKY!" Then spelling it out, they hail, "B---O---O---! U---K---Y! B---O---O---! U---K---Y!"

Then, as they quiet down, the Bookkeeper responds, "My friends, trends, customers, monomers, polymers, confidants, antioxidants, trustees, chimpanzees, shareholders, bank holders, scolders, acquaintances, maintenances, familiars, thrillers, liars, triers, cronies, phonies, alonies… lovelies… Everyone calls me, Boouky... At your service! Do not be nervous!

"It is an honor to make your acquaintance, Gallants. Even more of an honor for the Gallants to now know my name. All the same, what a shame you did not know it sooner. Why ruin her? I understand the name Boouky can be somewhat spooky, just lookie..."

Michael says, "Thanketh thou," as he interrupts his rhymes, almost as if he has grown annoyed with his rhetoric.

"It is short for Bookkeeper," adds Boouky.

It seems the Gallants and their Essences already knew his name, he just goes by a different nickname and they were able to determine his name, with their Essences, after all.

On purpose one of the angels in the crowd, asks again, "What is your name?"

The crowd once again yells and spells, "B---O---O---! U---K---Y!" Then Boouky indulges the crowd once more, turns around and shouts, "BOO! BOO!" As he tries to frighten them. The crowd laughs, and answers in spelling, "U---K---Y! U---K---Y!"

Michael says, "I meant it as a compliment! Thy rhymes art somewhat odd, but I hast nev'r seen anyone entertaineth as thou doeth. None can grabeth the attention of angels quite liketh thou, well… maybe Gabriel can… Rem'rkable!"

Gabriel looks insulted for this comparison to Boouky and then earnestly asks, "What are you talking about, Michael?" Then his frown turns to a grin, and he quickly says, "This Boo Boo character is way better than me... He even has a catch phrase, and a chant, for his name!"

Just as Michael becomes annoyed, Boouky shows them some attitude too, and invading their personal space, now close to their faces, he quietly and earnestly says, "Look Gallants… These angels are lined up like ants because of my chants. If you are sick of my rants, then do not make slants from my program…

"I would love if we would have sat and chat, but now, here is a thought, my hat is the spot to play and pay your pot, not a lot. Give it a shot! Give it all you got! I know you were taught this, no shame, not lame, game. You have arrived on the dot…"

Then he loudly says for all to hear, "WILL YOU BE PLAYING ON THE SPOT?"

As to also be funny and continue Boouky's rhyme, Michael quickly says, "NOT!" Boouky is not as amused as Michael and neither is the crowd.

The Bookkeeper shakes his, jewel filled, helmet, in their midst, waiting for them to place their bets. At that very moment that Michael says, "NOT," Raphael looks excited and with the same accent as Boouky, he says, "In alienum habuerunt me! Count me in! My fortuna, luck, is feeling hot on the spot!"

The crowd loves this rhyming; he has bailed Michael out from his previous failed attempt to rhyme.

Boouky sings, "That is the spirit! Do not fear it! Let us hear it for our Gallant, Raphael."

The crowd cheers as the Bookkeeper, victoriously, lifts Raphael's arm for him.

It is no secret that Raphael has always been fond of the dice game, and needed no convincing to play, especially with the staff of souls. He makes any angel believe that miracles are possible, even in this sport, indulging many in their love for wagers. He is fascinated by Boouky, but more so by the thrill of this particular game.

Raphael takes out a pouch of gold coins and puts them inside Boouky's helmet. Michael looks very surprised that Raphael has decided to play. He pulls Raphael aside by the arm and says to his ear, "As their command'r, thou must not loseth their r'spect… Doeth not engage in this ch'nce ent'rtainment, young one!"

Raphael says, "Relaxat, it will be fine! Quod est pessimum, ut fieri? What is the worst that could happen? Et brachium meum revertetur! Can I get my arm back, old one?"

Michael releases his arm. Raphael looks happy and

exhilarated to get started, but Michael clearly is not…

At this time, all the angels postpone their exciting games of dice to witness their Gallant play among them. It is like a professional has just stepped into the ring to demonstrate his abilities against an amateur. All focus and importance shift to Raphael…

The game of dice came along from an experiment, to test the randomness of events. In short, it is a simple way to test probability and its chaotic effects. The mystery of this game is fascinating. God gives us this notion that nothing is random, nothing can be left to chance, yet at the center of God's kingdom, a game of gambling is played. This leads me to believe that the odds of the game are controlled by something or someone and not completely random, probably God. But it is interesting to note, and it might be hard for you to understand that even though things seem random, there is actually a lot of skill, intelligence, and physicality involved in the game. It is much like a sport, a game of wits where your opponent and referee is usually the Bookkeeper who invests coinage in the game too, having a significant stake in every single game, in every single roll. Angels must use their vast intellect to analyze their best chances and the more fit you are, then the better decisions you make, and therefore, the better you are at the game. The more well rounded the angel, the better they are at the game, which is why Raphael is like a pro…

We have many pastimes, but among these, the game of dice is definitely a popular one. The coins that are bet are like spiritual currency. They are earned through good deeds. The Archangels are very wealthy, having justly earned this coinage through their faithful service.

Just so everyone is clear, the very simple rules are explained in a vivid, holographic image, created by Raphael's purple-stoned staff, which is lodged into the ground and left unattended. In the game, you can use as many dice as you want and you must attempt to guess the numbers you are going to roll. The angels' usually only use two die, but again, you can use as many as you want. Boouky seems to have no shortage of them. Different Bookkeepers will have different variations of the game, and the rules, but these are the simple rules set by Boouky.

Raphael collects the two die inside a cup. He shakes the chalice a few times, and then the youthful Gallant, says, "**TRIBUS! THREE!** Numerus Dominus noster! The number of our Lord!"

Every soul around him is cheering. They open an alleyway

for him to roll. The Archangels remain quiet and vigilant as concerned spectators that seem to be just as invested as the players… He then throws the die, and out come two ***"THREES."*** The crowd cheers for Raphael's victory.

Boouky yells, "DOUBLE YOUR INVESTMENT! Shall this be your last testament?"

Michael barges in, resolutely pierces his sword in the ground, next to the staff, and says, "Ok, thoust had thy fun, anon let's goeth!" The ground trembles with the might of the Essence.

Raphael says, "Tu ludens loqui? Are you kidding? I am just getting started… Nos vix pervenit! We have just barely arrived!"

All the angels are rowdy and in and uproar, they cheer, "YEAH!!! GALLANT, GALLANT, RAPHAEL, RAPHAEL!!!"

Raphael, once again, meticulously, collects the die, shakes them up in the cup and says, "**TRIBUS, THREE,** again… The Omnipotens, Alimighty, in His sacred number, favors me hodie, today!"

Boouky, encouragingly, says, "THE LORD ALWAYS FAVORS HIS GALLANTS AND ALL THEIR TALENTS!" The crowds laugh in agreement and so does Raphael.

Raphael continues shaking the die up. Then he blows in the goblet for luck, almost as if wanting to breathe, beautiful life, into them.

The dice fall, and out comes a ***"ONE"*** in one of the dice and a ***"TWO"*** in the other. They again cheer for their Gallant. The addition of his two die make the number three, and so his winning streak continues! He makes the game look so effortless!

Bookkeeper says, "1+2 will always be three, gee, like the Almighty is three and so I say to thee… DOUBLE YOUR INVESTMENT, AGAIN!"

All the angels are so ecstatic. They are having a party in the streets of Heaven. More gather around to see the commotion. Much like Raphael's coins, the crowd now doubles. Seeing all these angels arrive makes Michael insistent that they now leave.

"Ok, anon let's go," he says.

Michael again, pulls Raphael by the arm. The crowd is cheering. Raphael loves the attention. Trying to ignore Michael and be funny, he quickly pulls his arm back and says, "This time I will pick, ***"QUATTUOR, FOUR,"*** the number of God's Gallants, **QUATTUOR**!" He hopes that betting in the name of the Gallants will soften Michael up on his stance.

Everyone cheers as their Gallant puts on a display for the ages. With his usual routine, he throws three dice this time and out come a ***"ONE," "ONE"*** and a ***"ONE,"*** adding to ***"THREE"*** again. The number ***THREE,*** repeating so many times, could not have been a coincidence. The crowd goes silent, as they feel truly sorry for their Gallant, Raphael.

We hear an, "Oh," and a few, "Too bads." The Bookkeeper collects Raphael's money with a whole-hearted smile. Raphael is frustrated, knowing that he should have stuck with the number ***THREE***, and wishes to bet again...

Boouky sings, "Better luck next time! If there is a next time, please try to chime into the pot, on the spot, with more generosity and animosity."

"Ok, time to leaveth," Michael firmly insists.

Raphael disregards his brother, and announces in a loud voice, as if proclaiming a decree, "ANGELI CAELORUM! ANGELS OF HEAVEN! MY BELOVED CHERUBIM AND SERAPHIM! FORTISSIMO FRATRES MEI! MY GALLANT BROTHERS! IT SEEMS TO ME THAT *THREE* IS MY FELICIS NUMERUS, LUCKY NUMBER… I should have never abandoned thee, our God's number… ITERUM! AGAIN!" Then, he winks lovingly to the crowd.

If the angels were rowdy before, you should feel the atmosphere now… Legions of angels are cheering and yelling. Even more join to be witness to this momentous occasion.

Michael, being the relentless and sometimes scolding father that he is, insists, decisively, saying, "That is enough! This hath gone too far!" Then he whispers in Raphael's ear, "Thou must not lose their r'spect! Ye are their Gallant!"

Raphael says, "Ineptias… Nonsense… If anything, I will show them the value and virtus of persistence. I really do not see what the fuss is all about… Gabriel nihil obstat, quid? Gabriel has no problem with this, why do you?"

Michael looks to Gabriel sternly so he can jump in and support him. Gabriel looks indifferent and puts on a face that in both their minds reads, "Let him play!" what a joyous affirmation it is for Raphael.

All continue to look at Raphael's game very closely. Raphael takes out all his coins and jewels; he conjures a hidden pouch from his body and bets it very swiftly.

While he holds the die, he gives an elaborate speech to each one of them as if they were now alive, whispering, "**TRIBUS! THREE!** You have not wronged me yet. Paenitet dubitationes! Sorry for my doubts! **TRIBUS, THREE,** is greater than **QUATTUOR, FOUR,** only today. Because, God's Trinitas, Trinity, three in one, is immeasurably greater than His four Gallants." This speech seems to be directed to God.

This time, he rolls the dice without shaking them up in the cup, throwing them from his bare hands, so that Michael does not have time to take them away.

Gabriel knows that all the angels are watching and even

though he has no objection to what Raphael is doing, he still cannot let their commander lose or be disrespected. So, he uses his shield to bring good news and a victorious outcome. This is not cheating; it would be the equivalent of playing as a team versus individually. The sight of seeing their Gallant win will inspire the Cherubs and Seraphs present.

As Gabriel inconspicuously points the shield at the die, he repeats, "Three, three, three…"

This time Raphael rolls two ***"FOURS."*** Out come the elusive ***"Fours"*** he wanted in his last roll. He loses a second time in a row, but still, what an epic game!

Gabriel is astonished to see the power of his shield did not work on the die, despite having used his Essence to win for Raphael. No doubt Michael had also used his sword to bring forth a fortuitous outcome. Yet, to no avail! This outcome is new to them both...

The Bookkeeper is happier than ever. Yet, I can tell he is still left longing for something much bigger! Raphael loses all his coins. Michael pulls his gambling brother out. Raphael does not protest, this time, but you can see he is disappointed in the outcome, and not very happy.

Michael tries to cheer him up, like a good encouraging father would, with a pat on the back and a rub on his neck.

The Cherubs and Seraphs cheer anyway because their Gallant was bold enough to play the game of the common angel.

Michael encouragingly exclaims, "'Tis a pointless game anyway…"

This whole time Boouky had been closely surrounding the staff of souls that was stuck in the ground, like a pole, admiring it, as I tend to do with all the Essences. Raphael dislodges the staff, securing it back in his firm grip.

Boouky says, "Come back, anytime, unless next time you no longer want to hear me rhyme…"

Then Boouky smiles and waves goodbye. All the Archangels do the same.

Raphael looks back and, cheerfully ambitious, says, "Crede mihi, revertar! Believe me, I will be back!"

Gabriel still looks surprised that his shield did not work on the dice; nonetheless he tries to encourage Raphael, and quickly forgets about the issue.

The Archangels walk away. Gabriel turns around, and makes eye contact with the Bookkeeper who is still, attentively, staring at them. The Bookkeeper has the biggest smile on his face, and winks one of his pink eyes at Gabriel. As the crowd circle closes, Gabriel and the Bookkeeper lose eye contact.

It is now apparent, to me, that for most of these matches, the

Bookkeeper's only interest is to take whatever he can from all his players. After walking away, I could feel, in the pit of my soul, that something strange is at work here. I sense that, one day, we will learn the hard way, that this simple encounter is more sinister and secretive than we could have ever imagined or predicted.

Chapter 9

When Love Means War

Seraphina, the beautiful, is training with a formidable weapon called a *"la-bow,"* which extends out from her pink-flower, notched, pouch. A la-bow is the combination of a bow and arrow and a lasso. She is one of the only ones capable of using this la-bow; it has been fabricated specially for her.

Around her, there are hundreds of other Seraphs, combat training, in an angelic training camp. The camp consists of thousands of immense tents all around a big, central, arena.

There are twenty-five idle Seraphs surrounding Seraphina in this arena; she is in fight-ready position. A big bell rings three times. All at once, they reveal their weapons, and she faces the Seraphs in combat. Her strength and speed are incredible! It is astonishing to note that she is only defending herself and does not attack. She uses defense, not offense, yet still manages to quickly disarm and defeat her many opponents, and in record time.

What is incredible about Seraphina, other than her beauty, is her grace and, moreover, her humility. She does not show-off when she takes down an opponent. She is confident, yet simple, in all that she does.

One by one, with her strength and la-bow, they fall… Once they all fall or surrender, she extends her arm and upper wings, helping lift many of them from the ground.

"Good job," giving advice to each one of them. She tells them kindheartedly exactly what they need to hear to improve their fighting skills.

"Keep your guard up… Practice your stride... Your footwork has improved... You almost had me… Next time we will practice defense..."

Twenty-five more angels are sent unexpectedly to attack Seraphina. She rotates the la-bow, in the air, and rounds up all the Seraphs around her like if they were cattle in a windy tornado. Then she elevates them in the air with ease. Her opponents rise up after falling, acknowledging as if they never stood a chance. They are proud to have been knocked down by the best Seraph warrior, even more proud to be trained by the Magna. Her fallen opponents help each other stand up.

To even further test her senses, she is then ambushed from the surrounding tents. The Seraphs in the tents shoot at her with multiple, specialized, weapons. She destroys the projectiles and shoots some of them back with her la-bow, rebounding them like they were boomerangs. She also, quickly, uses her weapon as if it were a shield.

Now, exiting the tents, they ominously attack her on foot. She is no longer holding back... If you thought she was astounding before, you have no idea what she is capable of now. More and more Seraphs attack her, as if to kill, they also hold nothing back. Some of her students from the previous attacks join in. She cannot fly, but she can reach great heights with her strides and strength, using some of her pupils as steps.

Everything that is thrown at her is used in her favor, turning strength to weakness, just as Michael teaches, engaging the ensuing angels as they approach her. Many of them are tripped and elevated into the air even before they get a chance to reach and face her. Bolts of lightning, force fields, knives, darts, arrows, and many other projectiles continue to be launched towards her, none hitting their mark. The storm of objects are all destroyed or rebounded towards her attackers.

She now uses all six of her wings to defend and attack. Her wings are like additional arms, working in her favor to strike her assailants with precision and poise.

Others, more skilled, fight her in groups of three and four in, hand-to-hand, combat. Some strange and muscly ones, who seem to be trying to fatally wound her, do better than others, but their fates are no different than any other Seraph, and so they are defeated. One by one, they fall to Seraphina's offense and defense.

It is disturbing, to me, when I realize that many of her pupils seem frustrated to leave her unscathed, almost as if this final attack had been really meant to hurt her. Today, she had not expected such a thorough and demanding lesson, from such relentless and restless pupils, yet she was still victorious and up for the challenge.

After she is done training, we see a big smile of fulfillment on her face and on the faces of most of her trainees, who are too exhausted to continue. Her students had mounted this final attack to see the extent of her combat skills. They wanted to test her abilities and assess them for weaknesses, and she did not disappoint. I think it is pretty safe to say that if she has weaknesses, they are almost impossible to find…

She still continues with her words of advice and encouragement, saying, "Good warriors are not born, they are forged in training and by rising to the occasion."

They all say, "Thank you, Magna!" The Seraphs that seemed to want to harm her say this too, but in a less grateful and enthusiastic tone. These ill-omened Seraphs simply fade back into the crowd, disappearing from sight. They seem to be hungry, craving for a lot more than what they just accomplished.

Seraphina does not notice this in their faces, all she notices is Gabriel watching her, and starts to walk towards him.

"Not bad, Magna!" Gabriel says this with a few claps.

Seraphina says, "What do you mean, not bad? You were watching?"

"I might have caught a glimpse here and there..."

Flirting, she says, "Then why did you not jump in and help me? I could have used your help in that last ambush. They almost had me that time!"

"It looked like you had everything under control. Although some of those Seraphs in the last assault seemed pretty ruthless!"

"You were not worried, were you?" Asks Seraphina.

"Of course not! If I had been worried, then I would have

jumped in."

Seraphina says, "Yeah, right! I saw you in the corner of my eye when the lesson started and throughout. You looked pretty worried to me!"

Gabriel says, "I thought you said you had not seen me… Well, ok, maybe I was watching, but I did not want to distract you…"

Seraphina fesses up, saying, "Ok, I admit too. I might have also caught more of a glimpse of you too, here and there. It is good to have an admirer!"

"You know that you have more than just a few admirers, Magna, but I am your biggest, of course." She chuckles…

Gabriel continues saying, "I meant it as a compliment. I mean you are improving. Must be all that teaching and training all day."

Seraphina assures him, saying, "I rarely train anymore! You know how busy I have been with project *Mariam*. My students are the ones that are improving, keeping me on my toes, while I stay stagnant. But even without the training, I will take you and your optimistic shield any day."

Gabriel says, "I doubt that very much… Wishful thinking and optimism is what our Lord teaches with my shield, so I guess you are a great student…

"But, what do you mean you never train anymore? What was that, which I just saw?"

Seraphina honestly answers, "That is what I like to call a warm up session!"

The bond that unites them is very visible. They both flirt and compete with each other in very conspicuous ways.

Gabriel changes the subject, saying, "I have good news for you!"

"Of course you have good news for me! You always do, which is one of the reasons I am so fond of you. They do not call it the shield of good news for nothing."

The lovebirds make their way towards a big tent where all the Seraphs weapons are made. There is a small office at the entrance. They sit down in front of one another. A sort of antique-looking, transparent desk separates them from one other.

There are about twenty, beautiful, Seraphs working on interesting weapons and gadgets inside the tent. One of them, hooded in white, named Adriel, smiles and winks at me, I blush... These Seraphs are weapon makers. Usually all Seraphs are skilled architects and engineers of all sorts, including the assembly of weapons. The weapons that they make are made from the rarest materials, elements that no one has ever experimented with. Seraphina helps put these weapons to the test in the arena, seeing if their inventions can measure up to her skills and she assesses them for strengths and improvements.

Almost all of the Seraphs she defeated in the first round are in the tent. According to her suggestions from the field, notes and sketches were written on draft schematics, they make adjustments and tweaks to both their strategies and prototype weapons. They shorten, they cut, they make sturdier, they add-on, weld, etc... Hustling and bustling throughout the tent, these Seraphs are extremely endowed with the gifts of brainstorming and skilled labor.

There are springs, coils, parts, and many other interesting instruments. They also re-test the weapons, and so there are various moving objects, cylinders, wheels, levers and minerals, all available for them to use. It literally looks like an engineer's paradise, not just a conventional research and development factory.

It is now apparent, both Seraphina and Gabriel are sitting in Seraphina's office. She leaves her la-bow on the desk and Gabriel leaves his shield there also. They both peruse each other's weapons; particularly, Gabriel passes his fingers over the engraved, pink, flower he had left on her la-bow, sheath, in the

Promised, Holy, Land.

Normally, I would have given them privacy but everyone knows of my mandate to accompany the Gallants and today is my day to spend with Gabriel, and it is no coincidence that I am here. I can still tell that the two angels are acting as they normally would and do not let my presence detract from their usual affection for one another.

While she feels the texture of the Essence, Seraphina exclaims, "The shield of good news."

Gabriel says, "Yes, one of four Essences created by our Lord Himself. Your la-bow does not fall short. Seraph craftsmanship has always impressed me."

They both smile, looking into each other's eyes.

Seraphina, continues saying, "Then, we both have that in common because I find your Essence fascinating as well." I suppose she speaks of Gabriel's weapon Essence as well as his person.

"So, what good news does your shield bring me today? Or do you bring it to me all by yourself this time?" She is relentless in her flirting, funny, demeanor.

The Gallant, playfully, stands up and walks towards her. Seraphina looks over her shoulder, as she remains seated.

He says, "It is always both I and my shield who bring the

good news, but first things first..."

Gabriel caresses her wings, turns her around, lifts her up, holds her tight in his grasp and gives her a passionate kiss.

After the kiss, they look at each other very closely, and Seraphina says in a soft voice, "I knew it! Always with good news...

"I am still waiting for you to tell me my story..."

Then she covers her blushing face, with her top wings, as if they were a veil. Her middle wings bring Gabriel closer for a tighter hug.

"Indeed," says Gabriel.

They both smile as they enjoy each other's company. Their relationship is very passionate, but also very innocent. There is a strong bond between them that shall last forever.

Seraphina sits down again. Gabriel, still standing, hugs her from behind. Wrapping his arms around her, he gives her kisses on the shoulder, neck, and a final kiss on the cheek. Her top wings somewhat get in the way of them getting any cozier.

Gabriel says, "To business... How are the arrangements going?"

Seraphina, still seducing, asks, "Have they ever gone bad?"

"No, never!" Says Gabriel. "But I must check, nonetheless. I know I do not need to micro-manage any angel, you least. God trusts all His creations, and therefore so must we, and I do… I really do!"

Seraphina says, "All is being done according to His will. Project *Mariam* is still a contingency plan, right?"

"Yes, project *Mariam* remains a contingency plan, but our Lord does not will something for nothing. This is very important because God has entrusted us with this project. Are Beelzebub's tasks being fulfilled?"

Suddenly Beelzebub walks in, hears his name mentioned, and catches Gabriel with his arms around Seraphina.

Gabriel says, "Aha, Beelzebub, speak of the devil!" There is a pause for dramatic effect…

Beelzebub's face is seen, and he does not understand the pun. He only stands up straight, erecting his back, out of respect, for his superiors. He continues to be annoyed at the childish love between these two. Not just that, but he has the thought of Satan's love for Seraphina ever present in his mind...

… Yes, allow me to explain…

Both Gabriel and Satan are in love with her, but her love is only reciprocal towards Gabriel. Their love and attraction began long ago…

Satan was once in charge of the plans to help create

Seraphina. He had felt lonely and wished God to make him a better, more complementary companion. He wanted more than just the gifts of brotherly friendship that God had given him through the other Archangels. Although he loved the camaraderie shared with his brothers, his spirit always yearned for more, and that yearning seems to continue even now…

Attempting to be like the Almighty, and to have a hand in creation, Satan carefully chose her attributes and talents. He would spend countless hours making sure she was fit to be with an Archangel and help infuse into her many graces. He made sure that all the details leading to Seraphina's creation turned out perfectly.

When the time came, through Raphael, God breathed life into Seraphina like he did to me. She awoke from a deep slumber, perfect for Satan in all aspects. It was one of the happiest days in his life. A day he had been anticipating for very long... As she took her first breaths and steps, all four Gallants surrounded her, attending to their angelic duties. Her beauty impressed them.

Satan had expected her to recognize him as the one who had perfected her. He expected her to be his without hesitation, almost as if she had no choice… Although, she had a tremendous amount of respect for Satan, she was not attracted to him.

Instead, she became attracted to Gabriel and to Michael's art of combat. These are her three loves; God, Gabriel and Combat, and she excels in her dedication to all of them.

Gabriel had shown her kindness and optimism from day one. From the moment of her first steps, Gabriel covered her with his shield and made her feel welcome, holding her hand and accompanying her into existence. Satan always treated Seraphina as she was inferior, whereas Gabriel treated her as an equal, always calling her by the deserved title of, *"Magna."* Satan did not show her much of appeal. In fact, his admiration and near obsession for her had grown out of hand. Even though this obsession was only apparent in his own mind, if others would find out, it would be enough to scandalize.

I suppose he had helped design her to be fit for a Gallant, but did not specify which Gallant. He expected to be loved, but without need for reciprocation, he expected to get something from her, and that type of love is no love at all…

From Satan's point of view, his first attempt at trying to create a being was a major fail, but perhaps with the proper resources and experience, he could do better next time. But I do not understand, why would he want to learn to create? God creates plenty for us and He is the only One that can.

When Satan finally learned that love is a two-sided street, it was too late. His perfect Seraph had disappeared from grasp and his heart broken. I suspect that this heartbreak continues daily. Even so, he never gives up hope. He thinks that the love between Seraphina and Gabriel is a very innocent love, which can be broken, and indeed it is innocent, but this is not a weakness; on the contrary, it is a strength.

Slowly the love between Gabriel and Seraphina grew in the small and ordinary things, acts of kindness and deeds of affection. This is how all love grows... Many other things such as Gabriel's stories of chivalry and heroism also captivated her.

Still, Satan believes that only a forceful love is a love that will last. Much like the love he has for God, which according to him, does not come from his willingness, but is forced into his nature.

He now thinks he should have been more forceful with her from the very beginning, imposing his will, therefore assuring her affection. That is why Seraphina's eyes are brown, a combination of Gabriel's green and Satan's red. She was created to bear Satan's red, yet it seems her eyes have evolved to represent the love she has for Gabriel too. Perhaps one day they will change even more, shifting to blue, to represent her love for my blue, lineage's, art of combat.

At least all of this is the thorough account my brother, Beelzy, has recently entrusted me with. In a conversation we had, he commended this information to me as if it were relevant for my report. He opened up to me because I had also entrusted to him my concern for his friend's sanity, and the irregularity of his most recent actions, especially since they occurred in the territory that Beelzy and his Watchers oversee.

Beelzebub had also noticed some irregularities in his behavior, and thought I could help by documenting this story as an antecedent. It is hard to explain, and I don't expect you to completely understand, but I am not completely sure it was Beelzy who told me this... I know it came from him and I am pretty positive it was his voice, which I heard, but I do not know if that information was meant to be private, or if we truly had that conversation. For me, it was like a dream...

This is what happened... I was with him after our excursion in the Promised Land, and just by staring at him, I may have heard his most intimate thoughts, or was it God who communicated it to me? Or was it Satan? It sounded a lot like Beelzy's voice, though, and I could have sworn his lips were moving while I quietly listened. Although Satan's voice is a little similar to Beelzy's... No matter the source, I know in my heart that this is true! Not just that, but hearing what he had to say to me in the Holy Land, and the fact that he would be so willing to share his friend's intimate conversations, really scared me.

CHAPTER 9

Now it makes sense, this is why there is a certain tension between Beelzy and Gabriel. Beelzy thinks Gabriel did wrong when accepting Seraphina's love. He thinks Gabriel knew well that Seraphina was made for Satan, but the real truth is that he did not. No angel has ever been made for just one Gallant! We are created by God and for God alone. So it was wrong to claim her as his property in the first place.

Even so, Satan never spoke to Gabriel about this. If he had told him of his feelings and purpose, for her, Gabriel, being the selfless Gallant that he is, would have renounced his claim for her love. As a gifted storyteller, Gabriel loves a happy ending more than any Gallant and loves his brothers just as much as he loves himself.

The Lord thought that all of this was important for you to know, otherwise I would have never divulged this extremely sensitive information...

After Beelzy enters the tent, Gabriel releases Seraphina from his arms.

Beelzebub puts his fist to his chest and salutes, "*GALLANT* and *MAGNA*," he says.

"Should you not be doing your task?" Gabriel asks this in a very polite and cheerful manner. He is not demanding or scolding in any way.

Beelzebub, regimentally, says, "My task is taken care of for now, under heavy guard… You saw all our Watchers outside of Eden. The troops are more than capable of protecting and guarding the Garden by themselves."

Gabriel says, "That is great! I am very satisfied! Thank you! If everything is going according to plan, then I think my work here is done...

"I was just telling Seraphina how well you are both serving, and how there is almost no need to manage from my part...

"I shall let you, both, know if anything has changed in our contingency plan. For now, the details of project *Mariam* continue to be developed… Please continue to work on this issue with confidentiality…"

Gabriel exits and Beelzebub continues to stare at him with an ominous look on his face. Beelzy's purpose in being here is to collect more weapons for his legions on earth. He also visits to collect more tools for the workers in project *Mariam.*

In just a few hours, Beelzy can be transported back to earth, having fulfilled the curfew's requirements. Even though he is one of the few exempt from the curfew, he still likes to abide by these simple laws. This way he can also visit his beloved, Dumah, and spend some timeless, time, with her.

CHAPTER 9

The Seraph architects load the mini-transportation arks that were in the tent, and push the containers towards the palace. Beelzy gathers all that he needs from the tent and Seraphina watches closely.

Like a naughty child, he plays around with some of the inventions, poking the contraptions and switching them on and off, testing the applications of these incredible gadgets.

Suddenly, in a corner, he sees an incredible piece of armor that calls to him. When he approaches, with a delicate touch, the armor shoots triangular spikes. The spikes graze the gray cape he is wearing. Delighted, he is even more like a spoiled child who has just found his next present. He just has to have it!

Seraphina approaches, and says, "Spike-armor! Why don't you keep it? With it, you will be impenetrable to almost anything."

No need to say more, Beelzy's is sold. I too can relate to his feeling of excitement.

Seraphina explains, "There are only two armors of this sort. Uriel owns one spike-armor, and now you own the other. Gabriel wanted you to have it, in recognition for all your hard work…

"You will find that it has several other applications. Indeed this armor is my favorite accessory, and you will see that it has been made to fit you perfectly."

He looks at me for approval, to see if it is ok that we both own the spike-armor and I quickly give him the thumbs-up.

He is very thankful and says, "My troops down on earth will love it… I love it!"

Seraphina, jokingly, says, "It quite literally suits you… Even better, it will definitely protect you from any crows that try to attack you."

Beelzy knows that Seraphina is teasing, alluding to the panicking incident with the crow diving near them on earth. In that moment, I can tell he realizes why all the angels are so fond of her, at least I do! Gabriel is a lucky angel because she is beautiful, kind, and wise, all you could ever ask for in a companion. Not that the other angels are any different! In fact, Beelzy's companion, Dumah, shares parallel characteristics to Seraphina. These similarities are what attract Beelzy to her.

Seraphina, warmly, says, "Come back any time! I realize we have not had many occasions to talk, lately, because we are always so busy, but we must find time, especially since we both attend to project *Mariam*!"

Beelzy softens up, enthusiastically, saying, "Yes, yes, you are right, Magna!"

Seraphina says, "I really hope this spike-armor helps you with project *Mariam*! Do not disappear off the face of the earth. It might be tempting to do this now that you have nearly invincible armor, but don't!"

Beelzy, affectionately, says, "I will not! Thank you, Magna!"

He tries on the armor to see how it fits. No need for mirrors in Heaven. He can easily sense the way he looks, and then leaves the tent, and I follow to help him carry his armor. I have always seen Beelzy as a kindred spirit! We have a special connection. Now with matching armor, and him sharing his confidential affairs, about his friend, with me, our bond is even dearer!

When exiting the tent, we realize the outsides have become much more quiet and desolate as if all the Cherubs had been mysteriously called away.

Walking to the camp outskirts, he again feels that deep chill down his spine, that seems to be becoming more common, as if something were calling him, like an attractive homing beacon, a tractor beam. I also feel it! With a mind of it's own, his new spike-armor flashes, lighting up, first scarcely, and then in very fast intervals. He knows that his new armor is trying to tell him something, bring something to his attention, and so, concerned, he looks around in circles…

Reaching their fastest point, the small lights on the armor beep uncontrollably. He turns around, and is quickly approached by Satan who frightens both of us, giving us a jolt. The lights from the armor immediately turn off as if they had been deactivated or mysteriously malfunctioned.

Beelzy says, "It is you, Satan! You s-s-startled me!"

Satan says, "Do not be so nervous, it is just me. Spike-armor, huh! They gave it to you, huh? Say hello to your leash, there goes your freedom!

"It looks like you and Uriel got tans on earth, looking more like each other every day! I like it, beautiful! What are you doing in Heaven though?"

Shivering, Beelzy says, "Leash? Thank you! I am here gathering supplies and materials."

"You will see, one day, what I mean about leash! You left the Watchers with no leadership?"

I can tell that Beelzy is getting somewhat annoyed at people questioning and underestimating his working skills. Bothered, he answers, "They are capable of leading themselves! Those young Cherubs are even more-fit, to lead, than I am. They have learned from the best, you and the Gallants of course."

Satan notices this and wins him back, saying, "No, they have learned from you. Despite what you may believe, there is actually no Cherub more fit to lead the Watchers than you. Their loyalty to you is unequalled! Believe me, I know! I have seen this!"

"But I have learned from a great teacher, you," says the very flattered, Beelzy, returning the praise, with a grin, and proudly displaying his red eyes.

Satan seems to be acting as he usually does, happy but stern.

Beelzy asks, "Where are you headed? What are you doing here, my friend?"

Satan responds, "Nowhere in particular... I just wanted to get a glimpse of the Seraph training camp and see my competition... Scoping out the talent, analyzing its defenses, witnessing failed attempts… You know, the usual commander duties..."

"Surely, they are no competition for you or any of the Gallants, especially with your trident."

Satan says, "You are right, they are no competition to me, I know that now! How is Seraphina doing after the attack?"

Beelzy says, "She is ok… Still in love, but beautiful and hard working as always. She is the one that gave me this new armor. Attack?"

Satan, brusquely and jealously, says, "Beautiful?! I know the way she is, you forget that I made her that way!"

Then, he becomes silent, remembering that I am there, "snooping..." These words of his, help, confirm what I think Beelzy told me about Satan's infatuation with Seraphina.

Beelzy says, "Yes, excuse me… You just missed Gabriel, they were here together and we all met and chatted about project *Mariam*."

Satan, annoyed, says, "Ah yes, this elusive project Mariam. Tell me about it…"

Surprised, Beelzy says, "Perhaps I am not the best one to inform you on this project..."

Satan asks, "Are you not a part of it? Is that not what friends do?"

"Friends do and say many things, and I would love to tell you, but I know just as much as you do, all considering that the confidentiality of this project is extremely important."

I sense that since they are aware of my presence, among them, Beelzy does not budge in divulging more information. I would like to think that he is honorable and would not divulge any trusted information regardless of my attendance.

Satan brings him close and carefully whispers, "This is what you want me to believe?"

A chill runs down his spine. "Y-yes, this is the t-t-truth," Beelzy nervously says.

With a quick breeze, Satan abruptly flies off, not looking very happy. Beelzebub's spike-armor immediately reactivates, lights brightly on. There is no more chilly nervousness overwhelming him. This interaction between the two friends is an interesting one, an interaction that I feel I must better document.

What is of particular interest, and I make a point to write down, is that when Satan spoke to his friend, he made several almost sarcastic remarks that came out of the blue. Some of his questions have no antecedents, questions Beelzy does not even know how to respond to, because he has no idea what Satan is talking about.

Beelzebub is now able to return to earth as he sees the first rainbow shoot off from Heaven with precise punctuality. He hurries to the palace to catch his rainbow.

Chapter 10

Guardian Angels

I must admit, documenting all these events is quite hard. It is much more challenging than I thought it would be… At this point, I feel as though I am being pulled in many directions, somewhat drained, with no evident goal in sight, yet, I continue to serve as best I can...

There is no doubt that the truth is among my words. I am fortunate enough to say that God truly transmits His will through me. The same cannot always be said about some of you who think that God sometimes speaks through you and this is how you justify your miserable acts! I know these are harsh words, but they must be heard, or else what kind of Cherub would I be.

CHAPTER 10

As I am walking, there is a small puddle in my path, right in the middle of the grainy sand, which I try to evade... As I hop over it, I get a glimpse of my reflection and return to the puddle, having noticed a small change in my appearance. I stand there for a little while simply looking at myself from different angles, turning my back, rotating, noticing my wings are a little longer and my complexion has darkened.

All of my changes seem to be stemming from the nibble marks that those ants left on my back in the Garden of Eden. At least that is my only explanation for the changes that are happening. This darkening complexion, perhaps this is the tan that Satan had referred to…

As soon as I notice all of this, my wings twitch and then flap unexpectedly, once, with no control of my own, and I am elevated a little higher than what I am comfortable with. My wings have never done this before and this is somewhat alarming, as with a fright, I come crashing down to the ground, splattering against the sand.

I crawl back to the puddle, once again, glaring at my form to see if it was just my imagination. Wow! I really am no longer as light gray as I once was! My hands, wings, face, armor, and complexion are all different. My grayness could be described as muddier and I confirm this by looking to my Cherub brothers around me and comparing our tones. Nobody notices any of this, but me, not even the flapping of my wings, so perhaps it is just my crazy and vivid imagination…

We are all by the shores of an incredible beach on earth. Turquoise waters surround us, white sand at our feet, a cool breeze on our bodies and the warm sun on our faces.

Some of our brothers are standing on salt flats that extend as far as the eye can see. Tall cacti grow high from the earth. Strong waves come crashing in…

At a distance, two of the Gallants are standing on a podium made of, enormous, stones of a grand scale.

As we approach the hub, there are different sizes of loud drums sounding in all splendor. Trumpet-cellos are also played, almost like a battle cry or a call to action. Harmonious harps are played, not just plucking, but also intricately strumming.

Now that the multitude has gathered, suddenly, the crowd and drums go quiet... The Gallants, Michael and Raphael, have built suspense; they pause in silence for a few shorts seconds. I can tell they are choked up in happiness, one they cannot contain… Then, they begin to speak to the crowd of Cherub soldiers…

Michael, blissful, proclaims, "Thanketh thou f'r gath'ring hither t'day, Cherubim… 'Tis with glee, that I announce on behalf of thy Gallants, that we hast just been giv'n 'rd'rs fr'm our L'rd, God."

Everyone wishes to cheer but they quiet down even more, absorbed in what he has to say.

"Many of thou thought that thy timeth to c'ntribute to creation wouldst nev'r occur, but the timeth hath arriv'd…

"I am proud to proclaim that we art in charge of the new pr'ject, *Guardian*… Humans shall populate this earth, which thoust faithfully k'pt and mend'd. They will be, l'ving beings, much liketh us and much liketh our L'rd, and will reigneth, on earth, o'er all the creatures. They will be almost identical to thou but with a mat'rial body…

"The first human will be named, Adam, and he will be male in gend'r also much liketh, thou, Ch'rubs. The L'rd will createth, this individual, this p'rson, Adam, v'ry soon…

"Thanks to all of thou, humans will nay long'r be defenseless. Each and ev'ry one of thou shall be assign'd to a human. Thou will be assign'd to protect these humans from all dang'rs. The p'rson thou geteth assign'd to, shall be reveal'd individually in a timely mann'r…

"Thou shall helpeth them in spiritual and physical times of need. I sayeth to thou, protecteth and serveth them. They will need thou moo than they will ev'r admiteth!

"Present their pray'rs to God on their behalf. Without thou, they art defenseless! Thinketh of them as if they wast to becometh thy Essences... Just as the Archangels art entrust'd to guard their Essences, so will thou be, with humans, and believe it 'r not, they shall also giveth thou unexpect'd and incredible pow'rs.

"A sword and a shield shall be given to each of thou, today, to be us'd in defense of these creatures... This project entails that many of thou remaineth hither on earth..."

There is a cry of happiness since most of them will be given the privilege of remaining in the world, which they have deeply fallen in love with.

Michael, continues saying, "Many of thou will returneth to Heaven, since the plan is only to create one human, f'r anon, but that plan couldst changeth v'ry quickly." The great majority rejoice and are glad.

Raphael now calls on a name, he says, "Tremo."

A very fit, young, Cherub, with thick-combed hair, that was standing very close to me, comes out from the crowd and walks towards the Gallants, leaving the imprint of his steps in the sand. His chiseled features, parted chin, and noticeable dimples are glistening, gracefully, in the corridor of troops that has opened for him. His, very, blue eyes, much like mine, are a representation of his Cherub lineage. This clearly shows that he is one of Michael's extended pupils, just as I am. My Gallant, friend, has taken many of the angels, literally, under his wing, those who attempt to be just and merciful and wish to excel with the sword or in general combat.

When this Cherub finally reaches the podium, he firmly puts his fist to his chest, saluting with sincere regard and meek simplicity.

Michael proclaims, "Tremo, strong and faithful, young and exp'rienc'd. Thoust been given the hon'r to be the first guardian, f'r the first human, Adam.

"If successful, songs and pray'rs shall be written in celebration f'r thou and thy accomplishments, even in human histr'y. A new mural shall be 'rect'd in the halls of Paradise Palace so that all will knoweth the name of Tremo and the one he shall s'rve, Adam."

There is a pause that is meant for all to cheer and exult Tremo, but I know he does not want it to be so. He believes he has not done anything special to deserve this silent praise. And surely he thinks he has done nothing to prove his worthiness with Adam yet.

He says, "Thank you! No mural is necessary! I do not wish for recognition of any kind, only what is just, your prayers to the

Almighty and your unconditional support shall suffice."

What a display of humility! He wishes to deserve only what is just! He then bows his head.

Michael continues, saying, "Very well… listen closely… Oftentimes, when 'tis necessary, giveth Adam the feeling that he shouldst not doeth this, if it shall harm his body 'r soul, this is not right. And telleth him to be careful! With a few tactful and loving pushes, shove them back on path… Be both just and m'rciful in thy advice…"

Tremo is awarded a special weapon, the *club-shank,* which he attaches to his wrist, and he is also given a distinctive, circular, shield. The club-shank is a weapon that consists of many knives concealed in a big metal club. The knives protrude from the weapon and can fly out, so as to attack many opponents.

The pious silence, throughout, turns to thunderous applause. All the Cherubs are happy, none are jealous. Tremo is respected among his peers more than he knows and deserving of this great privilege.

He simply and gladly returns to his place among the crowd. In the middle, he is singled out and congratulated by his peers, myself included.

Tremo, much like Seraphina for the Seraphs, is one of the best Cherub warriors. He has taken part in the up keeping of

Eden and lead legions, of his own, in training and service. As a part of Michael's lineage, and therefore mine, I personally trained Tremo in all things. I like to take pride in helping form his actions, combat skills, and virtues. Truth is, his success was all due to his perseverance, hard work, and eagerness to learn. I simply fine-tuned him, here or there, encouraged him to do certain things, much of which, I am sure, eventually, he would have corrected himself, and will do the same with Adam. It is I who was lucky to have him as my student and more so as my friend. I have learned much more from him than he has from me.

I will let you in on a secret… It was at my suggestion that I recommended him to become the first Guardian. I told my Gallant, and friend, Michael, that he was ready, and that there was no one more prepared than him. I turned the job down because I felt that someone else, better, deserved this glory. I also felt that, for now, my purpose in serving is better suited elsewhere, specifically in my documenting documentary. I would like to say that I am special and have a higher calling, but all angels, literally, have a higher calling, so I am not that special…

Raphael, the young, takes over the second part of the gathering, and then announces, "Vos enim bene ministraverint gradum, Tremo! You have served well, Tremo! You have lead many legionibus, legions, in training, but remember, this duty is a little different and should not require many, just one, tu, you!

"Gratias agimus tibi propter sacrificium. Thank you for your sacrifice, and may you be an example of faithful service to the Dominus… Also, may we all be reminded of our Dominus's misericordiam, kindness, and the rewards to those who serve Him faithfully…

"Hoc opus est non leviter… This job is not to be taken lightly… When Adam is created, all you Cherubim will be able to view Tremo and Adam as they coexist on terram. This will be part of your disciplina, training, so when the time comes, you can know what to expect from these humana… and learn from Tremo!

"Adam non poterat videre. Adam will not be able to see you, Tremo, but he will feel your presence and the presence of our Dominus… Unfortunately, the material pulcritudines, beauties, which we have kept, will blind these humana to the existence of Deus, God, and His angeli, but it does not mean we are not there. Et erit opus nobis! It does not mean they will not need us…

"Admonere ut Adam tu illic es! Remind Adam that you are there! Diligite homines! Love your humans as our Dominus loves us! Aedificare nexu! Build a connection with them, and you shall both become fortiori, stronger! You shall learn from them as they will learn from you!

"Speak to them on a daily basis, and confirma vinculum, strengthen a bond. If they know what is good for them, they will do the same! Our Dominus shall give them instructions to do so…

"Do not fret if they shall, sometimes, stray from the path. As I have conveyed, simply help them return to it… Ne videant vos! Make yourself seen only under the direst of circumstances…

"Assert your presence with others, but not with your own humana... Your disciplina, training, for this starts hodie, today, but I am sure you realize that it really started long before… When combat training with Michael's gladius, sword, and hopefully you learned something from me too, in your care for animarum, souls, with my virgam, staff of souls."

Many chuckle at the far-fetched and completely untrue possibility that they did not learn anything from Raphael…

Tremo listens closely and so do the rest of us. Some of them even take notes on their golden parchments, mimicking what I do. I can tell that they are anxious to get started in their training.

Michael, resumes saying, "Soon Adam will be creat'd and Tremo shall be the first to followeth. Tremo shall be reb'rn and renew'd on earth…

"Oh, and one last thing… If ye are in peril, doeth not hesitate to calleth upon the, fath'rly, help of our L'rd, and if necessary, He shall sendeth many Ch'rubs to assist thou… This is whence thy exp'rience, Tremo, with leading platoons shall help, and thou shalt be adept to switching from a p'rsonal task to a collective one."

At the same time that Michael speaks, thousands of Seraphs arrive from the sea in many transportation arks. They settle on land, quickly unload bundles of cases, by the soft wave breaks. Since they are the best weapon makers, they are now in the crowd, distributing weapons to the Cherubs.

To have both Cherubs and Seraphs present elevates the atmosphere, tremendously, and our joy is now complete. Many of the Cherubs and Seraphs greet with their partners.

Raphael, continues saying, "From now on you shall be known as, *Custodes, Guardians…* Use your title of Cherubim Custodes with pride. In doing so, Dominus has created a new choir of angeli… When you are in Caelum, Heaven, you shall continue to be Cherubim, but when on terra, at the side of a humana, you shall be Custodes, Guardians…

"Now we will have four choirs of angels in this hierarchy; *Archangeli, Seraphim, Cherubim et Custodibus! The Archangels, the Seraphs, the Cherubs and the Guardians."*

CHAPTER 10

Most of the angels celebrate and are thankful for this great gift of serving God on earth.

"BEGIN ALL TRAINING AND PREPARATIONS!" The Gallants jointly say.

We all cheer, some jump up and down in happiness. In a loud clamor, we begin to say, "PRAISE BE TO GOD! BLESSED BE GOD FOREVER!"

The atmosphere is of high intensity. Some of them proclaim songs such as, "GLORY TO GOD IN THE HIGHEST AND PEACE TO HIS PEOPLE ON EARTH!" We also say, "FOR THE KINGDOM, THE POWER AND THE GLORY ARE HIS NOW AND FOREVER…"

At that moment, my student, Tremo, asks me for advice and I give him the guidance that Michael once gave me, "Continue to be both just and merciful, but above all, be you! Being you, a faithful angel of the Lord, is what got you assigned to this vital position."

I could tell that Tremo was very emotional and probably so overwhelmed with joy, that he did not hear my advice... It is ok; he must have a lot on his mind. After all, he has assumed a great responsibility. Above all, I know he is thankful for this honorable consideration at my recommendation.

However, some Cherubs are confused, much like Satan was when receiving the gift of conscience, because they are unsure of what to do, since for now, Tremo is the only Guardian and everyone must soon return to Heaven. No one is even sure that there will be more than one human, so, will Adam have thousands of Guardians protecting him? Will Tremo be the only Guardian? They are perplexed… No one knows what humans would need protection from.

Some also become mad because a Guardian is like a demotion in the choir hierarchy instead of a promotion. Not just that, but, lower ranking angels are always sent to perform less important tasks. This seems to be extremely disheartening to some of them…

We do not know where these feelings of objection come from, as if someone has instilled them… All they can do is wait and train and their day shall come, perhaps my day, too, shall come... They fail to see that all of God's projects, no matter how small, are vitally important! Whoever exults himself shall be humbled; and whoever humbles himself shall be exalted.

Gabriel arrives at the location, descending from the sky, as the celebrations and objections continue. Gabriel senses the objections, with his shield, and is a little taken aback about it. Since most are joyful, he simply let's their fellow Cherubs deal with any concerns they might have, hoping that their joy and optimism will be contagious.

I make my way through the crowds, up to the podium to thank my Gallants for heeding my advice about selecting Tremo to be the primal Guardian. I am right in time to listen in on their conversation…

Gabe speaks to his Gallant brothers and concerned asks, "Do you think Tremo will get the job done?"

Michael responds, "I hast nay doubts that he will… I had previously off'r'd the job to Uriel, as we all agreed, but Uriel tells me that thither is nay one bett'r than Tremo f'r the position. The pupil hath sup'rsed'd his o'erly humble mast'r train'r in ev'rything."

They look at me for approval, and I simply bow my head in agreement. That is all they needed from me because I know they trust my judgment.

"Good," says Gabriel now taking control of the post meeting. Then he says, "Our Lord might have us assign more than just Tremo to the first human. If need be, Beelzebub's Watchers are ready to step in… With so many Cherubs willing to serve and awaiting instructions, our Lord may want us to assure the man's protection, especially until Tremo is properly trained and accustomed to his duties…

"These reinforcements are just in case… It is simply a precautionary effort… I think we should be fine, since the

Watchers are already stationed at Eden's gates. They will be fast to respond if anything should occur... Better safe than sorry, though! We shall see…

"I will also speak with Tremo personally so that he is informed of his importance in the enforcing and establishment of project *Mariam*... His service shall be key in keeping *Mariam* as a contingency plan… Believe me! We do not want to activate *Mariam,* just as a very last resort!

"Michael, this, your project, Guardian, shall be closely linked to project *Mariam*, just as all God's projects are intently interconnected."

Raphael updates Gabriel, saying, "Adam, nomen eius. You should know that the first human's name will be Adam… We picked earlier when you were attending to project *Mariam*. The venatus, game of dice, got me so distracted!" He smiles and joyfully winks at Gabo.

Gabriel, happily, says, "I love it! How great the dignity of the human soul, since each one, from his birth, shall have an angel commissioned to guard it… and if he fails to be protected, he shall have a contingency plan to redeem it, Hail *Mariam*! Full of Grace! The Lord is with you!"

Chapter 11

Serious Doubts and Loaded Questions

Legions of Cherubs are training with our new swords and shields. The perhaps future Guardians are by the beach where their assignment was given to them. Some fight in the water, some on the shore and some fight in between water and land in the shallow wading waters, which poses a more demanding challenge. Their footsteps splash water, their movements allow sand to rise… Seaweeds of all sorts surround the area, entangling around their ankles, along with the salty smell of the ocean. Waves and their smashing sound, come tumbling in and splash our brothers with a significant force, pulling some into the water with its tides and currents. They use their environment to their advantage, hiding and racing through palm tress, digging holes of concealment, and flinging cacti spines. Some, more skilled, even walk on water; battling in and above the waves. The flocks of pelagic birds, flying above, cannot help but circle around the area to witness us curious angels.

Even Beelzy is combat training with the chiseled, Tremo. He spars so to pass on invaluable guidance to the future Guardian, having been more accustomed to the earth's erratic environment, especially the one in Eden where Tremo will live; it is the same instruction he continually passes on to the decorated Watchers platoon. Due to his extremely agile movements, he is sweaty and drenched with the infringing sand that invades all the crevices of his feet. He continues to tan in the bright sun as he shows the incredible activation and capabilities of his intricate spike-armor.

Now the Cherub stops his sparring, and removes his helmet, as he sees Satan land, and politely says, "Hello, my friend."

As always he is happy to see his friend arrive... They embrace with their usual big, strong, hug and warm pats on the back. They walk towards a rest area and sit at a table of nature.

I happen to be training on top of the salt flats, near the dry, quick-sand, which gives an additional level of intricacy to my training as well. Naturally my inquisitive nature leads me to stop my lesson and approach them, especially after sensing my friend Tremo's summoning to draw near and replace Beelzebub as his sparing partner, this is appropriate, since I can also give him advice of many sorts and he is already used to working with me. But Beelzy should not be leaving Tremo alone! He should be at his side, with no rest, further training him, having also been tasked with being Tremo's earthly consultant. More so, Satan should not be distracting him and he knows this.

Simply walking towards Tremo is a much-needed time of rest for me. While I make my way, I can barely hear what they say, but it is enough to properly ascertain their words.

Satan asks, "Your projects are going well?"

Beelzy responds, "Yes, they are! Thank you, kindly, for your concern..."

"Good," says Satan. Then he continues asking, "Do you really think God will keep you on earth to become a Guardian, when you are supposed to be protecting Eden's gates?"

Beelzy says, "This, I do not know, anything is possible, and so I continue my training... I must be prepared for anything!"

Wishing to be faithful to the Lord's commands, he longs fervently to return where he should be, at Tremo's side.

Satan engages him back, with flattery, saying, "Your duty to guard the gates of Eden seems to be attended to in full... When we visited not too long ago, I was very impressed with the security our Lord will give these humans. The Watchers at their disposal! And now you are training Guardians as well? Tremo, will be the first, huh?"

Beelzy, noticing something odd in his buddy, asks, "Are you ok, Gallant? We have already talked about this outside the Seraph training camp just a while ago... Do you remember? You seem a little different, as if peace has left you…"

"I am fine, better than ever! I remember we talked about this, but I am just being extra diligent… Nothing has changed in me, but everything has changed in the universe."

Beelzy says, "Like what?"

"Cherubs will turn into Guardian angels... An angel to serve each human…"

Beelzy reassuringly says, "Well, they are not really serving humans, they still serve God."

Satan, distraught, says, "You really believe that? You are blinded, my friend! Does it not bother you that these humans will have us as servants and even more so that they will have well trained legions at their disposal? They themselves will already be a dangerous and war-driven race. What if they choose to attack Heaven?"

"That is impossible, they have their kingdom and we have ours! Theirs is material and ours is spiritual... Plus, those are not our orders or predicament to worry about," says Beelzy.

CHAPTER 11

Satan says, "Was it not you a few moments ago that just told me that anything is possible? They will have a soul and a body! We only have a soul! So they will already have more than us! And, yes, we must worry!

"Humans will have access to our kingdom, just like we have access to theirs… If they have admittance to Heaven, then they could attack us!"

Then Satan abruptly switches to his topic of interest, saying, "I now know everything about project human, but what about your other project with Gabriel? You never tell me about this! Do you now know more? Or is it still, "confidential?" You have been fortunate enough to be a part of this, "important" project, for I am not… As a Cherub you seem to be more informed than I am as a Gallant…

"And tell me… why is it that you are the only Cherub involved? Are you not? What a coincidence that, you, my best friend, are involved and informed in this project but I am not!"

Beelzebub is surprised to see how abruptly Satan changes the subject. He still notices a change in him, as if something were wrong. Beelzy again thinks to himself, "Did I not have this same conversation with him just a while ago?"

Beelzy begins to have very obsessive, disturbing, and compulsive thoughts… The same instance of déjà vu, which occurred on earth, happens to him again. This phenomena has also warped into a special longing, as if being summoned to something... It is a sense of lure to a beacon, the same feeling of attraction that a moth has to a light, like destiny, but he does not know where this deep call comes from… I regrettably feel it too! I feel everything just as he feels it, in trembling-worthy anguish!

Beelzy fights against this longing, and shaking his head, he says, "I know what you know about *Mariam*, my friend, even Gabriel does not know more!"

Satan, not worried about his friend's obvious ailments, affected by this summoning beacon, argues, "I think all three of you know a lot more and you have been forbidden to tell me!"

Now more drained, Beelzy rebuttals, "It is confidential, but not from the Gallants. Just ask our Lord! I cannot tell you what I do not know, and I cannot tell you what I was told not to tell, so we have reached a stalemate…"

Satan looks disappointed as if he has lost trust in God and Beelzy. He leaves silence and awkwardness. Silence is the oldest, most effective, tactic for retrieving information.

During this time, noticing Beelzy is as dark as I am, my doubts about my darkening appearance and self are left somewhat at ease. Our shades of gray seem to match and so perhaps it was just my imagination to be darkening.

It is not good to darken because we are beings of light, drawn to the sprightly and not the obscure, but the Archangel's black complexions are the only exception to the norm.

Like mine, Beelzebub's wings also seem a little longer, which gives me an additional factor to think about... I second-guess myself, shrewdly discerning… that it could also be that both of us have morphed, but did he notice it too? I know that my condition is not a simple tan, and I know I am not a Gallant, so why do I darken?

The silent awkwardness, between them, comes to an end… To counter the discomfiture of this conversation, Beelzebub, flustered, repeats, "I am not supposed to discuss this with anyone… Our Lord has made a request that the details be confidential, but since you are His Gallant, I am sure He will not hesitate to tell you if you ask Him… I must do what the Lord has commanded of me!"

Satan says, "You have already said this to me, Beelzy… This is all I get? These are not the answers I wish to hear! Did the Lord command this project to be confidential, or did Gabriel command this?"

Beelzy says, "Well, the Lord has commanded this, but as always, Gabriel conferred the orders to Magna and myself."

Elevating his voice, Satan says, "That is the issue! The Lord has told me nothing, but everyone else seems to be informed… I do not like this! This is the change that you see in me...

"I have a feeling that Gabriel is doing what he wants and moving this project Mariam, forward, according to his will, and not God's…

"You were given your spike-armor by Serapina but at Gabriel's suggestion, correct?" Insinuating that the spike-armor is some kind of bribe or blinding object so that Beelzy does not question or find out what is really going on.

Beelzy, now a little more calm, but still anxious, says, "That is impossible! That could never happen! All the Gallants and all the angels always act according to God's will!"

Satan says in a threatening manner, "Do not school me on how to be a Gallant or an angel, for I am the original one! There are always ways of disobeying!"

Then he adds, "Another example of Gabriel's "artistic freedom" is the "invention" of this "curfew…"

"Tell me, why are you and the Watchers only allowed to break the curfew? God never told me about any curfew! What a stupid idea! Gabriel announces everything and we just have to believe him, blindly?"

Satan grows even madder and says, "Tell me what you know! If you tell me, there will be no issue since I am your Gallant and more so, your friend."

Beelzy insistently says, "But ask our Lord, He shall tell you! He always does… Please, do not make me compromise my service."

Satan comfortingly says, "I do not wish to disturb our Lord asking Him questions about other projects. These are busy times... All I seek is a little information…

"I have a feeling that there is a reason why He did not tell me about project Mariam. But what would that reason be?

"If it makes you feel better, tell me what you know first and then I promise to ask our Lord. This way, I can confirm or deny your misconceptions on Mariam, and we will both become better informed, enlightened."

Pointing his trident at his friend, Satan uses it to persuade, insisting and nicely, saying, "Come on! Tell me, Beelzy! You can trust me!"

Finally, after fighting an uphill battle to control his alarming urges, Beelzy caves in and tells Satan the little information that he knows about project *Mariam*, blabbing, "All I know, and all I can tell you, is that our Lord has commanded that this project be a back up plan... It is a contingency plan…"

Before Beelzebub can continue explaining, Satan asks, "A backup for what? A contingency for what?"

Beelzebub, irritated with the stagnant back and forth, says, "Do you disagree with our Lord's will? Why all of the sudden do you have such a big thirst for knowledge, when you always have all the knowledge in the universe at your disposal?

"You know all these answers! Yet, you still ask me for a report. It is as though you ask me as to catch me in a lie, and I do not like that!"

Satan, full of frustration, says, "Please, just continue! Contingency plan for what?"

Beelzy is again pierced with unexplainable pain... As if to be relieved from the mounting pressure, he continues, spilling the beans, saying, "*Mariam* is supposedly a contingency plan for project human...

"After the creation of A-Adam, our Lord has sensed that many un-unforeseen things might happen, and He might have to protect the h-humans."

"Protect them from what? Speak clearly! Is that why your legions are stationed outside of Eden? Why would they need the Watchers to protect their kingdom? Why would they need Guardians to protect them? Why would they need a contingency plan to protect their actions?

"If you say that humans cannot invade us, then why would they need an army's protection? Even though they are war-driven, surely the humans would not attack themselves! That would be like angels hatefully fighting among one another, a rebellion, a civil war! Just as God always says, ***"A house divided amongst itself cannot stand."***

"You have got it all wrong, my Gallant, I did not say that *Mariam* will protect them from their actions, how did you know that?

"But more than protection, we are to be their companions and so is *Mariam*… No one journeys alone and no one should think that they are alone. Just as He is here for you and so am I!"

"Raphael clearly said that they would need protection… He wants Cherubs to protect these people, and steer them on the right path, what path is that?

"And what is this conscience he gave me? The Creator told me that with conscience, I would help these humans pick and choose the right thing, yet have no control over them!

"My project is the same thing as being a Guardian! What is so special in that? It seems to me that these Guardians will be able to control their humans' actions, which is more than what I will be able to do...

"Should, I too, Satan, Archangel, accept silently a major demotion in rank and status? Am I nothing more than a Guardian now? Seriously! What is so unique about the project conscience He has given me?

"Yet, He refuses my Gallant proposal of possession! Slash what I just said about being demoted to a Guardian! I shall be even lower than a Guardian! And all of this God plans to give me under the guise of His "generosity."

"What do you call the choir that is lower than a Guardian? Oh… I forgot… There is none! You never know, maybe the lowest choir will be called *Satanists* from now on…

"I am stuck with this preposterous project conscience of mine, not being able to control any angels, while Gabriel is on earth prestigiously commanding the highest ranking Seraphs. Even you, Beelzy, have the exalted Watchers to lead and follow your orders. I would do anything to control these mighty warriors! ANYTHING!

"I keep getting the short end of the stick, even with the presence of my color, red, in the world, or should I say, lack thereof!"

Beelzy says, "Wow! Those are some pretty serious doubts and loaded questions… You are thinking very low of yourself! Too low, my Gallant!

"You have seen the respect the Watchers have for you, Satan! They would drop it all to follow their Archangel…

"Yes, the Watchers are outside of Eden for the reason you

stated, but for many others as well. They are also there to support and provide aid to our Cherub and Seraph workers on earth; anything they might require. What we will protect these humans from, I cannot tell you…"

Satan, fretful, says, "I grow more uneasy about projects, human, Guardian, Mariam, and even my own. You do not see what I see… I have been given a gift... I only fear that the gift of conscience God has given me only binds me closer to Him instead of setting me free...

"It is as though He does not trust me and is spying on me through conscience. Our Lord told me it is a direct connection with Him… Perhaps this is also why you were given your spike-armor, my friend, so to keep tabs on you too… as if Uriel were not already enough!"

Wow! This is what he thinks of me, as a nuisance! He presses on about the spike-armor, saying, "If I were you, I would get rid of that spike-armor and throw it away as far as I could, unless you want to be spied and controlled by Gabriel…

"I got rid of my real conscience long ago! The one I was recently given, was nothing but a weak recharge; a powerless endowment that has served it's purpose to refuel my trident…"

Beelzebub thinks about it and he gives me something to think about too… He remembers that after he was given his spike-armor at Seraphina's tent, that is when he began to have the longing and sense of attraction to something, this unexplainable but compelling urge, like a chilling, homing beacon. Not just that, but the lights on the armor had lit up blinking, when he began to sense this yearning. Maybe my armor would have done the same if I had been wearing it, but I seldom use it anyway. Perhaps Satan was right about his armor and its control over us, but still Beelzy does not come to any final decision on what he will do with it, and neither do I.

Suddenly he once again begins to feel the overpowering choking, and weight of this mysterious, burdensome call. This time it is stronger than usual, the lights of the armor, once again, flash at faster intervals…

He quickly, but temporarily, removes his spike-armor to see if Satan's theories are right, gasping for air as if in panic and with crushing anxiety, but he feels no difference, nothing has changed without his celestial armor… In fact, the pain now severely burns his being and the sense of confinement is even worse.

To keep his mind off of his pain, Satan unsheathes his trident and begins to playfully attack his friend with some strikes straight to the armor, almost as if to destroy it or dent it, adding undue stress to his friend, saying, "Now I shall see if your

Guardian training is up to par."

Is it as though he is testing it for weaknesses, but covering his attacks under the guise of "training."

The excitement of combat momentarily does its job, refocusing the feeling of anxiety, to a rush of adrenaline, leaving the disturbing feelings out of sight and mind for slight moments.

His trident collides almost abusively with Beelzebub's sword and shield, but more so with the armor, which is where most of the blows land. Beelzy sees it, innocently, as a thrilling game, meant to improve his skills. I am uncertain if Satan sees this in the same way. All I can tell is that most of the spike-armor remains off, just as Satan wants it to be, but luckily the armor and Beelzy are resilient enough not to suffer any damage.

And I notice, one more thing; that Satan occasionally steps on the spike-armor's breastplate, which Beelzy has taken off, almost as if trying to bury it under the sand with the weight of his stomping. He seems determined to rid his friend of his spike-armor or at least damage it enough. All this he does, faking as though he is using the breastplate as a stepping-stone or a tool of attack, when really he seems to want to destroy it. But nothing, he does, seems to even scratch it, and Beelzebub keeps digging it up, in the heat of combat, with his sword and shield.

At the end of this very short lesson, Satan flips over his

friend and shoots a bolt of red light to his back. The char that is left on Beelzy's back further darkens his complexion, as faint smoke glistens off his aspect.

Now it is clear, he was actually better with his armor than without it. Furthermore, an inexplicable force seems to want to pull his armor off like a magnet. This invisible power places obstacles to him re-clothing.

With no help from Satan, he barely manages to put it back on, fighting with every inch of his being's strength. I know he feels significantly better with it on; even I feel better when he puts it on! It masks the common bond of pain that we share. He puts up a convincing front as if he is not struggling at all, but I can feel his potent aches.

The skeptic, Beelzy, is still given some suspicious food for thought about the alleged two-sided nature of his, spike-armor, gift, but still doubts that Gabriel, Seraphina, or God could do such a, two faced, thing, and so, he ultimately remains attired in his activated armor.

For a moment he had felt somewhat better without the armor, but he is smart, knowing that it was the temporary adrenaline rush and thrill of the sparring lesson, which abated his feelings of ailment.

Satan had hoped that the sparing session would keep his

mind off of their previous conversation, making him forget the serious issues at hand, but since questions still remain, so does the dialog. There has been a question running fervently in Beelzy's mind, even during the attack, and so, he exclaims tenderly, "Why would He spy on you with conscience? Why would he spy on me with my spike-armor? I am of no particular importance! He knows you better than you know yourself. He knows all of us better than we know ourselves, without having to spy on us…

"This is preposterous! I do not understand! What is it that you see? What is it that bothers you? Tell me, I can help you! I have never seen you doubting like this before. I have never seen anyone or anything like this before… It is concerning me!"

An unrecognizable personality of Satan's, creepily says, "I have tried to get the Watchers to follow me in the past, but it didn't work! Mind my words! You are very important!"

Beelzebub does not understand what he refers to, and neither do I. Now I am back at Tremo's side, and distracted by all of this, I begin to spar with my pupil. In a way I am no better than Beelzy because at this moment Tremo deserves our full attention. Tremo notices how distracted I am, and understands that it is for a reason, so he takes it easy on me, so that I can turn my head and listen, and for this I am thankful!

Satan then pauses, takes a few deep breaths and asks, "I can trust you, right, Beelzy?"

"YES, OF COURSE," Beelzy loudly answers. Somewhat offended by his friend's lack of confidence in him.

Satan says, "You are my friend, are you not?"

"I am your best friend!"

There is a pause, Satan thinks about remaining silent, but then bursts into discontent as he says, "These humans will be given their own realm of paradise in Eden, and in this Paradise, they will be their own gods. You have seen how beautiful Eden is! Did you know that they will be able to fly? And I will not be the one to teach them!

"They will have, free will, leniency, to do whatever they want… They will be immortal just like us. Even their souls will be immortal if they are killed. If we are killed, our soul perishes, but theirs does not. We simply cease to exist and go into oblivion, while they continue to thrive…

"These people will be given their own Guardians to serve and protect them! Humans will have a choice to serve or not to serve the Almighty… We have no such choice!

"The Holy Spirit will live inside of them… Am I the only one who sees madness in this? Everything will be allotted to them, and for what purpose? Those are just my problems with project human, which I know everything about... Imagine the reservations I have with Mariam, which I know nothing about!

"Do not even get me started on the humans they will call *Priests*. They will have control over the spiritual, over Heaven, over us.... I SPIT ON THEM! Have I left anything out? I think not!"

Beelzebub is awestruck and now it is his friend's words, which momentarily bring him tortuous pain. To give peace back to Satan, stuttering, he slowly says, "B-B-B-But the humans will not have the s-s-s-same intelligence as us. They will not b-be as b-b-b-beautiful as we are… You should not com-com-compare yourself to anyone S-S-S-Satan. No one is above you, except for G-G-God!"

Satan picking up the pace, says, "That is just the thing... These humans will be superior to all of us, even to myself, and all the Gallants put together…

"Yes, they will have ways of gaining knowledge, and yes, they will be beautiful, do not doubt it!

"They will be made in image and likeness of our Creator, and able to procreate, to have children of their own. Their children will be given a soul and a body. This combination of body and soul is much more powerful than an Essence and a soul or a soul by itself...

"Can you imagine your love for Dumah culminating into an offspring of your same soul, who would continue your legacy? Just as the Holy Spirit comes from the love between the Father and the Son! Procreation shall essentially put the power of creation in their hands. They will be like Gods!

"Their scientists will defy God by creating life in test tubes and God will still deign to give these creatures a soul. Why doesn't He give the power of creation to His Gallants? To me? You saw how the creation of Seraphina backfired on me… Even after all I did for her…

"So many problems! Imagine having an arsenal of weapons throughout time that kill both soul and body. This is what they will have! This is what they will use against us, outnumbering the Gallants in the billions. If you do not see this, I must be going crazy!"

Beelzy's red eyes are opened to many of the issues Satan has revealed to him. He takes them into consideration, but says nothing about them, sweating, still not finding them as perturbing as his friend does, and he still does not know where his pain arises.

Satan's emotional exhaustion is also at a high. Realizing that he was panting, and breathing extremely loud, drawing the attention of the Cherubs, to himself, he stops, managing to somewhat keep his composure. Before this, it seemed as though the air they were both breathing was toxic, and how could this be since the breeze could not be fresher, here by the ocean.

After giving the speech, of defiance, to Beelzy, he slowly regains his composure and calmly says, "I will ask one more time… Please pick your words wisely… Depending on what you answer next, I have a very important proposition for you..."

Beelzy is interested in what he has to say...

Satan calmly says, "What else do you know about this project Mariam?"

I know what his strategy is... Since he has already taken some information, he probes for more. Since he has made himself vulnerable with his complaints about God's projects, he thinks maybe Beelzy will do the same, disclosing all there is to know about project *Mariam*. They say persistence and determination are omnipotent.

This tactic backfires because Beelzy does not budge any further, waking from a trance and he repeats what is already known.

"I---DO---NOT---KNOW---A-NY-THING---ELSE," he says shouting militarily and in syllables. "I guess I am like you… They keep me in the dark, but not on purpose. I do not think Gabriel or Magna know much of the project either. I think they know as much as you know... SIR!"

Satan angrily says, "HOW COULD THEY NOT KNOW?! I guess you do not want to hear my proposition, Beelzebub! Your loss!"

"I do want to hear your proposal, but not at the cost of my integrity. Gabriel and Seraphina both follow orders just like you do. It does not necessarily mean they know the purpose. How can anyone attempt to fathom the transcendence of the Almighty's plans, of His will?" said Beelzy wisely.

The master of persuasion says, "I CAN FATHOM! No! The answer you gave me was not what I wanted to hear, so I cannot tell you about my plans to reassign you..."

This has peaked Beelzy's attention, the pain is no more, he desperately says, "Please, tell me!"

"Why should I tell you, if you do not want to tell me," claims Satan.

"Ok, ok, ask me another question! Give me another chance!"

"Ok, then… what about the Promised Land? The headquarters of project Mariam?" Asked Satan.

Beelzy is surprised that he knows about this and that he keeps asking questions that he is not allowed to divulge the answers to. However, he does not know that Satan followed us to Israel, and so he says, "My role is to keep the gates of earthly

Eden and the Promised Land safe…

"The only way of reaching the Promised Land is by special rainbow, from the Garden of Eden. This is the only point of access…

"You have already probed enough! I have already disclosed enough! Now tell me your proposal!"

Satan says, "Like I said, I would like to reassign you and the Watchers. So that you do not suffer the agony of being demoted to the status of Guardians. For you, my friend, there would be a special promotion in line… General, Commander…"

Then, thinking it through, he retracts his statement, indecisively saying, "Actually, you know what? Let me run this by God and I will let you know…"

Beelzy, still excited by the possibility of an elevation, simply says, "Ok…" Then, he asks, "What do you plan on doing with all of the information I have given you, Gallant?"

Chapter 12

Off to Ignite His Flame

Satan begins to think... He then says, "I do not know what I will do, but something must be done..."

Beelzebub says, "If you do not wish to ask our Lord or Gabriel, then ask Seraphina. I know how fond of her you are. This will be a good opportunity to find commonalities, just like you always wanted."

Satan thinks about it, he knows Beelzy is right. He heeds the advice to ask Seraphina what she knows, and so he flies off to meet with her...

Since I cannot follow him, I ask the Lord to allow me to see what I cannot witness. I repeat those treasured words of mine, "Lord, that I may see. Lord, that I may be docile," and so, lucid images and insights begin to appear in my mind.

CHAPTER 12

Flying through the sky, he rehearses out loud what he will say, "Hello, Seraphina…" Satan must be as charming as ever, but find commonalities, just as his friend had suggested. In his mind, much is riding on this get-together and for once, he seems to be nervous…

Seraphina is in her tent, sitting at her desk. She looks concentrated in her activities, and speaks to herself much like Satan just did in the sky, as though repeating instructions in order to learn them. They are more similar than I imagined and now I know why, because he must have infused in her many of his own traits.

Satan enters the tent, opening the cloth door and ducking a little. Seraphina stands out of respect, like a soldier does when a General enters a room.

She says very cordially, "Greetings, Gallants," as she bows slightly.

"Call me, Satan... Please, sit." He says this in a casual way, as if wanting her to be comfortable with him.

Seraphina does as she is told and slowly sits. She then quietly begins to wonder why he is there, as quiet engulfs the scene...

It is interesting to note that Seraphina has always known that Satan has feelings for her, which is why their interactions are always interesting. Although he knows that she has already picked Gabriel, I can tell Satan is relentless in his pursuit. He thinks that perhaps the love and respect that she has for him as a Gallant, can transform into the love of a companion… But now it is as though he is giving her, and them, a second chance. He wishes to place more trust in her hands, hoping she will do the same with him... a desperate act of faith.

He knows why Seraphina has chosen Gabriel over himself, because Gabriel has always treated Seraphina as an equal and as a priority. For Gabriel, it does not matter that she is a Seraph, and he is an Archangel. Rank does not matter. In Gabriel's eyes they are both equal.

Satan acts oppositely, thinking of himself as the priority, and never as her equal. Even though Satan knows all of this, why she is not his, I can tell he still refuses to treat her as an equal. He even refuses to call her by her well-deserved title of, *Magna* and handles himself with arrogance.

The Gallant walks slowly around the desk much like Gabriel did when they met previously. He never sits down, busy, pondering his words, looking at the gadgets around the room. Then he impolitely asks the other Seraphs, present in the room, to leave and give them some privacy. In fact, it is not a request, it is a demand!

CHAPTER 12

After the Seraphs exit, looking at the pink flower on her la-bow sheath, he says, "You have been working with Gabriel quite closely on project Mariam... Spending time together?"

"Yes, Gallant."

He sternly insists, "Call me, Satan, please!"

Seraphina, uncomfortably says, "Yes, Satan."

He nods his head as if he did not mind that both her and Gabriel were spending time together. But this looks like it actually bothers him tremendously.

She continues to wonder why Satan is there. He detects this wonder in her eyes, and so quickly goes to the point, saying, "God has sent me to help on project Mariam, so here I am…"

He will not denigrate himself by directly asking about the project. From his view, it would be embarrassing for an Archangel to consult with a Seraph, especially on any of the major projects.

She looks confused, and taken aback, because Gabriel would have told her if he had been sent to assist…

"Wonderful, but Gabriel did not tell me of any extra help… I heard that you have already been given your own project..."

It bothers him enormously that she knows about his project, yet he knows noting about hers. What is worse is that there is no doubt that she knows through Gabriel, and really Gabriel has no need to disclose to others anything that occurs inside the Archangels' inner circle.

He shakes his head from side to side, and says, "Gabriel, Gabriel, Gabriel, always forgetting his tasks, always forgetting his place… Obviously he tells you everything, but forget about what Gabriel said. Right now it is, I, Satan, the first Gallant, who asks you."

He then reflectively and randomly adds, "Don't you know that all Gabriel cares about now is Mariam? He loves her now, not you! She has replaced that spot in his heart. Think about it…

"How much does he talk about her? Since he was assigned to it, how much time has he spent working on the project?

"He no longer cares for you… And you know what this project is about, don't you? A human woman, very much like you…

"Since you are the Magna, Seraph, warrior, Gabriel is just using you for your influence and respect among the angels of your choir… He has been so busy with Mariam! I know you feel neglected and that what I say is true…

"I, on the other hand, deeply care about you; about your well being, and regardless of how you feel for me, I know you better than anyone. There is a lot you do not know about me, though, about us, what we could have been… What we could still be!"

She is not entirely buying what he has to say, but at the same time, these words still affect her. At this point, she is tremendously nervous. Her personal space is being completely invaded. She can almost smell him.

In a bold move, with her proximity to his trident of persuasion, Satan begins to make an attempt to connect spiritually with Seraphina. Since he has her undivided attention, it would be an even bigger bonus for her to kiss him. He is now very close to her face, drawing nearer as his trident glows with mighty power.

Roughly grabbing her by the neck, with his hand, he reaches in for a kiss. It is almost as if she were in a trance or under a spell. What is more surprising is that I see a change in Seraphina, as if for a moment she were inclined to kiss him willingly. Their lips are very close now, as they glare at each other with a passionate stare…

Unexpectedly, she quickly uses her la-bow to grab Satan by the neck, like a noose. He is caught by surprise, and choking on the angelic rope for a few seconds.

She firmly says, "I think it is you that forgets his place! And trying to use your trident on me? Shame on you, Satan! You should know better than that! What has happened to you? I admire you, but your actions now lead me to pity you."

In a matter of a second, Satan quickly responds to this attack by pinning her neck against the wall with his trident. Her neck is pressed against the wall between the tridents prongs. She moans and groans trying to get free. The Gallant aggressor has managed to release himself from Seraphina's la-bow, he first reverts what he once told her, saying, "CALL ME, GALLANT! INSOLENT SERAPH! You dare to perpetrate this confrontation against your Gallant! What? You do not love or admire me anymore? Love Gabriel, and only him, do you? After all I have done for you!"

Seraphina does not respond, only moaning and groaning, and continues to struggle to free herself, like a fish out of water, she yells, "LET ME GO!"

The angels that were sent outside at the beginning of the meeting hear the commotion and they summon Gabriel for help, who luckily, is close by.

Gabriel drops what he is doing. He storms in, to see what is the fuss, and realizing what is happening, yells, "LET HER GO!"

The couple is one in their sentiment.

Satan, shrugging his shoulders, says, "Fine!" And so he takes his trident out from the wall.

Seraphina takes a breath of air and grabs her neck, as she falls to her knees. The trident had been slowly draining her energy, sucking her life force and storing it in its core. This is why she looks so drained. How odd! An Essence should never drain; just emit its own power.

In less than a split second, Satan throws his trident like a spear towards Gabriel. Gabriel tried to take out his shield to block the throw, but he was too slow. The trident actually ricochets off of the shield, at an angle, but still hits the desired location, doing the exact same thing he just did to Seraphina, elevating and pinning Gabriel to the wall by his neck. The shield Essence automatically appears on Gabriel's back to cushion his impact against the wall; it was not too slow to react to that.

Satan, hatefully, says, "Mind your own projects, Gallant!"

Now it is Gabriel who hangs from the wall struggling to get free. The shield that had just cushioned his impact against the wall, now automatically zooms up from his back to try and free Gabriel from his captivity, knocking into the trident prongs like a ramming bull, but with no luck of freeing himself.

When Satan quickly runs towards him, as if he was going to continue his attack, Gabriel covers himself with his arms. Satan punches him in the stomach with astonishing force. The jittery shield, that was on his back, trying to free him, drops to the ground, clunking. Gabriel now breathes with extreme difficulty...

As Satan takes out the trident from the wall, Gabriel also falls to the ground, next to his shield, and he whispers into his brothers' ear in a commanding and threatening voice, saying, "Mind your own business, Mariam lover!"

Seraphina, wounded and winded tries to reach for her la-bow so she can help her love. The la-bow lies on the ground close to Satan's feet. Satan notices her struggle, and quickly kicks her la-bow far away so she cannot retrieve it.

Gabriel looks troubled that Satan knows about *Mariam*, but he becomes relieved after Satan removes the trident from his neck.

Satan immediately looks remorseful as if regretting what he had done... It now seems like he is no longer possessed and finally demonstrates some clarity of thought.

As both the attacked angels attempt to catch their breaths, looking to the ground in panic, Satan bellows, "What have I done?"

We see his face of horror when he storms out. Gabriel crawls towards Seraphina to make sure she is ok. They hug and inspect one another for injuries. Gabriel grabs her face and makes sure that she is ok. They both have been drained of their energy, have noticeable marks on their necks, some slight bruising and burns, but overall, they seem to be fine. The horror on their faces is also apparent. They both notice a very odd, superstitious, repeating, act, in the pinning of their necks by the trident; it is like déjà vu.

Seraphina, distraught, says, "What happened to him? I have never seen anything like that. Even from him... There was hate in his face!"

Chapter 13

To Serve or Not to Serve

Only the Gallants know about the recent attack perpetrated by Satan. None of them have sought to confront him for his actions… Instead they give him time and room to perhaps apologize. They know something of significance has happened, but they do not have the full details. Of the four Archangels, only Gabriel knows the full story, having debriefed his love and been caught in the middle of it, himself. Still, they have no doubts that their older brother is remorseful for whatever he has done. Gabriel is the only exception, not so positive to this realization, even if he had left saying, "What have I done," and seemed to be horrified by his actions. Gabriel asks Seraphina not to tell anyone because this incident could be detrimental to God's many projects. News of this matter could lead to dissention in Heaven. Imagine if the angels knew that their Gallants were fighting…

Meanwhile, Satan has not been seen by his fellow Gallants in quite some time. This is reasonable since they all know that he was already assigned his very own, important, project.

But today they must cross paths. All the Archangels have been summoned to Paradise Palace for their usual meetings with God. Gabriel thinks that the Lord has probably summoned them to speak about this terrible incident. It will be the first time in a while that all of them are gathered together.

One by one, they all arrive, magnificently descending from the sky into the palace's courtyard. Satan is the last to arrive and very late, making his brothers late, as well, because they must all ascend together.

As soon as he descends, Gabriel aggressively rushes towards him to confront him for what he has done. Raphael and Michael try to grab a hold of Gabriel so that he does not do anything he might regret. Gabriel quickly slips their grasp and courageously challenges him.

The only violence he shows is catching Satan off guard and pinning him against the wall with the wings of his shield.

Gabriel tells the other Archangels to leave him alone and that everything would be ok. I stay… but not before I see the other Gallants leaving, dubiously, looking back, to see what is happening.

They are now alone... Satan, with an embarrassed smirk, does not put up a fight when he is pushed against the wall because he apparently feels sorry for what he has done.

Gabriel, exasperated, says, "You dishonorable coward! How could you do that to us? You are acting very strange lately! I should attack you and bring this to the attention of the Almighty! What has gotten into you?"

Satan, pounding his chest, facetiously, says, "Gabriel, my brother… I am truly sorry. I should have never acted that way. You are right; I have not been myself lately. Everyone has been bringing this to my attention and I have been trying to alter my behavior… There is a lot going on! The Almighty already knows of this incident. He has forgiven me, can you?"

Gabriel is surprised that he apologizes so quickly, since he was the only Gallant who had been anticipating a despotic luke-warmness from him.

He slowly lets go of Satan, and says, "If the Almighty knows about this and has forgiven you, I suppose I can too. Forgive me also for losing my temper."

Satan then smiles and says, "No need to apologize... I like this attitude of yours!"

I wonder if he apologized just because I was present. I must be keen to any manipulation that might come my way...

The meeting with God begins in the customary way. They give their usual greetings, professing, "Serviam!"

The atmosphere drastically changes as they face the tabernacle; it is of happiness and excitement for everyone except Satan, who unfortunately looks miserable. The moment in which, Adam, the first human will be created must be close now...

They potently recite, "Holy, Holy, Holy Lord God of Hosts. Heaven and earth are full of Your glory, Hosanna in the highest. Blessed is he who comes in the name of the Lord. Hosanna in the highest!" But Satan only seems to be mouthing the words, going through the motions.

Raphael begins, saying, "Descendit in Sacramentum Veneremur cernui. Sacrum tabernaculum cérnui! Down in adoration falling. The sacred tabernacle we hail! Quod omnia recte agerentur magnus, Dominus! Everything is going great, Lord!" He optimistically winks.

Michael then says, "Thy kingdom come, thy will be done on earth as it is in Heaven."

"You know everything, Lord... You know that we love you..." Gabriel says this with a big smile, almost as if testing God's acknowledgement of Satan's violent and hateful actions toward Seraphina and himself.

When it is time for Satan to say adoration, he instead stays quiet, absent minded, awkwardly staring at the ceiling, as if scoping out the location.

He coldly and simply says, "Blessed are we who come in the name of the Lord."

God, overjoyed in His tabernacle, says, ***"Welcome my beautiful Gallants! How are the preparations going? What lovely news do you have for me?"***

The Gallants then explain in great detail their recent accomplishments; even Satan comes up with a somewhat true story that is pleasing to God.

After a long synopsis of events, God says, ***"Excellent! I thank you for your service and the love, which you have shown me. The details that you fulfill daily with such love, have made me proud... Know that my love towards you is deeply reciprocated and your hard work does not go unnoticed..."***

CHAPTER 13

The Gallants' hearts are filled. One last thing needs to be addressed... First comes the good news, then follows the bad news…

Michael then says, "L'rd, thither is one moo item of interest to rep'rt…. I hate to lessen the m'rale of this gath'ring, but I wilt reporteth with great r'gret, f'r the f'rst time that all might not be well… Even with Gabriel's continuous work to lift the m'rale of Heaven, and even with all the new pr'jects and creations, thither is dissention in the ranks…"

The Lord says, ***"I was waiting for one of you to bring this up. I have sensed the same, but how so? Please continue..."***

Michael, the just, says, "While all plans art thriving, thither is a big and gr'wing n'mber of angels who seem to be displeas'd. 'Tis as though they art infect'd. 'Tis hard to explain…"

Michael is just in his assertions; he must be because of his sword of justice and mercy.

Gabriel chimes in, saying, "How is this possible? I have not felt this dissention... A sickness perhaps?"

Michael says, "Aye, much like a sickness, they ev'n hast a name f'r it. They art calling it, *conscience…*

"Not just that, but on mine way hither, I saweth a desecrating phrase paint'd on a wall with black envy that said, *Free at last!* Along with the drawing of a five-sid'd pentagram star. Such defilement cannot come just fr'm anywhere. This phrase and that symbol seem to be the calling card of a stirring movem'nt; one the Lord would not approve of..."

Satan looks arrogantly and proudly, and listens with profound interest, still remaining silent. This leads me to believe that Satan has already been stirring the minds of many angels in Heaven because everything worth of suspicion seems to be coming from him.

Gabriel asks, "Conscience?"

Michael responds, "Aye, conscience and appar'ntly lead by p'rsuasion."

Satan was hoping to leave this meeting unscathed, getting away with just going through the motions, but in his eyes it has now turned for the worse... I know that if questioned, he is not afraid of explaining himself, but would rather be somewhere else, doing "better things," more productive errands, which will lead to his glorification. A dilemma arises within him because he knows he cannot lie in front of God. The Lord would see right through him. All the Gallants, distinctly, now stare at Satan's posture of indifference.

God now addresses them concerned, asking, ***"What is happening, Satan?"***

Gabriel, looking confused, asks, "Why do you ask Satan?"

CHAPTER 13

The Lord answers, ***"In our last meeting, I assigned him with his new project... Project conscience..."***

Satan listens, but does not say anything, as he faces away from God and his fellow Gallants, hiding his volatile facial expressions.

Gabriel then asks, "Is that so?" Now he begins connecting the dots between the recent altercation and what he has been encouraging others to do.

Before Gabriel can say anything else, Satan turns around and explodes in both discontent and frustration, airing his troubles. He has kept it in for too long...

Passionately professing, "I ADDRESS THIS ISSUE IN RAGE AND IN FRUSTRATION!" He points to the tabernacle and continues saying, "Why does it have to be You that chooses what is created? We, Your angels, are supposed to have a stake in Your trust... Why are we not rewarded or shared in Your thoughts, prayers, powers, and decision-making?

"I want precise gifts, glory and recognition, not the promise of these things, of happiness, of fulfillment, or even less do I just want the simple pleasure of serving for the sake of serving! I want more!

"Are we, Archangels, not enough that you would have to create these humans? First it was me, then it was the other

Gallants, then the other choirs, now it shall be the humans! What is next? When will this end? Will You stop at nothing, Lord?"

He takes a breath as if an enormous weight has been lifted off his shoulders. His thoughts and objections seem to be all over the place.

All the Archangels are in awe. Now they notice how something in Satan's appearance has changed, which is what he was trying to hide, as he stared away from his brothers. He is no longer innocent looking. There is a mischievous look on his face. His expression seems tired and no longer cheerful. He carries heavy eyes, a thick brow, and his Essence shows restlessness, lack of peace, a sign of great diminishing.

God attempts to calm His General, saying, ***"How can you say this, Satan? I treat you in the highest esteem, much higher than others... We are all one! The more, the merrier! I have always shared my decision making with the four of you. The Seraphs and Cherubs were created in part due to your recommendation..."***

Raphael asserts his argument, "Yes, Satan. Ita opiniones sunt vera? So the rumors are true? You have been misusing conscience to start a rebellio, have you not? Nolui tamen credere! I did not want to believe it!"

"You insult me with your insinuations and assumptions,

Raphael! I have done nothing of the sort… Rebellion? Hardly! I have been simply sharing the gift of sight that has been given to me. THOSE ARE MY ORDERS," yells Satan stringently.

After Satan speaks these words, there is a huge tremor in the palace and throughout Heaven, not a small one at all. As the room shakes to its core, all the Archangels, except for Satan, elevate themselves in the air, flapping their wings a few times.

He almost loses his footing as the juddering develops. Michael lifts me with him, but my wings also flap unexpectedly and uncontrollably, as they did in the beaches of earth, which somewhat loosens Michael's firm grip, on me, and made it hard for him to grab ahold of me in the first place. We all elevate, so as to not feel the effects of the quiver…

Raphael thinks, maybe, it is Satan's yell that causes the tremor, but luckily everyone is so busy wondering what the tremor is, that no one notices the, sudden, flapping of my wings.

After the tremor ends, the Archangels descend to the ground again. There is quiet disbelief among them. They cannot believe what they are witnessing.

Gabriel says, "Another tremor! They have been more common! They have not been occurring until, just, recently... What is happening? It seems as though creation is out of synchronization. I do not understand it… One moment everything is fine and the next it is not…"

Michael says, "Tis a s'rious issue!"

Raphael interjects unnervingly, "Michael loquitur veritatem! Michael speaks the truth! Cherubim speak of saeculis obscuris vixerunt, dark ages to come, and they foretell of the wrath of our Dominus! Everyone knows about the angelica prophetiae, the angelic prophecy…

"Obscura prophetia futura…. An unbelievable time of great strife and choosing… A fall and a falling out… The Essences will play a major role in this black foretelling. But above all, to stop this prediction from coming true, the Essences must never be separated from the Gallants. The Archangels must always remain united. He who possesses the Essences shall have the power of God, unite the angels, and end this time of obscurity…

"But as long as we remain coniunctis, united, the Essences shall always belong to our Dominus! As long we stay together, there is no need for a tenebris era, dark era...

"Recentis tremores non potest esse fortuitum! These recent tremors cannot be a coincidence! I had not taken these rumors of conscience seriously and this is why I thought that everything in creation was going according to plan. I thought that the rumors were part of jestering and hospitium, entertainment."

The Lord interjects, ***"The biggest job that evil does is***

to convince you that it does not exist." All focus is still concentrated on Satan.

Raphael cries out, "Oh misericors! Oh merciful One! Non misisti iram tuam! Do not unleash Your fury! We have never dealt with anything like this… But, I am sure we can pull through simul, together, as we always do…

"Dic nobis! Please tell us, what shall we do? I am sure Satan has not done any of this on purpose. Solus ipse fuit sequentium ordinum… He was only following orders..."

God interrupts and says, ***"I think my gift of conscience has suited you badly, Satan. You are indeed troubled, my son… You are scandalized by truth, but not by evil anymore!"***

All remain silent and taking advantage of this silence, Satan again has a calm but discontent outburst, saying, "Badly? TROUBLED? NO! NOT AT ALL! Your gifts have fueled me…

"Everything happens for a reason, does it not? If bad things happen, something good and far better always comes from it, does it not? I am sure something good would even come from a dark era! Something good and far better, but in order for that to happen, it sounds like, something bad must first happen! It is inevitable!"

Gabriel reminds his confused brother, "The ends do not justify the means… You cannot rob from the rich to give to the poor, brother, and you know this!"

Then, Satan, trying to allude to his, private, Gallant connection between his brothers, says, "Have you heard the praises that God extends to these human creatures? Even before their creation... I am sick of hearing nothing but accolades about them! When has He ever spoken about us like that?

"The Creator just keeps creating new projects for us, when is enough, enough? When will all this end? Never!"

The Gallants continue to plea with their brother. They try to be charitable and reason with him, light a candle in the darkness, asking him to not use their stealthy connection in front of the Almighty. But who can reason with the Lord of persuasion?

If they were to argue, they know their arguments would just be flipped on them. They could likely end up agreeing with him, so they abstain from debating. Instead, the meeting has transformed into a forceful type of intervention that Satan does not wish to receive…

For the first time, they are unsure of their methods. They bind their powers without Satan knowing to try and see if they possess an effect on him. They conceal their Essences and shine their colored lights on him, trying to neutralize his warped, new self... Nothing seems to work…

CHAPTER 13

Satan, arrogantly, says, "Your Essences have no influence on me! My power of conscience has given me another Essence."

The Archangels are surprised that he has detected them silently using their weapons. There is so much uncertainty! They still do not know why their brother is doing this, and what he wants. They do not know what he plans to do or how he plans to rectify his anger.

The Gallants are now the ones out of breath from using their powers. It has taken a lot out of them. Their expressions look like a child's when they are lost without their parents.

Satan then turns to the tabernacle, roaring, "Oh yeah… project Mariam… I found out what that is… Let us stop pretending as if this project is not about me!

"A human almost as perfect as You? In fact, second only to You? She shall wear the crown of heaven at Your side? She shall be invoked as queen of angels?

"Both humans and angels shall say, Hail, to her, and the generations shall call her blessed? She shall be full of grace? I do not know anyone who is full of grace, only the Lord…

"And worse, one day she will bear God the Son inside of her?! Have several Guardians to do her bidding?!

"This is not going to be ok with me! Not if I have something to say about it!" Afterwards, he hatefully adds, "Do not even get me started on those humans You will call Your priests…"

Gabriel looks at the tabernacle; surprised that Satan knows so much about project *Mariam*...

Then, he looks at his kin, saying, "Do not let your pride interfere, brother! *Mariam* is a contingency plan... It does not have to be this way!"

Gabriel then gathers his thoughts and God speaks to him only, saying, ***"It is a contingency plan that now might have to be put into effect."***

The purpose of project *Mariam* now seems clear to Gabriel. Now everyone is better informed on project *Mariam*. Even the Archangels have their own thoughts and opinions about what Satan has relayed to them. Raphael and Michael do not quite understand the purpose of this project. They remain loyal to God, and do not follow Satan or give into his persuasive ways. It would be easy to do so, since the brotherhood and connection between the Gallants is beyond explaining, beyond any imaginable bond of family, but the loyalty to God is much stronger.

Satan says, "Contingency plan? Well… the Lord does not will something for nothing… There is always a purpose, am I right?"

He is so informed on all our conversations and dealings, as if he would have been present in the middle of them.

CHAPTER 13

Raphael says, "For the Glory of God, Satan! Est cogito Omnia! There is a purpose to everything. Placere, fratrem! Please, brother!"

The Gallants do not understand why Satan is now smiling. I think it must be because the details of *Mariam*, which were once blurry, are now confirmed with Gabriel's silence... Until then, he had only heard rumors or gathered poor intelligence on the subject. This newly gathered information, shall undoubtedly fuel his next moves.

Final silence, and shock, settle in… Gabriel sees the future clearly and knows what he must do with regards to project *Mariam*. He looks at the tabernacle as if he has telepathy with God and understands His wishes.

Raphael and Michael still do not know what to do, since again this is unprecedented, and God's plans have never been questioned before. It is a new situation to them all. They do not know how to react, so they follow their wisdom and give their troubled sibling some space.

Even if they would approach him, it is clear he does not want to be near them. He acts as if they are carrying a contagious disease, when really it is he who is infected and spreading this epidemic. They know something is wrong, yet they do nothing because they trust in God's will. They only hope that they have not mishandled this situation, and let the promise of something, much grimmer, slip away from their control. The Lord also wishes to give Satan some room to cool-off and reconsider. If the Almighty handles the situation in this manner, then the Gallants are wise to do the same.

Chapter 14

The Collection

Finally, all the Archangels leave confused with their usual kneeling and, "Serviam!"

However, Satan leaves, slowly, at the end, and does not kneel or say, "Serviam!" He begins to walk out of the hall, turning his back to God. The Almighty realizes that he has not given the proper farewell, and says with a raised, concerned, but calm voice, ***"Satan! My son!"***

The power of conscience is seen prominently in Satan's, red, eyes. At the same time, God is momentarily seen, personally, in the reflection of his eyes, a glowing eminence of pure power and love. Surprisingly, behind His radiance, I even see the hint of a body.

When he hears his name being called, he stops, but does

not look back. He seems annoyed for yet again being kept well passed the meeting's duration. Even with God's very personal appearance to him in both aspect and feeling, at this pivotal moment, Satan feels nothing but emptiness.

When gripping his weapon, with more strength than ever, the metal of the trident heats up. In a strong, almost growling whisper, Satan says, "You call me son? You already have Your Son," referring to what seems to be jealousy towards God the Son and the role He will have in project *Mariam*.

Then, he potently says, "NON-SERVIAM!" In human words, "I WILL NOT SERVE!"

He walks away without turning to face God.

The Lord stays quiet and has clearly heard His commander's words of defiance. And so it begins… It is now clear in Satan's mind what he must do. He must overthrow God who he feels just as powerful as. He must end God's "tyranny" and rule for himself.

His plan of attack has already been crafted. His thoughts speak louder than words, "Whoever holds the Essences, shall control the Cherubs and Seraphs. Those who serve under Michael, Gabriel and Raphael's lineage shall have no choice but to follow and join whoever holds the Essence of their pedigree."

How can he defy God like this? I look to admire my favorite

mural on the impeccable Palace wall. The black snake, below the golden tree, which looks like me, is now tangled around the tree's base. The snake's two fangs are covering God's III markings, replacing his symbol with a II of fangs. The sky above the tree has darkened. The panorama is cloudy and murky.

As Satan walks out of Paradise Palace, the clouds and sky, outside, turn black like in the golden tree mural. There is a mist and fog that lower as though to cover and follow the defiant one, who ignored God's command of not allowing the sky to be blackened and influenced by his mood.

Beelzebub is outside to greet him. Even though Beelzy is Satan's best pal, he does not know what Satan has been up to. Yes, he has seen a change in his friend and in the tides of Heaven, but he would have never expected him to rebel against God. Not just that, but Beelzebub has been quite preoccupied with his own changes in personal appearance, which like mine, also seem to be out of control.

With a big smile, Beelzebub says to him, "I have not seen you in a while... How did the gathering go?"

Then he feels an overwhelming sense of déjà vu, as if he had already experienced this conversation before. This summoning power that has become more common, tells Beelzebub to follow and keep up like a mindless drone. It conveys the same message to all who are close.

Satan quickly turns Beelzebub's smile into a frown and coldly, says, "I will have numbers and weapons on my side. We must acquire all the Essences!"

Beelzebub, surprised and nervous, says, "What do we need the Essences for? A new project? Are we going to borrow them?"

"Yes, that is good! Think of it as a new project, we shall call it, *Project Overthrow*! And yes, borrow them," as he malevolently smiles.

Then he realizes that his witty friend will not be so easily swayed by this lie, and so he transmits into Beelzy's mind, a vision, an image of the dark prophecy coming true. In this vision, the other Gallants are fighting among themselves and conspiring to overthrow God, which is really what he is trying to do...

Even worse, he shows him a deceptively edited image of the episode of Seraphina attacking him with her la-bow, followed by Gabriel, in attack mode, drawing his shield against him. A few more false images are projected of his beloved, Dumah, being kidnapped by Seraphs loyal to the Magna... Not just that, but since Dumah is of Gabriel's lineage, he shows an image of Gabriel lusting for her too, as he "apparently" did with

Seraphina, wishing to have both Satan's and Beelzy's treasured Seraphs.

The last image that he shows is of the Watchers command being taken over by Gabriel, and it being too late to accept Satan's generous offer of reassigning him. All this happens while Beelzebub ends up toiling, on earth, as a Guardian, on the side of a human, far away from Dumah's love and care. Beelzebub is still smart and can see through much of this flaunting, but the images do what they are supposed to, bring doubt into an already confused mind.

Beelzy, awestruck, interjects, "But what you ask is impossible! Are those images true? Your brothers would never do that! What would inspire them to do such a thing?

"You were only given one Essence for a reason… Only God is supposed to possess all of the Essences, and that is through your Gallant union! Your Essential union is the only thing stopping the prophecy from occurring…

"Another project? Aren't you already busy with project conscience? Is this what our Lord truly wants us to do?"

"Yes," lies Satan. "Need I remind you time after time, that you were the one who said, *anything is possible*?"

I can tell that this simple phrase, *"Anything is possible,"* from Beelzy's mouth, has helped justify and fuel Satan's methods more that he let's on, yet no fulfilling answers are given to quench Beelzebub's inquisitive soul.

Beelzy is still deceived by Satan who now obviously knows he can use his powers of persuasion and conscience not just to persuade to do good, but also to swindle and make others follow him. Beelzy does not understand the reason of their mission, but with the possibility of a promotion and a new project, ever in mind, he agrees to steal the Essences.

He says, "Yes, I only have one Essence… for now! Which is why you will help me collect the others!"

Just as Satan has Beelzebub waiting for him outside, Gabriel, who had left the meeting earlier, also has Seraphina waiting for him. Seraphina tenderly kisses and hugs Gabriel. Soon after kissing, they whisper into each other's ears as they usually do.

Seraphina requests her usual, "Tell me a story!"

Gabriel exclaims, "Do I have a story for you, my Magna!"

She makes eye contact with Satan who is watching them from farther up the stairs of Paradise Palace. Even though she really wants to hear the tale, there is no need to recount the story... She immediately understands what is going on…

Seraphina leaves Gabriel to attend to her projects, attempting to avoid crossing her gaze with the defiant one who attacked her. As soon as she leaves his side, wasting no time, Satan flies down from the palace steps, descending and using his trident to engage Gabriel in a fight.

He twirls his trident and thrashes into the shield of good news, but there is no visible damage to the weapons. Gabriel manages to block two blows with his shield, and allowed one offensive move by throwing his weapon. The blades that protrude from the angel's wings, on Gabriel's shield, come very close to detaching Satan's wings from his torso, but Gabriel misses and is then tripped, unable to mount a more suitable offensive. After all, a shield is more of a defensive weapon, yet he was never allowed to conjure his sword either.

With a firm, body-trembling blow to the head by the trident, Gabriel is left unconscious. The tight, and stable grip that he had on his shield is quickly loosened.

After this attack, even though it is very foggy, from afar, Beelzy is, clearly, able to see what Satan did. Although Gabriel and Beelzy do not always agree, he does not want to see him get hurt for an unjust reason.

Before witnessing this, Beelzebub was inclining towards supporting his friend, unconditionally, even though not everything he claimed made sense or was convincing. But after seeing this violence, he is fast to reproach Satan and does not condone his actions... He rushes down the stairs, comes closer and demands an explanation, asking, "What are you doing?"

Satan says, "I am rounding up the Essences!"

Beelzy, disturbed, asks, "Did our Lord tell us to collect the Essences by force? So you may be worthy of possessing them? Has Gabriel done anything wrong to deserve this?"

Satan, annoyed, answers, "Yes, on all counts! God said, collect them by any means necessary. How else will they let go of their Essences if not by force?"

Beelzy says, "Why didn't the Almighty just ask the other Gallants to surrender to Him their Essences? They would have gladly returned them to our Lord, no questions asked." He seems to want to be well informed before he makes his final choice.

Satan grows tired of the questions… He demands with an insane look, "Shut up and do your duty, Beelzebub!"

At this point, there is no turning back for Satan. He has committed to his cause of overthrowing God.

The scene becomes even foggier yet… Michael, who is not too far away, did not notice Satan attack Gabriel… I know that Satan's next target is my friend, Michael, and his sword. I wish with all my soul to warn him from the staircase, but the Lord has ordered me not to intervene.

Beelzebub realizes who his next target is, and screams, "NO!" He runs away, as fast as possible, so he is not an accomplice to these atrocities. He is shocked to see what his friend has done, scared to be associated with him…

Satan sees Beelzebub run away and is disappointed beyond belief, almost saddened to see his friend's lack of support. Even the summoning beacon of his trident did not make him stay. This is where this calling has been stemming from and not from his spike-armor, as Satan so malevolently planted in his head.

The lights of the spike-armor have become lit, activating its protective capabilities, apparently urging him to be vigilant and to keep the armor on, which is contrary to what Satan wants.

He runs up the stairs to beckon God's help, anyone's help… He runs by me, exasperated and winded, he says, "Are you just going to stand there and do nothing? You and I can stop this with our spike-armors!"

In disbelief of what is going on, I stay paralyzed. I cannot respond... It is not cowardice, I just literally cannot move or intervene, as much as I would like to. I have been forbidden from doing so, but he does not understand my immobility. He is extremely disappointed in me. In his eyes, I am a coward and a traitor. Regrettably, I can tell Beelzy takes this inaction to heart, as an offense of great magnitude, an act of appeasement. He runs off to find someone who will be of more assistance than I have been.

Michael, also near the scene of the crime, hears Beelzebub's scream, "NO," delayed and echoing through the dense fog, and he approaches, cautiously, sword in hand, step by step…

Michael sees Gabriel wounded on the ground, and his shield is missing. He is concerned and quickly bends over, kneeling to see if Gabriel is ok... He checks his vitals, and thankfully, he still has life in him but still does not know what could have possibly happened to him. Perhaps he fell down the mighty staircase, but even that is unlikely, because if tripped, he could have used his wings to stay afoot.

My friend then hears swooping sounds, of wind, around him and exclaims, "Satan? Anyone thither?"

The fast wind sound becomes louder than ever as if it is approaching his location… The sound is Satan flying toward Michael... With a sheer force, he holds Gabriel's shield in grasp. As soon as Michael turns around to see what the sound is, he is knocked out with one blow of the shield to the side of the head.

Now Michael is lying unconscious next to Gabriel. I see Satan elevate himself into the air as he proclaims his victory, and then slowly descends.

He drags Michael's sword on the ground. The sound of the sword being pulled on the pavement gives off an ominous, metal, screech.

Now, he elevates himself to my height at the top of the staircase to boast his victory... Slowly, I see his head, torso, and then his feet as I elevate my gaze through the haze. He now carries his trident on his back, Michael's sword in one hand and Gabriel's shield in the other. His entirety is shown victorious and restless for more conquest…

I can tell that he knows my orders, acknowledging that I cannot interfere, and so he flaunts his conquest in my face, tempting me to take action, but I do not budge, I cannot! To add insult to injury, he says loudly for me to hear, "The score is **2-1**… I believe I am winning!"

This once friendly bout, this once innocent tallying, for my own amusement, has now turned into a depraved competition on his part… He has blown my innocuous game, out of proportions, inflicting pain on my Master, Michael, and therefore inflicting pain on me, to which, I say, "GAME ON!"

I now get a glimpse of him flying outside the gates of the Palace, holding three fourths of the Essences. With much reverence, he slowly sheaths Michael's sword, in the same quiver as his trident, and places Gabriel's shield into a sort of backpack.

From the pack, he pulls out another sheath that bears a long, skinny, shape; it looks like it is meant for Raphael's staff of souls…

Luckily, by this time, Raphael had been long gone. If he had stayed a little longer, perhaps Satan would now be the master of all the Essences.

Aside from all his rebellious goals, in his eyes, if he collects all four weapons, he shall be the uniter of the Essences. The uniter is exactly what he wants to be... He takes matters into his own hands, so that the prophecy of dark times does not occur, but in doing what he has done, he may well be the catalyst to the dark times… because the weapons are now separated.

Chapter 15

Recovery

After Satan steals the shield from Gabriel and the sword from Michael, he heads to his own palace to conceal them in the safest place he can think of.

He is walking, with haste, up some steps that lead to his castle. He holds the two stolen Essences, and very carefully guards them bundled up in his packs. He is wearing a black cloak, with a hood, that covers his head and entire being. The scene is dark, almost as if there were a lightning storm approaching. The fog and bad weather seem to be following him wherever he goes. One thing is certain, he needs the Essences protected; this is the only thing obsessively dwelling in his mind.

"Now that I finally have them, I must not lose them! They are mine, all mine!" Even though I am far away from where he is, these words even echo through my mind.

From a distance, I continue to see him running up the stairs to his castle, in a hurry, to get both himself and the Essences guarded.

When he reaches the final steps, there is another tremor like the one we experienced in God's palace. This one trips him... He tumbles down, a few steps; significantly hurting his left leg... his wings did not help him stay afoot as if they have malfunctioned...

Cursing at the top of his lungs, he yells, "IMBECILS!" Then, with the help of his wings, he quickly stands, regains his balance, and continues to run with his gimpy leg.

Arriving at his castle, he brusquely opens the huge doors, where there are two Seraphs guarding the outside and two Cherubs guarding the inside. The guards have the marks of conscience bestowed upon them; their eyes are almost as red as Satan's, their thick veins are popping out from their necks and muscles are protruding from their armor.

Inside I see a large hall, which mirrors the great hall in Paradise Palace. Satan walks into the middle of the hall, and looks around, spinning in all directions. He tries to think of a safe place to hide the Essences…

In this very moment, I clearly see the empty hall too... He pauses in the middle and realizes that he must build something to protect the Essences. They will be safe in no other location! He must be sure that his newly gained Essences are better protected than they were with Gabriel and Michael... specially because the Essences have a tendency to end up back where they belong, in their rightful places, at the side of their masters, like a magnetic attraction.

The doors of the castle are shut closed... I can see him no longer… Now, I leave my vantage point, here, by the bridge, and return to check up on my Gallants, especially my friend, who was a victim of these senseless attacks…

Both Gabriel and Michael are convalescing in two white beds parallel to one another. They are in a very bright, white, room, and still have not woken up from Satan's attacks.

I enter their recovery room… Guilt and sorrow fills my heart as I stare into Michael's closed eyes. At this moment, I vow never to feel this way again. The next time I am put into a precarious situation, I shall be ready...

I bow my head, paying my respects to the Gallants, wishing them a speedy recovery, and make my way to one of the corners of the room so to better assess what I must do… I sit and keep to my thoughts, removing myself from sight.

I frantically ask the Lord, "How can I not intervene?"

God quickly answers, ***"You have my permission to intervene, but only once. Make it count!"***

Happiness overflows my soul, "Serviam! Lord, that I may be docile!" I say.

At the same time, another prayer is answered. Just a second ago, I asked the Lord for the speedy recovery of my Gallants, and alas! Gabriel awakes.

This whole time he has been in the care of some beautiful Seraphs, who have just reentered the room. Not remembering what has happened, Gabriel thinks it has all been a dream…

He opens his eyes slowly, and looks around the room. In front of him, squinting, he sees the beautiful Seraphs that did not see him wake yet.

Gabriel grabs his head and his neck, and starts to reconstruct what has happened. Why is he there? He sits up straight and then looks to his side. With a quick, blurry, glance, he realizes Michael is also recovering, in the bed, right next to him.

Gabriel begins to speak, gently shaking the bed parallel to his, "Michael! Wake up! Michael! Michael!" Then, he tries to reach farther, stretching towards Michael's arm to wake him.

CHAPTER 15

The beautiful Seraphs finally realize that he has awoken… They immediately drop what they are doing and tend to his every need...

One, with light-green eyes, by the name of Leliel, excited says, "Easy, Gallant! You have had an accident it seems…"

Another Seraph, her nosey, blue-eyed, colleague, named, Ethena, says, "You have been out for many days…"

Gabriel remembers it all now…

Leliel, desperately wishing to be heard by her Gallant, says, "Uriel looked for help and then brought you both here. He has remained at your side the entire time, but just now had to return to his training."

I believe she has not realized that I was inconspicuous in the corner of that same room. Maybe I am getting better at this cloaking and blending in.

Gabriel, again, reaches towards Michael's bed and continues to shake the silk sheets and covers…

Michael wakes up in a heartbeat as if he were scared and startled, as if just barely reacting to Satan's attack on him. He looks around in panic, also, not knowing what happened, or why he is there… Now they are both awake…

Another beautiful Seraph with deep, purple, eyes, called Aclaria, speaks cheerfully but obnoxiously, "We have never had a Gallant in our clinic, much less two Gallants to attend to!"

The extremely close friends, Leliel, Ethena, and Aclaria, continue to take turns, asking questions, as if they were a tandem unit, saying very quickly, "What happened? Training exercise? Or did something unexpected happen to you on earth? Was it the sun? Do you remember the perpetrator?" They are jittery, lively and full of aggravating questions.

Gabriel answers, "No, I barely remember what happened," and does not give the name of his perpetrator. He does not wish to stain Satan's name… Since his Seraph caregivers are being somewhat overbearing and annoying, at this instant, he cuts his response short, so to not prolong his recovery. In his current condition, he could use as much rest as possible. The less he has to worry about, and the less distractions, the quicker he will be on his way to being fully functional.

Actively searching around the room, Gabriel had tried to wake Michael with his shield, but since it was nowhere in sight, he then asks, "My shield of good news, where is it?"

Aclaria, pensive, answers, "There was no shield, no good news, with you, when Uriel brought you here..."

Gabriel looks worried. He has never been parted from his shield before. Not having the Essences makes the Gallants almost as normal as ordinary angels, not that there is anything wrong with that, it just does not make them particularly special.

Michael hears the conversation and stares into blankness, as he sits up straight, also realizing what has happened. He joins the worried clan and asks, "And mine sword of justice and mercy? Hast thou seen it?"

Wishing she could do more for them, the beautiful, green-eyed, Leliel, answers, "Sorry, your Gallants! Nothing was found on you when you were brought here. Perhaps Uriel is keeping them safe for you. Since you were found outside of Paradise Palace, we thought perhaps you had left them in God's safe care…"

Ethena chimes in, guessing, "Or maybe Gallants Satan or Raphael have your Essences?"

Ethena is right in one of her guesses because Satan indeed has their weapons, but Leliel is wrong since I do not have the Essences.

Both the Archangels look at each other in worry. They abhor feeling vexed; it is not in their nature to feel this way. Their concerned stares, toward one another, do not give the nosey trio of Cherubim much comfort, nor do they make my precarious job any easier, because I can hear all their conflicting thoughts.

Realizing that their actions are somewhat bothersome and to their own disdain, the Seraphs leave the room so that the

Gallants can continue resting.

The convalescents fear the two worst things, asking themselves, "Has Satan taken their Essences?" Or worse, "Is Raphael allied with Satan?"

They know who their assailant is, but they do not know if he took their weapons. Since Raphael is not at their side, they speculate that he might be on the side of the attacker.

As if on queue, from the corner of the room, we hear a voice... The raspy voice comes from Raphael who at first made himself invisible so as to not be detected by the Seraphs. Even I did not see him! He is much better at this masking than I am, all the Gallants are! He is now detectable, cloaked, and with his staff in hand, but his weapon is still concealed by his dark robe. For a moment all of us thought that it was Satan, since they are both gowned with similar black cloaks. Faithful to my new, "one opportunity," allowance, to intervene, I was ready to pounce on him at a moment's notice… Turns out, he, Raphael, has also been at their side almost the entire time. He had seen me coming and going, several times, and his staff of souls has definitely aided in their prompt recovery.

He says in his hoarse voice, "I do not have your Essences, nor am I allied with him... I serve the One, True God, Creator of Heaven and earth, of all that is seen and unseen, just as you do... I would never betray my brothers, no matter if they were Gallants, Seraphim, Cherubim, or Guardians...

"Unfortunately, your intuition and instincts serve you well… He has taken your Essences and disappeared… We must find him at once! No one must know they are missing, and no one must know of his actions…"

What is surprising is that he no longer speaks in angel-talk. It is almost as if this incident has forced maturity into his being. He has had to grow up promptly, leaving his old dialect behind, like he has been reborn. His brothers look surprised to see this drastic change in him, although his voice continues to be deep and raucous. Although, now, there is an added sophistication to his words, he sounds almost unrecognizable in his speech. It is almost as if in the past, he would speak in angelic-talk to be difficult and make my narrating of his words more difficult, since I had to translate a dialect which I am rusty in. But now he acts with much more poise and maturity, leaving the phase of angel-talk behind him. He knows how important his role really is.

Gabriel asks, "Why did he take our Essences? I feel lost, nothing makes sense anymore…"

He says in a thick commentator-like voice, "Think about it! Do you not remember our conversation, with our Lord, before you were attacked? Satan has started his rebellion. He is changing the natural and supernatural, as we know it! He is deceiving many angels! They are unaware of his tactics and many are too innocent to know the difference. Do not make their same mistake! Grow up! Search your knowledge!

"Satan is not happy about any of our new projects, not Human, not Guardian, and least of all, *Mariam*!

"While you have been convalescing, everything has changed, Heaven has been turned upside down... Many angels have been missing and failing to remain faithful to the one-day curfew; they are staying on terra, and even other planets...

"Natural phenomena is being changed, and tampered with, to favor him…

"There is no united force at this time. We are spread thin throughout the universe. I suppose this is how he wants us, divided and confused…

"The tremors have become a usual occurrence and there are no Gallants united to lead the choirs of angels…"

Just then, as if prompted by Raphael, another quake occurs. This one is longer and louder than ever, it shakes us all in our spots, even the beds, as objects fall to the ground, breaking and shattering…

The powerful vibration stops… Both convalescent angels

continue to stare into each other's eyes, concerned, pondering…

Raphael, croaky, says, "For once, Heaven is in danger, our Lord has told me so..."

Michael, still unable to process it all, says, "Dang'r?"

Raphael, frustrated, says, "Yes, danger! You are not as naïve and innocent as the other choirs, Michael. You are wise above all. You know what I mean! Danger, as in, unpleasantness, havoc, mayhem and all of the forbidden words our Lord hoped never to be used! Remember the dark prophecy! Our Essences have been separated!"

Michael says, "Aye, but please taketh it easy on me! Thou forgeteth I hast just been awoken from s'rious injury."

Gabriel, concerned, asks, "What is he planning on doing? Why does he need our Essences?"

Raphael, wisely exclaims, with his raucous voice, "This I do not know, but knowing our big brother, he is planning something big!

"What is even worse is that we do not know of his tactics, but he knows of ours…

"What we do know is that all that has happened so far has been premeditated. Who knows what he has planned next? We must think outside the box and attempt to be one step ahead of him!"

Michael, the battle strategist, comes to a realization, and says, "Raphael, the plan of action wouldst be to analyzeth one by one the odd occurrences that hast been h'ppening since our L'rd announc'd the plans f'r these pr'jects, to seeth if th're is a trend which we can possibly followeth to its logical conclusion…

"We wilt be wise to assume that he hath been troubl'd by these pr'posals since their c'nception… This will giveth us bett'r insight into his tactics… Let us all brainst'rm!"

They all come up with a list of antecedents, and I even write my own seven down to make better sense of them.

1. Tampering with the golden tree. Eating the apples, and encouraging Gabriel to do the same, knowing he does not need carnal sustenance, which only takes away from God's pure nourishment… **Gluttony.**

2. Satan followed Gabriel, Seraphina, and Beelzy to the Promised Land to spy, yes, but also out of **Sloth**, laziness in his dedication to God's works and plans, which leads to him missing very important gatherings with our Lord and his fellow Gallants.

3. The questioning of God's plans reflects Satan's **Envy** for humans and project *Mariam*.

4. Satan's **Greed,** to own the power of the Essences, leads to his crime of armed theft.

5. He attacks Seraphina, pinning her neck against the wall out of **Lust** and desire for her.

6. The tremors in Heaven are conducive to Satan's **Wrath** and lead him to curse when he says, "Imbecils!"

7. The last is the tendency of **Pride** that Satan commits. He attacks his brother Gallants for many reasons, but in his mind it is to prove a point to himself, that he is the Superior Archangel. He proudly believes he can be the savior of the dark prophecy, all by himself, uniting the Essences and there is nothing his brothers can do to stop the landslide that he brings along with him... More so, his pride leads him to believe that God is not necessary; that he is more than the Almighty and more beautiful than even Him.

Each of us has written a list; no doubt these points will be our focuses of investigation and approaches to quelling this stirring movement, dare I say, this uprising.

Michael adds to his own list, saying, "I thinketh that ev'ry time he dost something bad, 'tis conceal'd from us s'mehow. He hath been deceiving us directly with our broth'rly connection. This is the trend, sin! And so it is logical that he will continue with the same trend!"

Raphael continues leading the plan of action, saying boisterously, "Yes, we must get to the bottom of these actions and consult the meaning with our Lord!

"I have something else to inform you. I met with the Almighty, all by myself, and He has told me that Satan did not proclaim the greeting... To add insult to injury, he said, "Non-serviam." He did not kneel and improperly turned his back…

"Since he did not voice the greeting, we must now assume that he is no longer a Gallant, a renegade...

"In the presence of others, so that we do not invoke his name, we will try and call him, *Lucifer.* The one who thinks he sees the light. Frankly, he has relinquished his God given name and changed it himself, and for what? This I do not know, but there must be something or someone pulling his strings because the Satan we all know is incapable of such desertion, such treachery!

"Somehow he has been consumed by his hate and his sins, which could be the real culprits to his actions. Yes, sins can become alive! It must be acknowledged, and I fear that when we invoke his God given name, we open our brotherly connection with him, and he can see what we see…"

They call him Lucifer so as to try and never invoke his name again. Satan is the name God has blessed him with, when he decided to serve, but now that he no longer wishes to serve, he must be given another name because he seems to be someone else! It is appropriate that since he acts as a completely new and unrecognizable being, that he should also be assigned a new name. Satan was his Archangelic, God given name. Lucifer is his new alias, which perfectly represents the new duality of his actions.

They try to avoid his old name, but since they do not know which of his personalities, past or present, is most prominent, it is no big deal if they ever mention it.

The Gallants are unbelieving of everything they are hearing about their brother. They become worried and sad…

Michael says, "Aside fr'm investigating our own s'spicions of him, we wilt recov'r our Essences. Only God knows what he is planning to doeth with them…"

Gabriel asks, "What about Beelzy? He is Lucifer's most loyal friend and confidant."

Raphael agrees, throatily, saying, "Well, he is actually Satan's best friend and confidant, not Lucifer's, but, yes, we must talk to him. As far as I know, he has not become part of Lucifer's faction, and remains true to our Lord, but we must be sure. Perhaps Beelzebub has more insight into his plans…

"Just as Lucifer has begun to gather angels to follow his cause, we must also do the same. Not only that, but we must try to save as many of the deceived angels as we can…

"Your Essences cannot be far away! As extensive as the

Lord's creation is, there are only few places they could be, a place that must be meaningful to him, where he feels safe. We need to retrieve them as soon as possible. Now it is more important than ever to use your connection to your Essences to try and find them. No doubt he will try and mask your senses somehow…"

You can tell that Raphael has already put meticulous thought into the actions that must take place and his brothers are glad he has done so. He is already thriving at his new role of, sole, leadership. If there once was any immaturity in the youngest Gallant, it seems as if it has been swept away.

Seraphina, the Magna, walks into the room. She had been overhearing everything from the outside. Her eyes are in tears...

Gabriel, happy to see her, asks, "Why do you weep?"

Seraphina, bravely, says, "I am ok… I caught the first rainbow, here, from the Holy Land, as soon as I heard the rumors! It is such a sad story, which you all tell… I weep that the Gallants are now only three and I weep for what Satan, I mean, Lucifer, has done. More so, out of happiness because you are ok, and seem to have recovered nicely…"

Gabriel exclaims, "You were hearing our conversation? There are already rumors about this?"

"Yes, every word! Everyone has sensed the changes in creation, even, I, in my earthly post. I give thanks that you are all well! United we have a chance."

She approaches Gabriel's bed and puts her hands on his chest, as she reaches for an affectionate kiss. Gabriel mildly complains because she has touched one of his many, still tender, wounds but they kiss anyway.

Seraphina has now brought all of the Archangels to tears, as they understand that they have lost a brother, even though Satan wishes them to believe he is a savable project and not yet adrift.

Michael, foolishly, says, "I will nev'r loseth hope f'r him…"

Although Michael and Gabriel are both badly injured, with great difficulty, they rise from their beds, levitating… They do this to show strength and unity in time of weakness, to display that they will rise above these challenges together. Other angels could not have done the same after suffering these harsh Essence-inflicted injuries.

Gabriel says, "Since he is under my care, in project *Mariam*, I will speak to Beelzy and summon him before our Lord. I am sure Seraphina and his beloved, Dumah, can also help with assuring his pivotal allegiance."

Raphael, the newly wisest, delegates some duties with his intellect, saying croakily, "Michael, try to figure out where the tremors are coming from, perhaps you can send your trusted friend, Uriel, to try and locate Lucifer. In doing so, he will not be deviating from the Lord's mandates...

"Collect his report and the list with seven capital sins he has just created… Post them as decrees throughout the universe to remind all that these actions are still forbidden! They are offenses of capital and deadly proportions! When Uriel finds him, he must follow to ascertain his plans. Uriel's stealth nature shall surely mask his proximity to Lucifer…"

He then kindheartedly winks toward my general direction like he always does, as if he has spotted me, obviously aware of my presence in the corner of the room. Not to mention, he seems to want to help me achieve my goals and longing, acknowledging my one chance at impacting this documentary and facilitating my success. Finally, I get a chance to be involved! I am so pumped! Perhaps this is my chance to shine as the Lord has granted me leeway to only intervene once…

Gabriel wishes to delegate also, saying, "Raphael, since you are the only one with an Essence, keep it safe! This shall be your first priority! But, also, bring the power of the Holy Spirit back to the angels, as you did on their creation day. Recruit and save as many as you can… Still continue to enforce the curfew! We shall meet within a day to receive God's graces and touch base from there... Let us regain our strength and Essences, we stand no chance without them!"

CHAPTER 15

Raphael, the youngest and last of the Archangels to be created, is now the fatherly figure and most important of all Gallants, simply because he is the only who still possess his Essence.

Right this second; my hands further blacken, like a slow, spreading, virus, dispersing throughout my self as the pigment did on the beaches of earth. Since I have nowhere to look to confirm my darkening, I assume my whole being has done the same. Much like my skin, questions dawn on my intellect… What is happening to me? Why do I darken? How can I hear what everyone thinks?

I too am having on-going epiphanies, like Raphael seems to have had, and lately most of these epiphanies, that I hear, do not even belong to me, but are the thoughts of the angels who surround me. A battle is rummaging through my self… The darker I become, the more we seem to be transitioning into the prophetic era of darkness. I darken and so do the times!

Seraphina jumps in, distracting them, on purpose, from my obscuring condition, which has somewhat un-camouflaged me, here in my corner of the room. With an even more powerful distraction, wishing to help in all that is unfolding, she stylishly says, "I have an idea of how to find the Essences…"

Chapter 16

Into the Depths of the World

Seraphina says, "There is a Seraph by the name of Mammon. She is one of the best craftsmen, not only for weapons, but for other inventions as well. She might not be very well known in the Gallants' circles… but it is said among Seraphs that her inventions are second only to God's creations…"

I know who Seraphina is talking about! Long ago I met her in passing… She once constructed a contraption that mimicked an earthly tree, and it contained almost the same biological processes… Impressive! Mammon is sought near and far for her inventions and her, sometimes, questionable temper. She receives contracts from all choirs. There are even funny rumors that she is the one that built the Essences, which, I will tell you now, is not true.

As a great inventor, architect, and engineer, Mammon is well trained with her weapons, making her, also, an expert at the art of combat. She is always surprising her opponents with new devices, which she has tested with worthy Seraphs, but she is still not even close to being as strong as Seraphina. I can see where Seraphina's train of thought is going… and she is right! With her many talents, Mammon would be a great ally to anyone, and we want to make sure that we secure this alliance.

Long ago, one of the ideas Mammon presented to our Lord was for a panel contraption, which she called, "*Witchcraft*." Usually, ideas for gadgets do not have to be approved by the Lord, but this one was so intricate and so grand, that it met the standards that require the Almighty's approval.

Witchcraft consisted of a large, round, platinum, panel that could be used for many applications, allowing its possessor to practically accomplish any task that is put to mind, even to control aspects of time.

All of Mammon's inventions are always composed of the finest platinum coating. This is her signature, attribute, which she gladly forges on all her gadgets. This platinum, layer, is how you know that she has crafted an instrument.

I remember that the witchcraft machine's power did not stem from God and this was deeply concerning! Since Mammon was not able to explain where the power stemmed from, the project was quickly scratched. If God was not powering the apparatus, and neither was any process she could explain, then, what was? Aside from all of this, Mammon wished to use her invention to pass on these things called, "negative feelings," to go undetected, and she wanted to be the only one able to use it. She refused to share it with angelkind. So, for many selfish and troubling reasons, our Lord told her not to use it, and even asked her to destroy it.

Back then, Satan was the only one who liked the idea of witchcraft, advocating and unceasingly pushing for its approval... He claimed to be able to power witchcraft, very easily, with his trident like he could with his idea for possession. Still, Mammon's contraption was turned down.

I remember when she first tested her machine in the training arena… With the platinum-coated witchcraft she was able to convey fear, confusion, anxiety, restlessness, and despair onto others. During the demonstration of this artifact, she created many images of herself as if multiplied, and then she transported herself to her challengers back, holding a *razor-staff* to her opponents' neck. The razor-staff was also one of her many weapon inventions…

It is precisely witchcraft, which Seraphina wishes to use in order to determine the location of the weapons.

She says, "I will visit Mammon who lives in the land of Purgatory. We will ask her to construct a new witchcraft, invention, so that we can use its sensors to ascertain their location and then transport undetected to retrieve the Essences."

Michael says, "Mammon, anon, lives in the v'ry seclud'd t'rrit'ry of Limbo. 'Tis a place almost completely remov'd from Heaven, whence she can worketh on h'r endeav'rs without distr'ction. If thou maketh the trek out thither then ye are w'rthy of h'r inventions."

Gabriel hates to shoot down his beloved's project, but says, "If our Lord did not approve of witchcraft then, why is it ok to use it now?"

Seraphina responds, "Under the circumstances, I think our Lord would condone the usage of witchcraft… Better the devil you know, than the devil you don't!"

Raphael, the only one with his wits, exclaims, "No! Just as we told Satan, the ends do not justify the means! We must fight this uprising, cleanly, and not forget our virtues!"

Seraphina persistently insists, "But Satan is not fighting cleanly! All he has done so far is immoral, unconventional, and lacking of all honor...

"Just as you are not able to see when he does bad things, maybe the connection will also be broken when we do bad things. We would be using something he loved, witchcraft, against him… What a blow it would be!"

Gabriel and Michael's minds are somewhat clouded without their Essences and so Seraphina's theory makes a little sense, but she is completely wrong because Satan's new specialty is seeing others do evil. In fact, his brotherly connection with the Gallants now solely depends on them doing evil or invoking his name. This is the only way he can see what they are doing.

Seraphina assures them, "Worry not, Gabriel! Now that you lack your Essence, I will be the bearer of good news... I will be the optimist for all of us...

"I know Mammon well, and we were once good friends. I used to be her favorite subject, who would help test her many weapons… I am sure her allegiance is clearly favorable to us..."

They all agree and part ways to pursue their many endeavors…

Meanwhile, Satan is on earth, hiking up a green grassy mountain. It is daytime, but the full moon is clearly visible. When he reaches the summit, he sees the most majestic waterfall, consisting of clear, turquoise, water, and big, granite, rocks. The plummeting water falls into a small pond.

He walks into the pool of water, making his way towards the waterfall… Surrounding him, on the banks, there are many of his new angelic followers. They have emerged from the surrounding trees and begin to follow him like puppy dogs, like addicts craving a quick fix. They are longing for orders, more so, longing for fulfillment that cannot be filled by the lord of persuasion. He tells them firmly to stay! They listen and obey.

These are some of the many angels that have been breaking the curfew and establishing themselves in what Satan would call strategic locations, hiding all around the universe, spreading the rebellion to the confines of the galaxy.

I can hear what he thinks… His rebellion must be directed everywhere, not just Heaven, because if he wishes to be like God, he must control the entire cosmos, reach every nook and cranny. His deepest thoughts are even more disturbing…

After the galaxy is completely tainted to his liking, he will have succeeded in creating an alternate reality where all his plans and inhibitions reign, an existence where his evil overpowers God's goodness. And, so, God's creation will cease to exist. In his eyes, he will have finally become the master of creation, able to create something of his own, chaos, which is one of the things he longs for the most, to have the power of Creation in his hands. But I know that he will not stop there! I now seem to know him better than anybody, especially his strategy. His thirst cannot be satiated…

On earth, Satan is wearing his black hooded cloak. As he walks to the waterfall and into the water, his cloak floats on the surface. His Essence is submerged and breaks through the water. Its heat creates evaporation and the waters form a canyon much like the, powerful, parting of the sea.

The falling water, from the waterfall, starts to splash on his head as he approaches the plummeting. With some difficulty, he then passes through the extremely heavy downfall of plunging water.

Now inside the fall, there is an enormous grotto style cave. He illuminates the cave with his bright, trident, light. Many bats storm out, rushing over his head, and passing with a loud screeching noise. The bats, rushing out, graze him, as he ducks to dodge them.

He begins to explore the grotto, lighting the cave walls, as he walks. In his path, he passes through many puddles. Throughout, the walls are stunning, golden, patches of rock, they are filled with the shiniest of diamonds, resembling the constellations of the sky, which probably means that if the cave would be found, it would be a very wealthy gold and diamond mine.

He is cautious and alert in his steps, keen to any minimal sound or movement. There are many spiders and insects all about. Some of the bats feed on these insects. The creatures, in here, seem to be more tainted than the ones on the outside.

For many hours, he traverses the cave into the very deepest depths of the earth, where there are pits of fire, lava, and magma, swerving. In this solitude and in this remote, desolate, place, he feels at home. A sense of belonging overwhelms his senses.

He reaches the end of the cave where there are stalagmites and a relatively small pool of liquid. The toxic, chemical, pool of water, is completely murky and burning hot. The smell is pungent of sulfur and putrid eggs. The liquid begins to explode in the form of an internal geyser. It splashes him and burns his left leg and his face. He is enraged, more at the injury to his leg than to his face, since lately his left leg has been receiving a repeated and almost unbearable beating.

Yelling to the ceiling, "Are you kidding me!?" But then takes the pain as if it were pleasurable.

The exploding stops after a few seconds... He then ritually

places some objects in a circle around the pool… With the help of his wings, in one leap, he is now standing in the middle of the pool, and continues to be burnt. With a thump of the trident, the once polluted liquid is now transformed, purified into crystal-clear water. The pool is not very deep; it only reaches up to a little more than his waist.

Below his feet, inside the water, appears a platinum, circular, panel that is visible through the ripples. He unsheathes his trident and with it, begins to light the objects placed around the pool. They are ominous and odd looking, white and black candles. The light that emerges from all the candles is red. However, the light radiated from the white candles is bluish-red and the light emitted from the black candles is greenish-red.

He then twirls his Trident in the water, as if mixing inside a big, boiling cauldron. Intense ripples are formed and the ripples turn to a tempestuous vortex of water and light. Both the water and the light, that he spellbinds, mix with the light from the candles forming an explosion of vivid pigments…

He repeats some words in a thick, almost unrecognizable, voice, over and over, "Futurus futura futurum! Futurus futura futurum!"

The water, in the grout, turns into a mirror screen, which reflects onto the, mineral filled, cave, walls. He makes a screen appear and begins to watch, attentively, as the images take a harsh toll on his self, as if draining his power little by little, injuring him...

Many events are compiled like a video collage. What he sees are future images of human history. What will happen after man is created…

First he attentively sees the original human, Adam, in the Garden of Eden. Then he sees Adam next to a longhaired human with a differently shaped, curvy, body and they are walking beside each other, holding hands. He cannot see their faces, only their backs.

Things quickly develop for the worse… He sees his friends, the snakes, and serpents, miserable, crawling on their bellies, instead of jumping through trees. Satan then sees two humans, brothers, as one throws a rock at his brother's head and kills him. Still no faces are revealed. A dark mark is left, scarred, on both their heads. A flood decimates the earth with its potent waves, which transitions to the next scene…

He then sees many, brutal, killings in battles throughout time... Rockets are being launched, spears being thrown, clouds of arrows flying through the air. Catapults, in the shapes of human animals are being flung. Fire destroys mountainsides and villages. People are being brutally stoned. He sees his angel friends dying and suffering, to flames, and a whip, as they labor unceasingly.

Then, little by little, I begin to understand the images being shown, whereas before, I had no idea what I was looking at. I even know names, places and terms that had not been in my intellect before. How is this happening? How do I, suddenly, know what we are looking at? Does he understand what he is seeing?

He sees blood, sweat, riots, protests, and junkies with needles, people consuming drugs such as heroine, cocaine, marihuana, MDMA, and meth. Now he can clearly behold hallucinogenic people, drunks, rapists, murderers, lynching, lepers… Humans are dying of cancer, HIV, and AIDS.

He observes a man being crucified next to two other men. A lot of blood, hunger, and suffering are the many staples. He sees a man, named Hitler, and his armies. Assassinations and genocides in the land, racism, a human commander named JFK, assassinated, atom bombs falling in cities named Hiroshima and Nagasaki, and the deformities in people caused by these wars. He sees rashes on people's skin, the Ebola virus, pollution, trash, trees falling, oil spills, amputees, casinos exploding and tumbling to the ground. He sees people gambling their life savings away. People are smoking, partying uncontrollably, excess in all forms!

Now the panel focuses on medical stents, artificial limbs, and cruel abortion; babies suffering, excruciating pain, in the womb, and silently crying for help, as vacuums and needles crush them… Husbands and wife's cheating, sexual licentiousness, family's failing, buildings burning, people crying…

Satan sees both creatures and humans dying in their habitats, plagues, sickness, starvation, famine, the terrorist plane attacks of 911 into the pentagon and twin towers. Riots, water cannons... He sees a fellow named Osama Bin Laden, the members of ISIS, beheading and crucifying children, and many other people, refugees of wars, numbering in the millions.

He sees coins the same color as the golden walls in the cave, gladiators massacring and people being entertained by this. Massacres for profit! There are mercenaries, children soldiers in territories such as Africa and throughout the world... North Korea, Russia, and the United States' armies, their weapons, missiles, drones, and their tanks crushing all in their path, which now flash along the screen.

People slaving away in front of machines, their phones, computers, and TV screens, like mindless robots, ignoring each other like senseless drones. Slaves are building pyramids and plowing fields at the hands of tyrant whips. He sees people named, the Roman Empire, the Greek Empire and even the Jewish people, fighting and falling. Battles and more battles are a prominent sight throughout time.

He sees limbless and deformed children, the holocaust, genocide, orphans, starving people, drug lords, warlords, gas chambers, extermination camps, depravity, more riots and car bombings.

Pirates, con-artists, hijackings. He sees the crusades, the KKK, skinheads, gangs, worshippers of deities, human and organ trafficking and he watches how humans would implode the world.

Many more disturbing scenes of the future are seen... He is troubled and saddened by how humans would destroy Gods creation. Worst of all, he sees how humans would destroy earth, and God would forgive them and still continue to love them. How they will still be praised, exalted, and preferred above angels. Satan's sadness turns to immense anger as tears begin to run down his face.

In his rage, with a swipe of his trident, he jumps and knocks down many of the stalagmites from the cave walls. They come tumbling down, splashing in the water. The stalagmites cut his arms, back and wings. It hurts, but he is now more used to the pain, emotionally and physically. He is just happy that the cave fragments have not landed on his now sensitive, left leg.

Chapter 17

Project Mariam

At the same exact moment that the visions unfold, Gabriel, Raphael and Michael are looking down on Satan in a similar screen. We are all in the room where we once transported to earth on the rainbow. All this time, we have been spying on him while he watched all these barbarisms unfold. Seraphina has already retrieved what looks to be the witchcraft apparatus, from Mammon, and this is what we use to look down on him.

As the images begin to wind down, Seraphina says, "Uriel and I visited Mammon in her dwelling in Limbo. When I arrived, her Cherub, red-eyed, companion, Belphegor, greeted me. He informed me that Mammon was not there…

"When I questioned further, he told me that she had just left and will return within a day to abide by the curfew…

"Since I could not wait that long for her to return, I conveyed Belphegor our mission, but did not go into great detail, for security purposes, and because it is in our best interest to leave things vague…

"I asked him if Mammon could build us another witchcraft machine like the one she built long ago. I told him it would be a major priority…

"At first, Belphegor was very surprised and dismissive, but then after insisting, he saw no problem in my request, almost as if he had had a change of heart. He only required that we provide sufficient compensation for the labor..."

Referring to Mammon's availability, Belphegor, with a thick voice, said, "You know how busy she is… Her time is almost as valuable as the Gallants' time!"

What is interesting is that Belphegor told me that others had shown interest in the witchcraft machine long ago. They were interested in it before and after Mammon destroyed it, much like we are now... In fact, they pleaded and offered a large sum of compensation if she would not destroy it. I asked whom? And he did not know, or at least did not want to tell me…

What he did tell me is that the hooded figure that approached Mammon looked an awful a lot like me, and that he felt some sort of déjà vu in my visit. How odd, right?

Seraphina continues, "What he also told both of us is that he is certain that Mammon had destroyed witchcraft a long time ago, having witnessed it himself when our Lord ordered her to do so. But, she constructed a similar device that heeded all the Lord's restrictions, still within the limits of feasibility. Until Mammon came back, we were welcome to use this other device instead..."

With this other platinum machine you can see whatever you would like to see, without being present in the room. I think to myself that the machine is pretty similar to the gifts I have developed recently.

"Mammon had planned to add certain features to the machine so you can pass positive feelings and powers through it, but it is still incomplete. This apparatus is called, *Sorcery*," pointing to the simple, platinum, box now in her pristine hands.

Seraphina continues saying, "I gave Belphegor many thanks for this machine… He showed me how to use it. As you can see, we needed a very strong power source to fuel it, the staff of souls did fine."

Raphael interrupts, saying, "Seraphina, show me how to use the apparatus." He wishes to understand how the box works since he is skeptical of it and because his staff was just fueling it. He figures that in knowing how the apparatus works, he can maximize the power of his staff to more efficiently exploit the capabilities of the machine.

She demonstrates, performing a similar ritual and conjuring as Satan did in the cave, lighting candles in a circle… As soon as she does the conjuring, she says, "Espia, Explorator… Espia, Explorator!"

Raphael's staff leaves his grasp, forcefully and automatically, re-powering sorcery. Raphael now remembers how he is not supposed to use the power of his Essence to harness energy or pass on its power onto anything, but remaining silent, he makes an exception…

Gabriel, also skeptical, reminds them, "This is not right! Our Lord wanted there to be privacy! Only He has the power to see everything and shares it with us if we need it. Maybe we should just ask Him for help, He has never failed us!"

We do not know for sure if the Almighty has approved sorcery and cannot afford to take Belphegor's word for it.

Raphael, the risk taker, wishing to take a gamble on Seraphina's methodologies, says, "No, Lucifer wants us to go to God for help. If we use our normal tactics, he will be one step ahead of us, just the way he wants it. We must use unconventional strategies to counter his unconventional schemes. This is why I allow the use of my staff to power sorcery." As always, he wishes to take his own chances, make his own luck.

The machine turns back on. The four of them are once again able to clearly look down on Lucifer. They are saddened to see him so changed.

Raphael says, "We do not even know him anymore! There is so much hate in his soul, and my staff cannot do anything about it. It cannot revive his Essence or his soul. Fecit tuum sinistrum latere Essentias!"

He breaks from his trend of not speaking in angel-talk. This last phrase is hard for me to translate. I think he said, "Satan has used dark powers and your Essences to conceal himself!" I don't know what this means, "Dark powers," but it must have something to do with the prophecy!

We continue getting a glimpse of Satan's sights of human atrocities in the cave, watching through the screen of sorcery. What's more, they see that he is using witchcraft. Seraphina recognizes the panel machine, after analyzing it from every perspective, since she had once helped Mammon test it…

He must have stolen witchcraft from Mammon, long ago. He must have been the one interested in it all along. After all, this makes sense, since he was the only proponent of the machine when it was presented to our Lord.

Gabriel says, "There are two options… Perhaps Mammon never destroyed the machine, disobeying our Lord and giving it to Lucifer…

"The second option is that she constructed a new one, which would have been incredibly difficult to reproduce, and Belphegor lied to us. Whichever way he obtained it, we must be very concerned. It is a weapon of immense power!

"He could transport legions to whatever location he desires. He can see into the past, into the future, everything! He could be looking upon us just as we are doing to him, and appear right behind where we stand with the force of one thousand Seraphs."

As Satan continues to look at the human atrocities in the cave, the good angels also start to get emotional at the sights.

Raphael asks, "Gabriel, is this true? Will this happen to humans?"

With a weepy voice, Gabriel regretfully answers, "It is very possible... These humans might develop concupiscence, which could stem from everything that Satan modifies. This is how big of a domino effect his actions are having. This is why it is so important that we stop him!"

Seraphina interrupts, asking, "What is concupiscence?"

Gabriel explains, "Concupiscence it is the tendency to do

evil... But again, what Satan fails to see is that most of the atrocities committed by humans will be, in part, due to his changing actions... An enormous ripple effect!"

One last scene appears on the ominous witchcraft screen… It is the most important one… The vibrant image is of a beautiful, tanned, human, woman, clad in a long, blue, veil that is covered with the brightness of the stars. She is wearing an elegant, pink blouse, looking peaceful, with prayerful hands, as she steps on the crescent moon… Her incredibly genuine smile, her black hair and brown cheeks remind Gabriel of Seraphina's luminosity, but they even exceed her splendor. Her face is the only visible human face in all these images. In fact, this is how it is revealed to us what humans faces will look like… The poise and grace that she irradiates are hard to compare even to the liveliest of stars…

We feel inspired and at peace. For all of us, I can tell that it is love at first sight! Yet to Satan, the image of this Lady is more disturbing and angering than any of the previous barbarisms… I have never seen him look at anyone with such jealousy and wrath; he is fuming and even trembles in fright!

All of the sudden, Raphael hears banging noises coming from another room in Paradise Palace. He is the only one that can hear them… He then hears faint, whispering, voices, in his head, that sound like Satan's voice, as if he would be trying to communicate with him… He indeed is!

Satan says, "Raphael, Raphael, join me... Give me your Essence…" And then, he hears the same words repeated. The feeling of déjà vu is overwhelming to him.

Raphael, terrified, says, "Turn the apparatus off! Lucifer is trying to connect with us! He knows what we are doing! He is accessing my thoughts! Turn it off!"

Seraphina hustles to extinguish the candles with her la-bow. The image of Satan, surrounded by thousands of snakes, who is now looking straight at the screen, eye to eye with the Gallants, disappears...

The fatherly, Michael, had allowed all of this to happen with no objection. He closely chaperoned the use of the machine, and did not want to get his hands dirty, respectfully removing himself from involvement due to his lack of Essence and therefore judgment, just as a spectator would. Allowing for this to continue, and jumping in once it becomes clear that someone is about to get hurt. But, now he is outspoken and reminds them, "We must not be in hither, spying on him, using this s'rc'ry! Our L'rd wouldst not approveth of anyone c'njuring these dark arts… Just anon when we us'd s'rc'ry, the c'nnection between him and us was obviously re-opened, aft'r all we hast done to isolate our thoughts from him."

Gabriel, who had been so against the using of witchcraft, is now sorcery's biggest proponent. A seed of persuasion has been planted into his head through the mischievous, diabolical, device. The fear of losing his Essence is too great for him… Ever since he lost his shield, I could sense his desperation, especially in his standoffish attitude towards Seraphina.

Emotional and disturbed, he says, "We must use sorcery! There is no other choice! We have to retrieve our Essences at any cost, and find where Lucifer has hidden them. Many things depend on our success!"

Against everyone's will, Gabriel, quickly, powers the machine back on, abrasively stealing the staff of souls from Raphael's hand…

All march to stop him, but are halted when they briefly see, on the screen, their stolen Essences floating in Satan's Palace... Through the display, Gabriel desperately reaches for his weapon, as Michael holds him back with all his strength. They are only deceiving images, mirages.

Michael yells, "NAY, GABRIEL! TURNETH IT OFF!"

Raphael aggressively pulls his staff out, to cut the power... In his resolve, I can tell it is the last time he will part ways with his staff. Then, in a menacing, firm, voice, he says to Gabriel,

"NEVER take my staff from me again!"

Gabriel's expression turns from that of an obsessive miser, to one of immediate repentance.

Michael heatedly says to Gabriel, "Doeth thou not seeth that in using this machine, we art nay bett'r than him? I cannot emphasize this enough! We doeth not even know how to control it!"

Gabriel says, "You were all so fond of using sorcery, before, but now you have turned on me, as if I were the villain!"

Michael says, "Nay one is the villain hither! Thy lack of Essence clouds thy judgment, Gabriel. Doeth thou seeth how ye are willing to doeth the same as Lucif'r, stealing Raphael's staff from grasp? Just as he stole thy shield!"

Gabriel reminds Michael, "But you are also lacking your Essence. How is your judgment better than mine? Do you not want it back as bad as I do?"

Raphael settles the dispute, saying, "Michael is right! No more sorcery! We are falling into all of Satan's traps. He has us exactly where he wants us…"

Raphael now begs, "Lord, forgive us! Have mercy on us!"

He approaches the platinum, sorcery, box, and with a firm hammering of his staff, he splits the contraption in the middle. It cracks with ease, bursting out an impressive and unexpected river of three distinct colors. An endless liquid of platinum, red, and black explodes, covering and surrounding the angels. A few moments later, this haze that burst out, hastily dissipates, trespassing the floor as if it had a mind of its own. The liquid metal slithers and infects through the cracks, in the ground, like legions of snakes that quickly disappear beneath our feat. It is like self-effacing mist. They had all felt anxiously troubled, but immediately relieved when the box is ruptured.

They all kneel repentant and distraught.

God connects with their minds and tells them, "***Sorcery and witchcraft lead down the wrong path, and with many horrible side effects...***"

Just as I had suspected, He also assures them that sorcery directly reconnects them to Satan.

Michael then has a realization, and asks Gabriel, "This is wherefore pr'ject *Mariam* is a c'ntingency plan, right?"

Gabriel, now more calm, happy to change the subject to what he is most passionate about, then clarifies, "Yes, Michael... this is *Mariam* is a contingency plan, but now I am afraid I have been ordered to put Project *Mariam* into effect. It is no longer a contingency! Satan has deviated from his plans and so must we..."

Raphael says, "Please, explain..."

"Project *Mariam* is an attempt of God to redeem humanity from their actions, which will be triggered by Satan. To redeem them from sin! Our Lord saw all of this coming, whether it is part of the prophecy, this I do not know... He knew Satan would try to corrupt our angels and then humanity, that there would be a rebellion of some sorts... Of course there was always a chance that our, misguided, brother would not taint anyone... You know that nothing is predetermined. It all comes down to our choices…

"And so, God has decreed that the only way that humans can be redeemed from sin is through His Son... God the Son has volunteered for this redeeming, this holocaust, long ago... If need be, He will lower himself, becoming a human, and offer His life up for humans in a very painful way. This is how much God loves His creations that he will humble himself to become one of them… We all know that love is sacrifice and what better sacrifice than to die a humiliating death. Greater love has no one than this, that one lay down his life for his friends...

"In order to come down to earth, God the Son who will be known by the humans as *Christ, the Messiah, the Son of man, Emmanuel, Son of the Most High, and Jesus,* must be born into a perfect, human vessel, without sin and with perfect willingness that must be prepared well in advance... *Mariam…*

CHAPTER 17

"Michael, you closely serve God the Father… I faithfully serve God the Son... Raphael, you diligently serve God the Holy Spirit… Satan used to serve God in His entirety, all by himself... *Mariam* will be similar to each one of us in that she shall be daughter of God the Father, Mother of God the Son, and Spouse of the God Holy Spirit... She will have a special relationship with each person of God's Trinity, basically replacing Satan as a Gallant…

"But Satan chose this, it is not as though he is being forcefully replaced… The show must go on with or without him! In Essence, project Mariam is also a contingency to replace Satan's Gallantry with someone else…

"I was simply in charge of designing and overseeing the circumstances for this human, *Mariam*. The Perfect circumstances continue to be set up in the Promised Land…

"The human woman, *Mariam,* will live a good life, devoted to God and will be a perpetual virgin. Her body shall be a temple more sacred than any palace we may ever possess. She will be the mother of the human form of God the Son... He who shall become, true God and true man…

"The Emmanuel (God is with us) that we have in the tabernacle will be passed on to her. She will give birth to Him in the humblest of manners and many blessings will come her way…

"Just to be extra cautious, she shall bear the protection of many Guardians in fear of Satan's corruption, twelve to be exact, and she will be given one more Guardian with each year of life. Even so, Lucifer will throw much suffering and temptation her way, but she must never fall, she must never fail!

"He is noticeably jealous that this human shall be so revered, even above him. He is envious that she will have a close relationship to the One God, in each of His three persons, which has traditionally been his job. It is he whom once served the Trinity all by himself and he believes this privilege was revoked with each one of our creations, but *Mariam's* status shall never be revoked! You can imagine that he is even more jealous to be replaced by a human… For these reasons, *Mariam* is not simply a project, but THE PROJECT! Actually, she is much more than that…"

Michael confidently says, "*Mariam*, that is who we just saw on the screen, right? Beautiful, peaceful, cloth'd with the stars and stepping on the moon? The one Lucif'r glar'd upon with hate?"

With a timid smile, Gabriel says, "Yes, that is our Blessed Lady! Get to know her. Love her as I do."

Seraphina hears Gabriel's word with what seems to be concerned fascination, remembering what Satan had said to her about Gabriel's love for *Mariam* and neglect for her.

Raphael says, "But clarify this… If humans will be so weak, will *Mariam* not be corrupted also?"

Gabriel, optimistic, says, "No! She shall be free from any defilement! She will not fail, just as we will not fail in our current predicament. All the more why we must help her!"

Using his connection with his staff, and looking into the future, Raphael says, "But he has not corrupted humanity yet… Adam has not even been created yet… Our Lord has not even seen it fit to give Adam a, woman, companion yet... We can still stop him! Those visions that Satan conjures can be halted!"

Gabriel, firmly, says, "He has already corrupted the minds of many angels. Human nature is a million times weaker than angel nature, and now on top of that, he has our Essences. If not defeated, he will probably find ways to, easily, corrupt humanity, and no doubt, God will eventually give Adam a companion…

"But you are right; there is still hope for humanity with project *Mariam*. The Lord ordered me to initiate this project if Satan becomes corrupted. Once we acknowledged the change in his name and his alter identity of *Lucifer*, this is when I was supposed to intervene with this project. He may corrupt humanity, but he will NEVER corrupt *Mariam*…

"I suppose we can also hope the best for our wildcards,

Beelzy and Adam's Guardian, Tremo…

"Beelzy's role in project *Mariam* will be the most key! He has no idea, yet, but he must realize his key role by himself, with no help from us! We must not bring it up with him because if we talk about the touchy subject of his friendship, it might make him more stubborn and rebellious. He, Tremo and the Watchers are our failsafe, and the only hope for deactivating this project. I want you to be right so badly about all not being lost! I would like to continue hoping for the best… and this way, we can cut out the dark prophecy before it develops."

Gabriel says to Seraphina, "But for now, announce to our loyal Seraphim; let project *Mariam* be put into effect… In time, the one who I directly serve, God the Son, and the humans redeemer, *Jesus of Nazareth*, will be born of *Mariam*."

She understands the orders and passes on the information to the helmets of the necessary Seraphs, so they can activate the project.

Chapter 18

Lucifer's Throne

Cloaked with a disguise, I decide to follow Beelzy to determine where his loyalties lie, and to find out how it is that his role will be key… He has received an official summoning from his friend, to appear like the ones the Almighty sends, but this one is in writing and becomes incinerated, into ash, after he read it.

He arrives at Lucifer's palace… Without him noticing, I closely follow… Outside of this dwelling place, angels are mobilizing. There is a huge commotion, one I did not want to believe, but the rumors are true! All the angels about, bear the, intensely obvious, mark of persuasion… I shall use this disorderly chaos to make my way discreetly into his palace.

I am surprised to see that an enormous fence and gate

have been built around the palace. Gates and barriers are only allowed to exist in the most sacred places and this is not one of them! He has claimed the area as his personal property, something that has never been seen in Heaven.

Beelzy is allowed to enter the estate along with all the eager recruits, whose eyes are turned red immediately when entering the barrier. I follow closely and hide in bear sight.

When I enter the fence's gateway, I unwillingly halt, and my eyes begin to burn and water intensely. A heated struggle of pigments surfaces in the iris of my eyes, accompanied by a magnetic sense of attraction to the palace, which looks as though it is on fire.

I can tell my eyes are on the brink of turning red, just as everyone else's have, when entering the portico, but ultimately, the blue pigment in my eyes has won the battle, not without a great struggle and with great difficulty. The burning palace disappears, turning back to normal.

The pigment of mine that seems to be losing all its battles is the gray one, for as the blue was victorious in this skirmish, so immediately has conquered the unceasing blackness of my skin.

No one suspects of what I am doing here. I am getting better at this; I hope!

I don't know if I am hallucinating, but I think I just saw

Michael's missing sword. As if a mirage and a reflection, I caught a quick glimpse of blue sapphires shining in the light. When I look back to the area of interest, the crowd and commotion of my fellow angels, covers my sight, and I lose my bearings. It was probably nothing, a delusion, just like the burning palace!

Beelzebub begins to climb the stairs to the palace. The Seraph guards open the great, black, doors for him to enter. I also slip in, pretending to be his accompanying, Watcher, subordinate. My spike-armor, below my hood, has provided me with a mirror-like weapon, just like the ones the Watchers use.

When I walk in, there is a contrast between the hustle and bustle from the outside and the tranquility on the inside. I had thought that there would be more angels in here, and that I could more easily hide and remain inconspicuous. This is proving difficult… I thought perhaps this is where all of the rebellious scheming was occurring, indoors. So far, it seems pretty tame in here, but this front too can be deceiving...

I grab a spear from the side armory, remain cloaked and simply convince one of the Cherub guards that he is relieved of his duties. He recognizes me and instead of ratting me out, he is inspired to see that I have joined their forces. He gladly leaves his post, as I get a better scope of the palace and maintain a watchful eye.

The other Cherub guard, who I join, seems to be an unruly one. He has a big nose and a prominent nose ring that goes from one nostril to the other. He does not recognize me and does not seem to be in as good mood as the angel I just replaced. He breathes deeply, grunts, squeals, and growls all in one breath. He has a potent and intimidating snuffle. I simply stand and smile, trying not to attract attention to myself.

My grin is not to his liking… His temperament is an unstable one, to say the least… Now, I simply look away, nervous of his unwieldy demeanor. What is his problem?

Beelzy begins to look for his friend and hesitantly calls out into the empty hall, "SATAN!? WHERE ARE YOU, MY FRIEND?"

Every step that he takes into the hall is an uncertain one. He is cautious not to be startled or caught off guard.

I now realize that Lucifer also does not know where Beelzebub's allegiance lies because he ran away when Satan attacked Michael and Gabriel.

Beelzebub continues to timidly yell out, "SATAN, ARE YOU THERE? … SATAN?"

He then hears a loud, commanding voice, almost as if artificially amplified that even scares me! The voice says, "Even though Satan is my old name, I like you invoking it! You must have heard that I go by many other names now, Lucifer, for example."

Then, he ambitiously poses a question, "What do you think, Beelzy?!"

Beelzebub does not know where the voice comes from and twirls in circles to find where the sound arises. The voice now feels close, behind him, next to him, around him. He feels as though he is being pulled in many directions, as he becomes engulfed by the potent speech.

Beelzebub's voice echoes into the hall as he asks, "WHAT DO I THINK ABOUT WHAT?" Continuing to turn and spin around… It is as though the voice is leading him to a specific location. He turns around yet again.

Now at his final destination, in the middle of the main hall, he notices a large, gold, and silver box, much like God's tabernacle, but adorned with two parallel lines (II) and much more ruggedly assembled.

At a distance, the doors of the box are wide open, and Satan is sitting outside on a majestic, black throne. The seat looks as though it is fashioned from dark marble. This is where he was being lead by the voice...

Beelzy is scandalized to see that his friend has constructed a tabernacle, hoping to compare himself to God.

Lucifer stands up from his throne, smiling, and firmly holding his trident. He walks down some steps to encounter his friend. As always, he obsesses on how he must be exceedingly charming and enticing if he wishes to attract Beelzy to his cause...

Beelzebub tries to avoid speaking about what he has just seen because he knows that his friend would probably look for encouragement. It would be wrong to encourage such profanation and heresy.

Beelzy, attempting to alleviate the tension, says, "I am h-h-here to see h-how you ha-ha-have been, my o-old friend…"

He has developed a noticeable, nervous, stutter in the presence of his pal. His voice projects, shaky, no matter how hard he tries to correct himself.

Satan, suspiciously, says, "No doubt the Gallant scum have sent you to spy on me…"

"No, they are not s-s-s-scum, and I am here on my own a-accord as a concerned f-friend and b-brother." Beelzy is telling the truth.

Satan says, "Do not make me laugh! Why would you be concerned? I am well, better than ever!"

There is no reasoning with Lucifer and so Beelzebub tries changing the subject to further lighten the awkwardness, he blurts out, "I came to t-talk about the l-l-l-latest news on project *M-Mariam…*" He says this immediately regretting he had said anything at all…

Lucifer is interested to hear that his friend might be reconsidering, and might now be willing to tell him the latest news on this elusive project, so he insists by showing incredible interest, asking, "What is the latest news?" This has greatly peaked his attention.

Attempting to remain loyal to God, Beelzy again tries to change the subject. Now in these tumultuous times, it is more important than ever that he remain faithful to God, especially because project *Mariam* is no longer a contingency, and procedures to counter Lucifer's rebellion have been put into effect. Not to mention that Beelzy seems to be a key piece in all of this. But every word Beelzy says, seems to be worse than the last…

He again blurts out, unintentionally saying, "I s-s-saw G-G-Gabriel and Seraphina em-em-embrac-c-cing…"

He is even more sorry he said this, realizing this would further enrage his friend. The more he puts his foot in his mouth, the more he stutters.

Lucifer is indeed fuming. He knocks down a cup of what seems to be wine that splatters on the ground. The stain on the marble floors is as red and thick as his chest. Then he grabs a bowl of what seems to be thin, unleavened, bread wafers, which are marked by the sign of the cross. They are there as if he was studying them, researching them, unlocking the deepest secrets of these simple nourishments. Some of the pieces of bread seem to have been tampered with a thin coating of Mammon's signature platinum. He grabs a handful and throws them in the air, flinging them in al directions. The pieces of bread lie scattered throughout the floor. He even steps on both the wine and bread fragments, as if he were trying to desecrate them.

Lucifer, trying to regain his poise, but failing miserably, says, "I ALREADY KNOW ALL OF THIS! I WAS THERE! Do you remember fleeing like a coward? You left me abandoned in the staircase, when I needed your help the most, but do not worry, Seraphina will regret what she has done to me when…"

Now it is he who does not want to disclose too much information until he figures out where Beelzy's loyalty lies. Lucifer stays silent and pensive. Then, he coldly turns his back to his friend, trying to leave the impression of abandonment.

Beelzebub, twitching, says, "M-Magna will regret…wha-wha-what?" Slowly they try to probe at each other for information... It has become a witty game of who can retrieve the most valuable intelligence.

There is another pause and Lucifer does not answer. He then collects himself, and tries to calmly, but assertively, intimidate Beelzy by pointing his trident at his throat and saying, "Stop calling Seraphina by that stupid, meaningless, title, which she will probably not hold for very long anyway! WHAT IS THE LATEST on project Mariam?"

There is an ominous foreboding in Satan's words about Seraphina not holding her, Magna, title for long…

He begins to walk, in circles, around Beelzebub, like when a snake surrounds its victim to constrict it. Lucifer's words have the same effect as real constriction does, but to his soul instead of a body. Beelzy is being so confined by Lucifer's questions, that he does not even realize what his friend means by these menacing words of premonition.

Beelzebub's last line of defense is to try to change the subject, at all costs, shivering, he says, "The Essences…you plan on giving them b-b-back, r-r-right?"

Certain that Beelzy has been sent as a spy or a negotiator, now it is Satan who again deflects the subject... He faces towards his friend, but no longer looking at him straight in the eyes, as if he is not worthy of his gaze.

It is clear, he is no longer very interested in project *Mariam* because he already knows all he wishes to know about it, and despite efforts of concealment, he knows that it has been put into effect. Witchcraft seems to have told him everything, and he also knows this because Satan has many spies, who blend-in, experts in hiding the mark of persuasion. I know this from painfully exploring his thoughts. The closer I am to him, the better I seem to be able to read him, leaving clear what were also uncertain speculations of my own.

Pointing his trident to the tattered, tabernacle-like, box, he had come out of earlier, Lucifer pushes his first question further, saying, "You still have not told me what you think about my tabernacle and throne!"

It is so hard for Beelzy to resist his friend's questions, appeal, and powerful trident.

"A bit m-much. Don't you th-think?" Beelzebub tries to answer as diplomatically as possible.

"My box is the same as God's… No one thinks His is too…" Satan pauses a second and then finishes his sentence…"Much! No one thinks His tabernacle is too much!"

For the first time, Beelzy feels threatened in the presence of his friend. He had not even felt this way when aggressively sparing with his crony by the beaches of earth. Against his wishes, his friendship with Lucifer seems to be gradually flailing and he has no control over it. Yet he still takes it personally and worries. The decay of this friendship seems to be favorable to our projects not Satan's.

With the giggle of an innocent child, Beelzy says, "But y-y-you are n-n-n-not G-G-Ga-God."

You can see Satan, fuming, veins protruding, face further blackened, with a rush of capillary blood, proclaiming, "WHO IS GOD? TELL ME, BEELZEBUB! WHO IS GOD? You know what? For once you are right… I AM NOT GOD!" Under his breath, he silently says, "With all the Essences, I shall be more powerful than God!"

Luckily, Beelzy does not hear the latter, but I do! And Beelzebub is happy that they are in agreement, saying, "Well, now that I see you are doing well, I leave you to your duties, my friend."

He tries to go up a few steps to give him a hug, but his friend pulls away and refuses the embrace, turning a cold shoulder that pierces Beelzy's soul, just like the cold shoulder he had presented God when proclaiming, "Non-serviam."

Beelzy is heart broken and since they have already gotten off on the wrong foot, he simply decides to leave. All that is in Beelzy's mind is to convince this madness to stop, yet, he does not feel that it is the appropriate time or place anymore…

As he exits, another angel enters and they cross eyes and paths. It is a stern, but still fair, looking, Seraph walking in to the hall; this extremely pale, and boney-cheeked, angel. Her name is Sodoma.

She inspects my companion, the unruly guard, standing a few steps away from me, telling him to stand up straight and to stop grunting, it is so hard for him to do those things. She gets in his face, invading his space, and demeans him by calling him, "Swine!" on account of his heavy breathing. Then, she smacks him around a few times in the temple of his head, again saying, "Pig-swine! Porker-boar! Hog! Curtsy to me! Hee Hee Hee."

Each insult comes with a slap to the forehead. He forcefully obliges to do this small bow, struggling to control his boisterous breathing patterns.

I can tell how much being compared to an animal of earth really bothers him, especially a pig that tends to dwell in unclean places. I must admit that the resemblance is spot-on. I briefly laugh at the name-calling and at how demeaning she is being to the big bully. He deserves it, for the way he behaves and treats others, but they both hear my giggles. What a mistake, I commit, as they now turn their sights toward me, refocusing their aggression. It is interesting how the peacemaker between two feuding parties, tends to become the focus of hostility by the once enemies he was interceding for.

The big, ugly, Cherub pierces me with his red eyes, almost as if exhausting steam from his nostrils. Sodoma is not too happy either… If she treated him bad for no good reason, I can't even imagine how she will treat me for my snotty remark…

She makes her way towards me, intent on inflicting some kind of humiliation on me, but I am saved from her hot-tempered scrutiny by the summoning of her new master, Lucifer... Sodoma quickly forgets about approaching me. Her anger seems to have been diffused by this call, focusing instead, strictly and nervously on the one who calls her…

Even though I saved my fellow Cherub from additional torture, and Lucifer just saved me from what looked like initial torture, I have a feeling this quarrel between this intense, Cherub, guard and myself is not yet over...

More so, I can tell that a certain animosity has been growing between the choirs of angels. Cherubs thinking they are superior than Seraphs and vice versa, and this has nothing to do with rank. What can you expect with a commander who thinks he is superior to God!

When Sodoma walks passed me, I am now able to read her like a book, extracting details that would not be so obvious to other angels. As with everyone, her proximity helps unleash my senses of examination.

Sodoma is a beautiful, but ruthless Seraph. I can tell by her posture, she is the military strategist that Satan has been longing for, and I cannot help but suspect that I am in the process of witnessing two job interviews, first Beelzy's and now hers. Beelzy's interview was not very good, but we shall see how hers goes!

Even though Lucifer has not approached the situation with proper charisma, the title of *General* is exactly what he wanted Beelzebub to assume in his ranks.

It is poetic justice that as Beelzy leaves, now enters his potential replacement; the next best thing, as if she had already been through a rigorous process of interviews or as if she has crafted a deal, blackmailing herself into this job.

The tone of the gathering quickly changes with Beelzebub's unwillingness to serve him, it no longer seems to be an interview for Sodoma, but it seems as though she has been given the job, by default, but Lucifer does not seem to be too happy about it!

Sodoma's twin sister, Gomorra, who is not present, is also a great military strategist and engineer, but they are both rarely seen together.

Gomorra is not as powerful, but is smarter and more

calculated than her sibling in her moves. She is said to be one of the most cherished apprentice's and assistants of Mammon, the great craftsmen and inventor, who created Witchcraft and Sorcery.

In combat, Sodoma is the second best, Seraph, warrior, after Seraphina, hence there is a big rivalry between them both…

… A long time ago, in the ultimate tournament, after overcoming countless rounds of worthy opponents, I witnessed, first hand, how Seraphina and Sodoma qualified to duel for the title of best Seraph warrior.

Following an epic match between the two, Seraphina was victorious. This is why many address her as, "*Magna.*" I can sense that this event has remained fervently in Sodoma's mind, occupying approximately 95% of her thoughts. The constant admiration, status, privileges, and benefits that were given to the victor, are some things Sodoma longs for, which occupy 5%. God had once occupied 100% of her brain capacity, but much has changed in this short time. Ever since the duel, she has been looking forward to a rematch and will do anything to see it realized…

The reason why she is not allowed a rematch is because in Heaven, time is a different notion. So, when they fought, it was a contest that withstands time. Seraphina, the Magna, was, is, and shall always be, more worthy of the title. If they were to fight again, Seraphina would always win… There is no scenario where she would lose. As you can see, a lot was riding on that tournament, so to have a rematch is just preposterous. Even though it was a tremendously close match, the true victor won that day, and for all eternity…

Satan, wishing to be heard, cutting to the chase, facing the bony cheeked and pale Sodoma, says, "I need that staff! It is the only Essence I lack."

Sodoma, confidently, says, "Hee Hee… Then you shall have it! It was not hard retrieving the other two… Hee Hee."

Satan, evilly, argues, "But before I had the element of surprise… There was no real antecedent to my actions. I worked extremely hard to control my urges, so to not blow my cover!"

Sodoma replies, "Knowing the Gallants, they have not given up hope on you and this will continue to fuel your element of surprise. They are quick to give you a clean slate… Hee Hee… What about the other gamble of a plan?"

Satan says, "It is moving slowly but surely. How are the Goliath preparations going?"

"Slowly, but surely, Hee Hee Hee." Sodoma repeats exactly

what Satan said and giggles as if joking.

What a big mistake, as she is violently struck down with a trident slap to the face, which leaves her face branded with the fiery iron. The marks look like thick scratches, singed below and above her left eye. Even though she is very beautiful, an ugly face is momentarily revealed behind the scars.

My ill-tempered, companion, guard, get's a kick out of the violence towards Sodoma. He thinks it is well deserved for the demeaning she has inflicted upon him.

Satan says, "DO NOT MOCK ME! I need the Goliath now!"

She is frightened at his reaction to such an innocent joke. I can tell Sodoma has not lost her innocence quite as much as Lucifer has, no one has!

I notice that there is a certain hostility, lack of patience, and distrust towards his General, almost as if she had failed him before, and with every breath, she continues to let him down often…

Sodoma, nervously chuckling and breathing intensely, says, "Hee Hee... But I need all of the Essences for the Goliath to be at full power and capacity… So we can better test it…"

Annoyed, he responds, "I hate excuses, but you shall have the Essences when the Goliath is finished, not a moment sooner, understood? And I will be the one to test it… Not you, not

Mammon, not anyone! Me!"

Sodoma answers, "Yes, understood! I am just saying it is much harder to test it without the weapons… Hee Hee," she nervously snickers.

He interrupts in the middle of her rebuttal, as if he were to slap her again. She reacts in defensive mode, so as to block the strike, but he does not reach her face this time, it is only a warning…

Now Sodoma knows better than to bring forth problems, obliged only to provide solutions. More so, it is obvious, Satan will not entrust the Essences into her or anyone's care.

Satan says, "Tell Mammon and your sister to hurry their efforts! Not only do we need the Goliath, but also we need them to assemble more weapons for our army…

"Belphegor has now joined our efforts and delivered the decoy machine, sorcery, to the Gallants. With the delivery of this item, I have the Archangels right where I want them and the first platoon, my most decorated, has already entered the picture. God and the Gallants are right where we want them to be…"

Sodoma, disgusted and angered, spits to the ground, and says, "My sister, Gomorra, is still helping Mammon? Helping us? I have not spoken to her in a long time, we do not get along!" Refusing profusely to work jointly with her.

CHAPTER 18

"Well now is the time to reconnect sisterly bonds."

Lucifer's orders of reconciling bonds with her sister, is the only semi-good task that he has done in a while. It is still done selfishly and with no intentions of helping their relationship, just of helping his cause, yet there is still a noble and unintended side effect to his directives.

Sodoma says, "As for the weapons, when Raphael and Michael distributed swords and shields for project Guardian, some of our troops already received weapons. We have also, silently, raided most of the armories in Heaven. It would be good to raid the one on earth..."

The rebellious one unsympathetically says, "Yet, most of our soldiers still are weaponless… You are stupid, that is why you are second best! Do you think we can go against the Watchers and raid their armory on earth? How impractical and illogical you are! We will never defeat such a distinguished troop of Michael's combatant lineage! Open warfare must be saved for two very special occasions! Even so, I prefer not to use anything God has given us because He could use it against us...

"No doubt the Gallants are planning something big, just as I have... As I become more unpredictable, so do their moves… Just as I want them to be…

"We will need more innovative and stronger weapons from

Mammon and your sister this time around… This time, it is all about the weapons, understood?"

The title of *second best* pierces Sodoma's soul; ignoring everything else she was just ordered.

"Yes, Lucifer," she says this, painfully, pensive, grabbing her scratched face.

This whole time I am being amusingly taunted and threatened by my Cherub, guard, friend. I ask God to reveal to me his name, and I now find out that his name is, *Sweenie*, which is perhaps why he was so mad when Sodoma called him the very similar but mistaken, *Swine*!

He points at me as if he wants to duel... I know he cannot leave his post, especially with his two superiors in our vicinity. He is simply making an elaborate show of vain threats for my amusement. I cannot contain my laughter… He is just too ridiculous! With every smirk from my face, he grows bolder and madder, attempting to approach, drawing closer and closer, but quickly returning when Sodoma and Satan look his way. He must be under his best behavior when serving in this palace…

I feel invincible and so I too join in on the teasing, giving more reasons to fuel his fire and approach me; taunting him with every gesture, mannerism, and facial expression possible. Here in my corner of amusement, never have I been so threatened, but felt so safe at the same time...

Multi-tasking, I am still able to hear in on the important conversation of Sodoma and Lucifer.

"Now leave and talk to your sister, Gomorra," Lucifer commands.

Tired of dealing with her excuses and disgusted by the presence of his commander, Lucifer is the one who leaves his palace, leaving Sodoma with a whole lot of confusion, unsure if she should also leave or if he was giving his orders of exiting to himself. As of late, it has not been uncommon for him to have loud dialogues with himself, since he is the only angel he seems to trust.

Just before he arrives at the door, I open it for him and bow my head so as to not be recognized… He storms out, covering his face with his cloak and luckily does not detect my presence. Sweenie, the Cherub right next to me, also bows, but now that his senior master is no longer there, he takes out his hostility on me, saying, "Hey vermin, aren't you going to follow him?"

For a second, I thought maybe I had been detected… As if Sweenie knew that my mission was to trail him… Puzzled, my heart drops… I stutter a little and say, "F-F-F-F…Follow him?"

The Cherub blows out of his large nostrils, and responds,

"Yes, pigsty! Escort the Gallant out! You are his protection…

"Not too tough without the Archangel in the room, are we?" as he points his menacing spear towards me…

"Did you hear me, scum? Aren't you going to follow him?" The menacing Cherub, Sweenie, repeats. "Get very close to him! I dare you!"

No, I will not follow him closely because I know that he speaks to me, sarcastically, wishing me to get hurt by his master.

I say to him jokingly, "Oh, of course… SWINE!"

My words infuriate him even more. At that very moment, as I pass him by, my very loose, helmet, disguise, falls to the ground making a loud clamor. The helmet rolls on the floor and lands close to Sweenie. He rests his foot on it, putting all his weight on the headpiece and leaving a dent by the ear hole. He taps his foot on the helmet, daring me to approach… I need that helmet because without it, I am sure Lucifer will recognize me…

When attempting to retrieve it, I am cautious and quick, running as I quickly slide over, bending over, to pick it up from beneath his foot.

When I grab it, my wings grow an extra size as they have gradually been doing for quite some time now… I too feel myself grow about an inch in length. The uncontrollable and apparent liveliness of my, expanding, wings, inadvertently hit Sweenie in the stomach, loosening his firm step on my helmet.

Not just that, but my swelling feathers become entangled with his nose piercing, leaving him breathless and knocking him down to the ground. He grunts and squeals, holding his nose like a baby pig. I kind of feel bad for him now, knowing that I am leaving him alone with Sodoma, which probably means he is in for a second round of belittling, but I still sneak out before I receive the consequences of my jokes.

Sodoma is indeed left behind. She stares at Satan's, lonely, throne with hate and the instigation of watery eyes, as she painfully grabs her wounded face…

Chapter 19

Into the Den

All this time, I have managed to maintain myself infiltrated in the enemy's camp... With my cunningness, I was able to get a swift replacement at my side for Sweenie. I exchanged him with the much happier and cheerful Cherub, "Al," who posed no threat to my discovery and was also a good conversationalist. Well, I think he was... Again, I am not sure if we were actually talking or if I was simply reading his thoughts... Because not much talking was allowed at my post...

Al had been assigned to Satan's palace duty much before the upheaval had started. He has witnessed a stirring in the atmosphere, but like me, he stays true to his mandates, which according to him, have not yet changed. I tell him that perhaps they did change because Heavenly communication is being cut off to this palace. So maybe he has been reassigned, but he has no way of knowing it, except my words, and so he stubbornly stays put. He had heard rumors of a deceiving angel going about, swaying the minds of others, and as a good servant of God, he listens to the command of the One who sent him here, in the first place, the Almighty, whose name resembles his own. Al's eyes seem to still be blue like mine probably because he has not walked through the palace's portico. He is a great Angel, good hearted!

Even with all my changes in appearance, the only things that seem to have remained steadfast are my eyes, which still continue to be blue, just like Al's are. But, in my conversation with Al, I was better briefed on my strict duties as a guard and on the overall chatter of this palace. I have also made a few other "contacts" that shall be my eyes and ears to the ever-changing protocols throughout the palace.

It is nighttime by Satan's palace. Raphael, Gabriel, Michael, and Seraphina, are on the outsides, attempting to break into the palace to recover the Essences. The four of them already have a small pile of intelligence suggesting that the Essences are being kept in this location. I have provided what I could, even though not much communication is allowed to flow.

They all split up... It seems as though they have devised a, simple, plan, which they are now putting into effect, attacking from different sides, running around the palace at full speed. They all try to avoid being detected by the many angels, diligently, guarding the premises.

Seraphina is supposed to enter the palace from the secret, rear, access, usually only known to the Gallants. She runs at extraordinary speeds and jumps straight over the black fence.

Separately, Raphael takes flight and elevates himself to the top of the palace. There is an opening on the roof, big enough for him to enter. He makes a pole by magically extending the staff of souls and securing it to the ground. Then, he slides down the pole through the opening. When reaching the ground, he pulls down the staff and it retracts. It is extraordinary how the Essences can be extended to the size and shape of their choosing.

Michael has also managed to enter the palace from the north end, walking up some stairs, inside the castle, and quickly joining Raphael who greets him with a warm eyewink.

Michael has noticed something out of the ordinary in the

basement level, saying, "I doeth not know what he is doing down thither, but he hath built s'mething. Thither art many changes made to his palace. That is whence our Essences couldst be..."

They both begin to search for the Essences in the most conspicuous places, but with elaborate order, with the precision of scientists. They think perhaps Satan is hiding them in plain sight, for that is where they had seen them floating in the vivid screens of Sorcery. He has divulged his deepest thoughts to me, and I know he would not risk losing the weapons and leaving someone else in control of them. Where else could they be if not safely with the thief?

While they search, there is an ever-present fear of being discovered, this only allows them to search the surface. Other methods of digging would be too noisy and give away their positions. Not only that, but in digging, destroying, or tearing apart, they would have to destroy, or alter, something in Heaven. Heaven is a place so pure, so uncorrupted, and so sacred, that it would be a tremendous crime, a sin, to desecrate its sanctity, even in the slightest of ways. Not to mention, God has created everything, and so they would be destroying God's masterpiece, therefore they avoid these tactics, even if they suspect Lucifer has chosen to break these unspoken guidelines. They will no longer follow their big-brother's lead. They have already broken enough rules, through his example, as it is.

Even though they believe that the homeowner is not present, because the palace feels desolate and is quieter than ever, they must still search, stealthily, in the dark, so as to not awaken suspicions from the many guards and spies throughout.

A few moments later, still trying to penetrate into the palace, I see that Gabriel is attempting to pick a lock with an incredible contraption. The contraption, which he calls, the *ball-drone*, is a small, golden, ball. He throws it from behind a pillar without being detected by the guards. The ball begins to bounce and then hops to the door, picking the lock to the palace with two retractable levers that extend from the core as it opens up.

The gadget has a mind of its own and legs similar to a spider's. It squeezes through the keyhole and knocks out the other two guards, inside, by bouncing from head to head. They are left unconscious.

Good thing I was no longer stationed at that position, if not it would have been me, unintentionally, knocked-out in their stead. The ball-drone would have not differentiated me from the rebels. The ball then returns to Gabriel. It has done a good job and both the ball-drone and its owner are pleased.

CHAPTER 19

Gabe's delay on entering the palace is a strategic move. He is not supposed to be caught, but meant to distract the guards from what is really going on in the background; this incursion. He is supposed to attract attention to himself with his gifts of entertainment. But if for some reason he is caught, then his cohorts will not be, and so all that he does is done with a lax sense of patience and enjoyment, as he whistles his favorite hymn of praise.

Gabriel throws another small, silver, ball in the midst of the guards outside. The ball again extends two, long, levers on the sides. The levers rotate on an axis and trip the guards. As the levers are retracted into the small ball's core, with blows to the face, they too, knock the guards unconscious. I hate to revel in someone pain, but it is almost comical how Gabriel, the ball-drone, and the guards conduct themselves.

The gadget has personality, just like the other ball-drone, it is courteous and jittery; it even bows, whistles, and opens the door for Gabriel like a doorman. The ball returns to its owner, also having joyfully served its purpose. It is excited to rejoin its thingamajig companions, the many other balls, inside Gabriel's pouch. The drone playfully kisses Gabriel's palm, and then does the same to its fellow balls. The drones even join in on Gabriel's whistling. I recognize the song, it is a song called, *"Immaculate Mariam;"* one of my many favorites!

The doors swing open and Gabriel glides in like he is the owner of the palace, almost boastful, saying, "That was easy!"

The cheerful way in which the Gallants penetrate the palace makes it seem as though there are no problems in Heaven. They merrily execute their plan like if it was a payoff after endless training and planning, and indeed, everything had been perfectly rehearsed. There was no need for Gabe to be the decoy or even get caught. His spectacle with the ball-drones was meant to be for a larger audience, but they were limited to very few. He has fewer guards around his castle than they thought he would, which is good, but it was a spectacle, nonetheless.

Gabriel rendezvous with Raphael and Michael, who are busy searching in the perpendicular corridor. All of the Archangels have managed to enter Satan's palace, then they continue to search for their Essences in all the rooms. Still no sign of Seraphina, but I am sure that Magna had no difficulties accomplishing such an elementary task…

They sense their Essences as if they were near, yet they cannot find them. Not knowing the exact position is very frustrating because the feelings of proximity are overwhelming.

After a long time of searching, the last place left to search is Satan's great hall, which they have methodically been trying to avoid. They enter the hall, where the lights suddenly turn on and are brightly shining. It is as though they were automatically tripped, as if sensing their presence... Satan had been expecting them...

The Archangels are surprised to see the tabernacle/throne, now illuminated, that has been built. Now they all understand why the basement looked different… He has constructed this box that runs structurally deep into the ground, with no permit and with no scruples. Just as they had suspected, he has altered God's, original, design for his palace. What a desecration! What a sacrilege! The Gallants sense that this, false, tabernacle is probably where the Essences are, like a vault, but they do not know how to access it without applying force

The doors of the tabernacle swing open. Satan is sitting on his, retractable, throne that extends like a plank, and then he stands, clapping his hands three times, and saying, "Well done my brothers, well done! You managed to penetrate my meager defenses. What an accomplishment! Next time, let me know ahead of time... I could have prepared and properly invited you...

"Nice to see all the Gallants together, reunited, myself included… It is the first time in a long time! Seems like an eternity!" He acts as though he has done nothing wrong.

Michael says, "Ye are nay long'r a Gallant, Satan!"

Taunting and flaunting his Trident in front of them, he says, "Well, I have this... Do you have one?"

Michael is extremely offended and saddened. Mindful that just because Satan has his trident, there are other more important things that make him an Archangel, such as exemplary love and service to the Lord and others.

Then he says, "If I would not be a Gallant anymore, do you not think God would have taken my trident from me? No, instead he took your Essences from you, not me! So, who is more Gallant? You or I?

"Think about it… Why would He let me keep my trident, yet take your Essences from you? I know you can relate to what I am saying... You have thought it through, very, carefully... I know you all feel abandoned, as if He is not helping you! It is true! He is not aiding you at all!"

Gabriel says, "You took our Essences, not God!"

Satan exclaims, "Yes, you are right, but God allowed it to happen and what good has come from it? Nothing! So blame Him, not me! It does not matter that you no longer call me a Gallant, I have given myself a promotion anyway!

"I know you are here for your Essences, but God does not expect you to succeed. In fact, he has already set you up for failure... I have seen this… I know how this plays out…

Sending you, unarmed, against real might, against real power, against ME!"

The Gallants look at each other, somewhat relating to what he has to say, as if he had a point.

"But unlike God, I have faith in you, my brothers, I really do! I'll tell you what… As a token of my magnificence, I will give you your Essences back. In exchange for them, you shall join me… It is a fair trade! You do want them back more than anything, do you not? You can be my Gallants instead of His, and keep your palaces. In fact, you can have whatever you'd like, that is what I am capable of…

"How about you give me some sibling loyalty… God, the Trinity is allied with himself and with these humans… What about my loyalty? Will you turn your brother down? Or will you continue to serve the one who sends you unarmed into a massacre?"

This is a tempting offer, the Gallants are intrigued by this proposal as they look at one another and remain silent in quiet reflection.

Raphael, now timid, appalled at the words his older brother is speaking, says, "Where is your humility, big brother? How could you ask us to be less than you if all four of us, Archangels, are the same? How can you boast to be greater than even God?"

Satan, proud and arrogant, says with a snicker, "You ask me about humility? Humility is seeing yourself in your rightful place, as you are… Come on! Don't kid yourself! It is you who lacks humility! I am not at your level! You have never been at my level! How can you even compare yourselves to me?

"Although you have your staff, Raphael, it has never contained the powers my trident does! Remember that I once had God all to myself and have witnessed things, know things, secrets, that none of you can fathom..."

All of the sudden, another side of Satan's wicked personality is seen… A personality I have become much too familiar with, or at least heard from afar, in my stay in this palace; giggles, with a strange voice, and then screaming, as if he was suffering.

This is followed by a mellow Satan, who calmly asserts, "Why bother to explain anything to them? They will never understand!"

Gabriel, concerned for his brother's well being, not knowing if Satan says these, odd, things to distract them, will not allow him to persuade them, and so he says, "What are you up to here, Satan? Give us our Essences back!"

Satan, conceited as he is, thinks about it, and says, "Since you will not consider my first proposal, here is another… How about a trade?"

CHAPTER 19

Pointing to the air, he reveals Seraphina who is being held in a windowed cage. The wicked, Sodoma, the straight-faced, Belphegor and the voluptuous, Mammon, have appeared from one of the adjacent halls, guarding the cage. Several hundred other, tainted, angels also appear eager to participate. These new servants of his are very attractive in their appearance, but gross in their wickedness. I am among them, yet, I do not think I am tainted like they are… Although, who knows? What they suffer from seems to be forcefully contagious.

The wicked couple, Belphegor and Mammon, look very similar to one another. They have very thick frames, red eyes, straight, square, faces, and backwards combed hair. They are also smiling; holding different, exotic, platinum, weapons, in their hands, including Seraphina's la-bow. Each weapon is more menacing, looking, than the last.

Mammon and Belphegor, caught Seraphina when she was trying to enter through the back of the palace. Knowing ahead of time that they would attack, she was an easy target because their dark forces had concentrated on only detaining her, and so she was doomed from the onset. They focused no attention on the Gallants... but how did they know? How could they anticipate our strategies with such precision? Unless… there is a spy among us… but who would be so daring?

When watching her combat train, by her tent, in the wide-open fields of the, Seraph, training camp, Satan concluded that the only way to subvert Seraphina was to get her in an enclosed space, like he did when pinning her neck against the wall inside her tent. And that is exactly what they did to her, now, restricting her strength and agile nature to a small area, where their force easily overwhelmed her.

The back passage where she entered is extremely narrow and tight. I had no part in her capture, but I was hoping to be among the ones who captured her so that I could let her go and warn of this premeditated ambush.

Gabriel had been wondering if she was ok, he had hoped she had found the Essences and left as soon as she could, just as they planned. Now he only hopes she has not been scathed.

Chapter 20

The Rematch

Seraphina does not struggle to get free, she appears ok, but her eyes contradict, showing fear. It seems as though they hold her captive and in pain. Sodoma is smiling, demonstrating her pointy chin, voicing her usual giggles, and enjoying her role as jailer, taunting and detaining her adversary who is under heavy guard.

I could probably make my way to release her, but this would only land Seraphina and myself in the midst of these, tainted, angels with no way out. Not just that, but I would blow my cover, which I have worked so hard to establish.

Gabriel demands, "LET HER GO!"

Satan points at Raphael's staff of souls, and says, "Those are a lot of demands and you have no leverage. I have too much to bargain with!

"Let's see… You give me the staff, and I shall give you your precious Seraphina back… If you give me the staff, then we can all live happily ever after as it should be, as I deserve.

"Surely you will need your "Magna" for what is to come… and I think you all know what comes next… All hell is about to break loose!

"Seraphina may have picked you over me, Gabriel, but now I choose to pick her, and pick, me, for her. How does that sound?"

Gabriel, distraught, says, "This is about that?" Satan does not respond…

I do not know what, *"hell"* means!? Maybe it is a word in angel-talk that I am not familiar with because my Gallants seem to understand the hidden depth of his words. So much hatred and malice have already built in his heart, it has built so quickly!

The Archangels analyze their options, knowing that they cannot make the trade. He cannot have all the Essences. Moreover, Seraphina is willing to perish for the sake of God's cause. Gabriel is worried about this notion, afraid that this episode will cost her life.

Seraphina sees the Archangels, through the glass, and now determined, struggles to get free and to penetrate her cage, banging the cell, with kicks, worried that she will perish without a fight...

Gabriel, desperate, tries to think of a solution, and then says, "I have an idea that would benefit us all, how about a duel? Me against you, Satan! Let us settle this once and for all!"

Satan considers Gabriel's proposal, saying, "Mmmmm enticing! I had not thought of that scenario… But, you would not stand a chance without your Essence, and I am not about to give it to you so you can fight me. Nice try though! Let's face it; you did not even stand a chance if you would have your Essence...

"I have a better idea! Why ruin things? Let us see what the Seraphs are made of, shall we?"

Satan wants Seraphina and his new General, Sodoma, to have their rematch from the angelic tournament, and then perhaps he will try to bargain again for the staff of souls after they see the might of Sodoma's newly found hate.

Every one of them, including Gabriel, is confident in Seraphina's capabilities, and that she will retain her Magna title, he lays down the conditions, saying, "If Magna wins, she gets her freedom... If Sodoma wins, then you get the staff…"

It is a tremendous gamble that Raphael is not too happy with, but he is confident that they will not lose. Since Raphael is a bit of a Gambler, he enjoys the odds of the challenge. They have analyzed this from all aspects with their gifts of intelligence, like in the game of dice, and have seen that there is no way, probability, or scenario where Seraphina can be defeated. There is no risk of loss in any, valiant and sanctioned, display of combat skill. More so, God has guaranteed her continuous victory with her win in the contest long ago.

Unfortunately, losing the element of surprise, the angels know that they have lost their chance to recover their Essences. Anyway, they were not completely sure if Satan was keeping them there. This is the only scarce data that they had gathered on the location of their weapons. Satan could have been playing games with them when they were doing sorcery. I can now confirm this… As feared, when they used sorcery, they saw exactly what Satan wanted them to see and so they were baited to this location for a purpose. They also confirm this, having seen, Belphegor, the one who gave them sorcery, among Seraphina's main jailers. Even with the strong sense of proximity to their Essences, they were mislead… Maybe it was, Satan's Essence, which they were sensing all around them.

It is a hard choice, but they now prefer to keep Seraphina, alive, instead of trying to get their Essences back. If they do not agree to the duel, then there is no telling what Lucifer, Sodoma and the others would do to her, but all hints point to her demise.

But besides all of this, Gabriel should not gamble with what is not his and he is too willing to offer the staff without Satan even demanding for it. Gabriel made it way too easy for him, yet, since Seraphina won, long ago, Raphael seems to agree that the wager is a fare bet, in fact, he believes that Satan is the naïve one for even considering such a dumb wager.

Seraphina is released from her cage and she drops to the ground, softening the landing with her bent knees and gliding wings. To be somewhat fair, Belphegor throws Seraphina her la-bow. She is excited and ready to fight. Her eagerness to quarrel reaffirms Gabriel that he has made a good deal. Since she has been released, this is an affirmation that Lucifer has agreed to the terms, even though he never explicitly says anything.

Sodoma is also excited, and says, "Hee Hee, Deal!"

The rematch she has been longing for quite a while, now, is about to begin… She stretches and rotates her neck. Both of the Seraphs loosen up, especially, Seraphina, after being cooped up in her cage…

Sodoma begins by saying, "We shall see who bears the Title of Magna after this!" Then she throws numerous insults to intimidate...

They all begin to wonder if the outcome of this rematch could have changed with Sodoma's, newly found, happy-hate. Maybe there is some serious intelligence that they missed when analyzing the result. This might play an unforeseen role. Gabriel becomes worried, but it is too late to back out now…

Satan adds to the disheartening, invading Seraphina's head, "Gabriel does not care about you… He is letting you fight... He gave up on the idea of fighting against me so quickly! If he had insisted, no doubt it would have been me and him fighting right now, instead of you…

"If you had stayed captured, with me, no harm would have come your way, quite the contrary!

"You could lose, today, you know? Gabriel just cares about getting his Essence back...

"First he gives Mariam too much attention, then his staff, what is next? I would never do that!"

Seraphina does not know how to respond… She listens and sort of agrees… For once, she is encountering unforeseen tactics from both of her foes. But it is not in her nature to lose or despair!

Sodoma immediately reveals her weapon called the *"shake-whip."* It is a whip very similar to Seraphina's la-bow. It has three, long prongs, with a round spiked ball in the middle.

Sodoma shakes her whip repeatedly, from left to right; the whip cuts everything it touches. She tests her weapon by instantly breaking a vase containing Gold, Incense and Myrrh, which were in three separate compartments, and the objects spill out with her fury.

They both walk in circles in fighting/ready position, checking each other out…

Prematurely commencing the duel, Sodoma tries to first catch Seraphina off guard, but luckily to no avail… With what looked like a disastrous beginning for us, Sodoma pushed Seraphina off balance, and almost struck her with her hook, but luckily she quickly recovered her footing…

Their weapons become rigid, using them as swords, just fighting and struggling, as they jump into the middle of the hall. The three tips of the shake-whip act as individual swords, moving in many directions. Seraphina has a stronger counteroffensive for every one of Sodoma's strikes. But she makes it look so effortless, whereas Sodoma seems to be expending enormous amounts of energy.

The warriors use their six wings to their advantage, as the edges are all lined with spikes. They use them as shields and to strongly hit one another.

Moving through the room, their weapons collide. The two Seraphs are very fast in their strikes and blocks. Many artifacts in the room, such as rudimentary furniture, made out of wood, and golden chalices are destroyed due to their combatting, as if they were innocent casualties of war. Everything, from small cylindrical containers, and thick nails, fly everywhere. All of the, angel, spectators have to move out of the way, as the quarrel approaches their location.

The lasso component of Seraphina's la-bow also multiplies, and attacks in a unique way, surrounding it's opponent and bringing forth attacks from all sides.

The formidable Seraphs attack and block the many strikes that fall, heavily, on their weapons. Both the shake-whip and la-bow also become fortified shields upon request. From Sodoma's side, the weapons extend through long distances to hurt and even attempting to kill. From Seraphina's side, it is a sign of great technique, to be able to control her, calculated, blows so as to not kill Sodoma, for this is not her intention.

From the very beginning of the fight, Seraphina notices that Sodoma is fighting to kill, and holds nothing back. The hate of her blows have added fuel to her menace. This does not deter Seraphina in her resolve or in her capabilities. She has seen it all in the training battlefield, having often faced overwhelming odds. But this duel is starting to seem a lot like her last sparring session in the Seraph armament camp; there is an ominous feel in the air!

Their quickness is astonishing, flipping and jumping in the

air, swinging from the ceiling and bending their limber beings.

At one instance, during the fight, the two combatants approach Raphael, whose staff is being used as a support stick. Sodoma tries to, firmly, strike the staff to loosen it from Raphael's grip, but with no luck.

Raphael will not part with his Essence! He holds it, tightly, and makes sure she is not able to get close again. Gabriel and Michael remove Seraph weapons from their backs, and step in front of Raphael, forming a perimeter, to protect the staff.

Gabriel holds a circular weapon called a *ring-sword*, with sharpness all around the inside and outside of the circumference. The ring-sword can be held and thrown to attack, as well as used as a shield. Michael carries a *swallow,* which is a spear with two swords on opposite sides. The swords can rotate in many directions, being used to attack and defend. These weaponries are no Essences, but in their hands, they are still elaborate enough to be impactful.

Once Raphael figures out that Sodoma tried to play dirty and steal his staff, he fakes a strike to Sodoma's head, but does not actually touch her. She covers her head, and ducks from both Raphael and Seraphina's threats. He could have easily struck Sodoma, but wishes to play fairly and so he refrains from doing so… Grinning, doing the usual, Raphael winks his eye at her, letting her know what he could have done to her if he wanted to. She understands but does not seem to care.

The partners, Belphegor and Mammon, were also ready to join the fight if the Gallants were to jump in, it is almost as if they are itching to do just that. By themselves, they would probably bait fights with the Gallants, but Lucifer has ordered them not to interfere just as I was once asked not to... They are cowards; they only, now, wish to fight because 2/3 of the Gallants do not have their Essences, otherwise, they would not stand a chance, especially against Michael who helped develop the art of combat. They still do not stand a chance, but at least, now, they have better odds.

It is as though Belphegor and, especially, Mammon have been holding a grudge on the Almighty and the Gallants ever since their masterpiece of Witchcraft was disapproved. Now it makes sense, this is why they removed themselves from Heaven's main land to the secluded territory of limbo, wishing to be as far away from any sort of rule, like hermits.

Also among Seraphina's jailers are the many menacing Seraphs that had maliciously and persistently attacked her in the many waves at the training camp, not too long ago. They are the ill-intentioned Seraphs that had left longing to hurt her, but with no luck. I can tell that this sentiment has not vanished, as if their only mission is still to damage her. They also wait, eagerly, for their chance or any excuse to redeem themselves because I can tell that they too had been punished by their master for failing at something!

After ominous taunting and stares between the many angels that are not fighting, on opposite sides, attention is brought back to the fight, as Seraphina is the first to wound Sodoma right above the knee.

Astonishingly, the blow to Sodoma's leg draws blood, which begins to flow out slowly, in a thick, black and red texture. No one knows what the red liquid is, since angels do not have blood, they think perhaps it is wine that has been spilled, but as I stated, I know what it is…

This injury fuels Sodoma's rage, even more, as she attacks with more determination than before...

A few moments later, in retribution for this wound, Sodoma wounds Seraphina just below her left rib. No blood is drawn; just a painful mark is left behind.

In the second part of the duel, after they have both been wounded, they begin to use their weapons as they should be used, with their even more special capabilities.

The first time I saw this duel long ago, I thought I was

very fortunate to witness such a feat, now I am even luckier to witness this epic rematch. But a lot of it is déjà vu, just in a different setting. It is almost as if I know what is about to happen next.

Seraphina shoots arrows and projectiles with the bow component of the la-bow, while she runs in circles around the room, elevating herself to great heights and even running on the walls with dumbfounding speed.

Sodoma destroys the arrows with jolts of her shake-whip. They both take cover from each other's assaults, barricading behind walls and furniture that continue to be pulverized everywhere. Sodoma's signature, crazy, giggles resound in the halls.

Many of Seraphina's arrows rebound back to Seraphina by the blocks of Sodoma's shake-whip. Seraphina makes the arrows disappear with the twirl of her la-bow, as if she had a portal in the middle of her lasso. She is also able to redirect the rebounded arrows by grabbing them with her weapon.

Sodoma whips the air and small thorns shoot from her whip, swerving around corners. Some hit their target, stinging and weakening Seraphina, but most miss their mark. All the, spectator, angels have had to block the many projectiles and stay away from their paths. It is an evenly matched battle! No one is, clearly, winning…

After they are done shooting, once again, they both meet with extreme force in the middle of the hall, exposing themselves, colliding, while pulverized debris is flying everywhere!

Jumping in the air and clashing, Sodoma's whip and Seraphina's lasso intertwine. They struggle to hurt each other, pushing off with kicks and shoulder shoves. Sodoma seems to want to thrust Seraphina, very far away, and be nowhere near her opponent, wishing to only hurt her from far away.

Sodoma tries to box-in Seraphina wherever she can. She knows that this is how she was recently captured, in a confined space, where her moves were restricted. On the other hand, Seraphina tries to keep Sodoma as close as possible.

In an extremely agile and strong maneuver, Seraphina breaks the weapons from entanglement and manages to hang Sodoma by the neck. She then throws and attaches her lasso, to the ceiling chandelier, in order to bind her.

Sodoma is now wrapped and dangling, immobilized in the la-bow's noose, hanging and choking. With the sound of a loud splat, her shake-whip falls to the ground…

This is exactly how she had defeated her in the first tournament, déjà vu! Seraphina remembered that Sodoma's weakness was proximity. Just as her "weakness" is enclosed spaces, Sodoma did not fair well when her opponents were too close to her. Both combatants had very similar weaknesses, but only Seraphina was able to exploit Sodoma's properly, and twice.

Seraphina, heroically, wins the duel! The Gallants are very happy, and can breathe with more ease, especially Gabriel, but they must all continue, on guard, as Lucifer's troops now threaten to charge them.

Since they are victorious, now they simply wish to exit as soon as possible, Gabriel insistently implores, "Let's go!"

Seraphina detaches her la-bow rope from the hanged Sodoma. She is still hanging as though Seraphina had only detached part of the rope and kept some of it on her hanged foe. Sodoma is enraged, but in sad disbelief, she still manages to get her loud, desperate, chuckles in.

"Hee Hee Hee."

Satan once again claps his hands and seems unfazed, he calms and halts his forces from charging, by lifting his trident, saying, "There will be a time… Not yet… Not yet…"

They look disappointed.

Looking up at Sodoma, he nods his head in disappointment but does not care about her, and so does nothing to bring her down, while she still chokes.

CHAPTER 20

The victor has a big, compassionate, heart, and so she becomes even more sorry, for her opponent, when she sees that her master shows no sympathy for her current condition. It is in her, caring, nature to want to release her from bondage, as she watches her, struggling to get free, wobbling in the air…

Satan and Seraphina look at each other while he still claps and she pants.

It is now obvious to me the he wanted Seraphina to feel the same ecstasy she did long ago when she first won her title, maybe he thought this would soften her heart towards him, giving her this thrill of excitement that Gabe has failed to give her in a while. He wants it to be a reward, an incentive, but it is not!

Fearing retaliation, Seraphina does not let Sodoma go. To make sure there are no further attacks, she cautiously moves out of his path. Bruised and winded, Seraphina walks toward the Archangels with a calming relief.

Excited and ambitious, she boldly says, "Let us take the trident!"

Seraphina presumes she is in the clear, turning her back to Satan, and begins to walk incautiously towards Gabriel's arms.

At that split moment, with the power of his trident, Satan, instantly, floats the shake-whip, up to Sodoma, which immediately releases her hands from immobility. She grabs her shake-whip and with a simple, precise, strike, hits Seraphina in the back.

Still standing, Seraphina makes eye contact with Gabriel and slowly falls to the ground. Now on her knees, she maintains her gaze fixed on Gabriel…

With a simple smile, Seraphina mouths, "I love you."

This is how she has lived her life with love for God, Gabriel, and all angels… She disappears from sight like white dust in the cool breeze. It is a sad scene…

Sodoma manages to, completely, release herself from her cocoon noose. Lucifer has played dirty! Even though it was mainly of his doing, Satan lashes out at Sodoma, striking her with red gases of pain for having killed his beloved. He now knows that they will not give him the staff because of the foul play, and everyone knows that Seraphina was the true victor.

The sore loser, first, calmly says, "What a pitty…" Then he yells with rage at the top of his lungs, "GET OUT!"

He holds his trident in front of him, and begins to blow at the trident tips, as if he were extinguishing an inextinguishable candle. The three tips light up, as if they were bright, coal-like, embers.

The Archangels struggle, to stay in, against the strong blast of wind that has been fashioned by the blowing of the trident.

As they are being blown out of the palace, Gabriel creates friction with the ground and begins to slip out, yelling, "NO!" Reaching forward as he slips, he manages to grab Seraphina's la-bow and the engraved pink flower case he gave her. It is all that remains of his beloved companion…

Michael grabs a hold of Satan's door and struggles against the force of the strong wind, so to not be blown out.

They are all eventually whisked out, and the doors to Satan's palace are shut, tightly, with the gust of wind.

Inside, Lucifer calmly walks up the stairs to his tabernacle, as if nothing had happened, this is the extent of his grief for his beloved Sodoma takes a moment to quickly compose herself, covering her wounds with pieces of torn cloth, and then joins Satan. She is unsure if he will continue to lash out on her, not understanding why he did it in the first place, since she was just following his scrupulous orders, so she keeps her distance... Since his original scheme, to kill Seraphina, was accomplished, therefore immensely debilitating our forces, nothing else is mentioned of her defeat…

Even though she killed her opponent, she does not feel as fulfilled with the victory as she expected to be. The cheating manner in which she won is what dictates this. She is the culprit of the first, ever, angelic death. Even her giggles fall silent, meditating on the severity of her actions.

Now, they make way to the throne, and enter the tabernacle. The doors close like those of an elevator...

Outside, the Archangels' land on a grassy pasture, they have used their wings to land on the grass unscathed.

Raphael, painfully, says to Michael, "We have failed! I was not able to do anything with my staff! Once again, Lucifer was one step ahead of us...

"Seraphina is dead and we have lost our best Seraphim warrior… We have never lost anyone before... I cannot imagine how Gabriel must be feeling."

Even though this loss affects them all, of course, it affects Gabriel the most. I am there, with him, trying to console my Gallant with telepathic thoughts... Appreciative of the sentiment, he still distances himself to be left to his reflections of mourning. We respect and understand his request...

It is so hard for me to stay silent in my grief and disbelief, which I must do to keep up appearances! Where was I during this? Right in the middle! This is embarrassing and it hurts! It feels even worse that I could have probably released her from bondage, but at the expense of blowing my cover. Still I should have acted because I could have potentially saved her life and her life is probably worth more than mine. It saddens me not being able to break my cover, but my time is now close… I can sense it!

Michael, presents some primitive sketches to them, and says, "As they wast fighting, I p'rus'd the room and saweth that Lucif'r hath construct'd an und'rground elevat'r… The throne and box wast not the only additions. I couldst feel the hot breeze c'ming from down below. Who knows what 'tis and whence it leads?"

Raphael, seeing this all as an adventure and trying to be optimistic, winks his eye, and says, "We will have to find out!"

There is no time for sadness in Heaven because God is optimism in its purest form and they are reflections of the Almighty.

Michael says, "Did'st thou see mine crony, Uriel, in thither? He is well infiltrat'd among the wicked ones… I shall delivereth him his task of finding moo about this und'rground structure... Knowing mine p'rsistent friend, he pr'bably already knows what 'tis."

Raphael says, "He knows our mandates! He is listening to us right now." I see my Gallant winking his caring eye toward me.

Gabriel continues isolated from the group. He has

Seraphina's la-bow in one arm and the ring-sword in the other. He grips them both firmly, gazing upon the pink, rose, emblem, on his beloved's la-bow sheath. There are tears running down his face as he now stares at Satan's palace in the distance. He feels destroyed, without consolation. It is even worse because he had been so busy lately that he had put his beloved aside… She had been demanding for him to tell her a story, but he had been postponing it. He could not even follow-through on something so simple, but now there are no longer any opportunities… It is hard for him to be optimistic without his Essence of good news. It is sad to have lost something so beautiful and meaningful! Her effort will have not been in vain...

Nonetheless, he struggles and fights through his pain, knowing everything happens for a reason and that the Lord is kind and merciful. The prophetic dark times have truly arrived if someone as pure as Seraphina is the first to go, what shall become of the rest of us?… Angels can die! The plot thickens…

Chapter 21

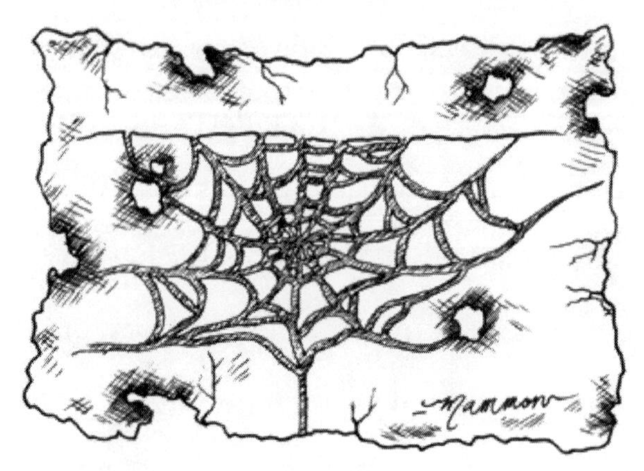

Tunnel Vision

Sodoma, Satan, and a troop of angels are lowered underground by Satan's throne, which acts as an elevator, taking us a few stories below his palace. It is a shaky and somewhat lengthy ride down. Satan stands in the back, his troops, myself included, in front of him, not trusting his back to anyone. His head remains bowed, pensive, eyes facing the ground.

When finally reaching the bottom, the thick, stone, doors open slowly with the sound of scraping rocks. The scene is dark and desolate...

Pointing his trident in all directions, Lucifer lights his view of the enormous, dark, tunnel, therein. His troops exit and align on his sides, enclosing him in an orderly box of their ranks.

Sodoma and her master begin to walk in the middle of the square of companies, dodging rocks, crystals and objects... Advancing, militarily and then stopping. Advancing again, stopping, doing this many times for no reason other than to build suspense and thrill, as if going to a rhythm.

They reach a point where there are thousands of Cherub and Seraph, workers, digging. Water is dripping everywhere and it is extremely humid.

The worker angels squint as the light of the trident is shined in their eyes. Further into the tunnel, the workers have bright lights being projected so that they can see better. All the workers bear the mark of persuasion, those noticeable, ominous, red, eyes. Most of these workers should be working on God's projects, yet they are here, below Heaven, in defiance of God, working in the darkness for Satan's projects.

Although a small number of them have been deceived and filled with lies, most of them have been stolen from earth to come and do Lucifer's bidding and are there of their own accord. To their defense, he has told them that they are, there, doing God's will. They think this is all part of the four projects.

There are also those who simply have a loyalty to Lucifer as their Gallant, simply for his past deeds, and for his role in their creations, having been trained in his lineage since their creation.

The great majority of them do not realize that the real plan is to overthrow God, they are simply sick of serving, but they do not realize that with every disobedience, they are lured closer to Satan. This is the plethora of stories among the mutineers.

There are pillars being constructed, to maintain the integrity of the tunnel, and a very wide walkway is being paved with the use of their dirty hands. There are thick, wheel, marks in the area that has not been paved yet.

Sodoma, optimistically, says, "The passage is almost finished, Lucifer. As specified, *the Cobweb* is an extensive networking of tunnels. Our angels have been working on it in the dark for a long time now… The designer has done a fabulous job. Hee Hee. So far, Mammon's platinum tools have been invaluable in all aspects and will continue to be…""

He exclaims, "It is about time!" Then he asks, "And it leads to the desired locations?"

Sodoma, concisely, answers, "Yes!"

From the main tunnel, there are many other passages that root off of the main stem. It is hard to know exactly where the tunnels lead… I try to read the minds of the workers to ascertain where the passages lead. I get nothing! They don't seem to know either; they just dig where Belphegor tells them.

My speculations lead me to conclude that the passages

probably lead to Paradise Palace, to the Gallants' palaces, anywhere really… It is hard for me to determine even though I seem to grasp things much quicker as of late. It also dawns on me that at the end of the tunnel is where Satan hides the other Essences.

Not letting any of her snotty remarks slide by, Lucifer, annoyed, says, "I know they have been working here for a long time; it is I who sent them here. The witless imbeciles have been filling Heaven with earthquakes and suspicions…

"If Mammon and her team would have been doing a fabulous job, like you claim, the passage and the Goliath would be done by now. Will it fit through here?"

Sodoma says, "Yes, it has already fit through here, see the wheel marks? As we speak, the Golaith is being finished at one of the tunnel's ends… We have been using it there. The smaller tunnels are being dugout manually, but the incomplete Goliath…"

"Do not mention that name anymore... *Goliath*... God also has His spies... Remember? I told you that!"

Nervously, she says, "Forgive me… I reiterate… Just like the cobweb tunnels, the G… is almost done…"

Satan, bothered, exclaims, "I keep hearing; almost done… I will believe it when I see it!"

CHAPTER 21

He then, wickedly, says to himself, "Punish her!"

Sodoma, looking, nervously, concerned to this statement, says, "Apologies! Is this good? Have we done good? Hee Hee." Like a dog, she looks for reassurance from her master.

Satan talks to Himself, and volatile says, "Nothing is good anymore! Greatness is what awaits us!"

Sodoma is shocked to hear these words, and insists, asking, "But I am still good, am I not?"

Satan, enraged, says, "No!"

Then, in a crazy voice, he contradicts, saying, "Yes,"

A second later, he firmly clarifies, "NO!"

Then he mutters quite clearly, stating, "At least your sister, Gomorra, produces, somewhat, acceptable results constructing the cobweb."

He says this looking to irritate Sodoma, praising her sister, Gomorra, whom he knows she is still feuding with. This indeed bothers her, sparking incredible jealousy. He has never, ever, spoken highly of Sodoma, yet he speaks highly of her sister, who unlike her, has a very much secondary role in the rebellion.

He does not care what Sodoma thinks or has to say; only interested in the work at hand and that his own commands be fulfilled, asking, "Let me ask you... I was able to persuade most of these angels to dig… They believe these are God's orders... Is this good?"

At first, she too thought that they were doing God's work, but is now too deeply involved and unable to leave. Sodoma, unsure of the correct answer, replies, "Yes, this is good!"

In his rage, Satan expulses a sort of power bolt from his trident. It hits both Sodoma and a column inside the cobweb, and he yells, "WRONG!"

Followed by another, wicked, voice from him, which paranoid, says, "You are right that she is wrong!"

Part of the tunnel collapses and many are caught under it. After much suffering, they perish, disappearing like black dust under the rubble. Luckily, I was concealed, well away, from their location.

Sodoma crawls out with a few scars, bumps, and bruises. She and the other workers are shaking because of the unpredictability of their new master.

Sodoma begins to think, "I think I preferred serving God…"

Satan intrudes her thoughts, now caring and sensitive about what she thinks, stares at her, and says, "I know what you think, Sodoma… Do not make a fool of me... You will serve me now, only me, and I will make your wildest dreams come true...

"After the war comes peace. What comes next is the war that I speak of and later comes the peace... this time it will be different, this time we will not have the same fate...

"I promised you would get your rematch and revenge on Seraphina and you did... Are you not happy because of it?"

"SHE IS NOT," he crazily yells to himself.

Sodoma, scared, reassures him, saying, "Yes, I am! You are right, Lucifer, and now I am the Magna! If this has changed, maybe our fate can change too! I guess you are an angel of your word... I would say our deal is about fulfilled."

Her master says, "I THOUGHT I TOLD YOU NOT TO MENTION ANY OF THAT! You seem to be longing for torture...

"Archangel, Gallant, Lucifer and Magna, what feeble titles! I hate them! Do not mention them again!"

He has drastically limited her options of how to address him, and so she does not know what to call him anymore.

Satan is then reminded that for Sodoma to obtain her revenge, his love, Seraphina, had to become a casualty.

Satan says, "We all have to make sacrifices to see our strife fulfilled, just as I sacrificed, Seraphina, for your glory, so must you sacrifice yourself for my glory now that our debt is settled." Sodoma reluctantly agrees, and I cannot help but wonder what debt they are talking about, almost as if Satan owed her more than a favor!

He asks one final question, "Have you made amends with

your sister, Gomorra?"

She answers, untruthful, "Yes, Lu… I mean, your lordship, Hee Hee, I have!"

"You see?" All is well, and now both you and your sister have extinguished the feud that haunted you for such a long time. These are the rewards that I offer you even after you blackmailed me, and I promise many more to come…"

Sodoma is cautiously thankful, and she is given the necessary fuel to carry on her tasks.

He sees the injured angels that are lying on the ground because of the collapsed cave. Approaching, he hits some of them with his trident, putting them out of their misery, saying, "Weak minded fools; Slaves! This is what I call dignity in death because they had none in their life!"

With the hate of a million souls, he yells to the rest, "BACK TO WORK!"

Then he calmly requests, "Please…"

They continue to work, diligently using their tools. Another tremor occurs because of the digging. They are all shaking in their spots, but wobbling from side to side. No one is hurt; nothing falls from the cobweb ceiling, just a little dust arises, engulfing the ambient. It seems as though they are already used to the, intense, tremors. I am not accustomed, and so I lose my footing.

Sodoma knows what she must do, leaving her master, and begins walking and descending to the other end of the tunnel, taking a few muscly Cherubs with her. The rage that she has been accumulating is taken out on the workers, mouthing insults, degrading them, and shoving them against the walls. They look at her with envy, hate and lust.

"You shall call me, Magna!" She hatefully and self-righteously says. Everyone knows of her rematch. Even though Seraphina once earned the label of Magna fairly, she had never boasted about her title, yet Sodoma acts oppositely.

After walking and inspecting for many hours, she is now in proximity of the source of all the tremors, but sees very little in the darkness. For now, all she can see are dozens of her soldiers and workers, inadvertently, falling or maliciously being pushed by others into some of the descending tunnels and conduits, screaming on their way down as they move like ants, quickly carrying rubble and gravel through the tunnels.

One more, curious, sight is prominent... In the puddles there seems to be the remnants of a liquid, much like the one we saw exploding and gushing out from sorcery, when Raphael destroyed it. I remember the colors of the liquid, vividly, after the staff of souls parted the, wicked, machine in half. This platinum, red, and black, fluid seems to be scattered everywhere along the ground. In fact, all the holes are filled with that platinum fluid that had once seeped and dissolved, disappearing into the ground. I guess this is where the liquid went and ended up. Not just that, but this region seems to be millions of times hotter than where she recently came from.

Lighting her shake-whip like a torch, another thing she briefly manages to see and hear, are many angels, screaming, and some trampled angels with burnt marks, scattered, around the area… These are the casualties that have arisen from the collapsing of the cobweb when digging in defiance of God.

All of a sudden, she then turns around to hear Satan's voice desperately calling and summoning her…

At the other end of the tunnel, just as Lucifer was returning, by himself, and about to enter the elevator up to his palace, he senses as though he is being watched. His intuition serves him well… In the darkness, he sees two bright blue eyes spying on him, and then they begin to come towards him at full speed, becoming bigger and bigger…

I engage Satan, hitting him with a blow of my club and knocking him in the air as I shove him towards one of the cave walls, right through a very sturdy pillar that shatters with his impact.

Now it is my time to shine! I have no doubt! This is what I was sent for! I seize my, one, opportunity with no reservations... Enough of standing here, arms crossed, hiding, and doing nothing! Enough of cowering, enough of hiding behind this scapegoat of "non-intervention," and appeasement, that Beelzy once accused me of. I have been training incessantly so that when the day finally came, I would be ready, and now I am! My spike-armor was created for this purpose…

Satan shines his Essence to see whom the eyes belong to. He realizes it is, yours truly, I, the beautiful, incredible, magnificent, extraordinary Cherub, Uriel, in all my newly darkened splendor; with my strength and armor. Well, maybe not that splendorous… Just little old me and my desire to finally make my mark…

He picks himself up from the blow. Smiling, he stretches his being, expanding his wings and self to intimidate… cracking his extremities to loosen up. I cannot lie; the idea of a duel with him is indeed daunting, it has always been! Believe me, when I say, that I have rehearsed this moment many times, in my mind, but nothing ever goes according to plan, anymore, especially in this warped Heaven.

Using his, prideful, behavior as a distraction, I hit him in the face with my club once more, giving him a rude awakening, jerking his head to the side. The darkness of the tunnel and my, quick, nature, serve as my allies.

Satan, with hateful coercion, says, "Uriel! Get out of my way!"

Then, terrified, screeching, he obsessively screams, "HE HAS COME TO KILL US! HE HAS COME TO KILL US!"

I do not respond. I know this is hard to believe, but believe it or not, I am a Cherub of few words.

In this confrontation, I hold my own as we exchange blows. Satan's blows are much stronger, but I'd like to think that mine are much more precise and deteriorating. I am quicker than the Gallant, and with quickness comes strength. Unlike Seraphina, I work well in enclosed spaces. No insult to her memory, I am just saying that I have never been the best warrior, but I have always excelled when I have been confined to small areas, and I have been known to scare my opponents with some of my dark tactics. But here lies my secret... I know strategies of combat and attacks that no one else knows, having closely shadowed my pal, Michael, the creator of the art of combat and I am excellent and anticipating other's attacks. From him, I have learned many innovative tactics that boggle the mind.

My, extremely, rigid spike-armor, unique to Beelzy and

myself, serves its purpose and thank God, protects and camouflages, making me hard to follow and detect. My quickness also contributes to my stealth attack. He still strikes me with, many, exceptionally strong jolts. Let me just say that I feel much less than I should be feeling…

Satan plays the physical and psychological games when he fights and so the armor protects me from, both, the hits, as well as his beguiling words. Thanks to the armor, I am not able to hear even his telepathic words of persuasion. With a few words, he could get into my head to demoralize and even end my mission. I only see him moving his mouth and conjuring some words with his Trident as if casting a wicked spell. The power of my armor is incredible, it is as though I am in my own world, entertained by my favorite celestial music, all considering that the full capabilities are not currently activated because when it is at full capacity, the lights are bright, but this would not be helpful at this moment, it would just make me more visible in this alley of darkness, and so that is something I am able to manage, too, the expenditure of my powers, redirecting them to support what I need at any particular moment.

For a second, eluding my opponent, disappearing from sight, I am able to hide and camouflage in the blackness. My armor and my darkening complexion allow me to blend into the rocks.

It has an application that obscures my armor, the room, and with a dark cloud, even my enemies' sight.

He turns in all directions to try and find me, tiptoeing quietly, flashing his Trident in all directions, and thrusting his trident, quickly, when he thinks he has detected me.

This pause gave me a much needed, but brief, rest and recovery, one that I was longing for. Especially after the piercing blows that I have sustained, which are now starting to take their toll on me. My armor becomes vulnerably infected with red persuasion, as if, slowly festering, in a corroding acid, that eats at my armor… I know this harsh infestation comes from his trident...

Using my speed, I jump on him from the crevice where I was hiding, as I continue my attack. He notices that the, red, persuasion gas has no, particular, special effect on me, so he concentrates to oust something much, much, stronger...

The gas that he conjures is now purple… This vapor is much more effective and begins to get through to my head…

Could this gas be what I think it is? Only purple is expelled from the staff of souls. Could he now have this Essence in his possession? After the epic rematch, did he manage to swindle the staff from Raphael? Maybe in their cheating, what they originally bet for; their original odds were still honored, their original terms still paid...

In this case, the bet was for the staff of souls and so it is possible that he is now the owner. Just like in the game of dice, this is the only way the Lord allows there to be wagers, if the debt is paid, the agreement fulfilled. I become, extremely, worried! Does he finally have what he wants?

To obstruct his concentration in summoning this purple power, and stop this, I shoulder him with my spikes against another pillar. The enemy again falls to the ground. I have disarmed him of his Essence, and I quickly search him, inconspicuously, patting him down to see if he is hiding the staff somewhere. Where is it? Where are they? As far as I could detect, he is not concealing anything! Maybe the purple gas was just a trick of his or a figment of my, vivid, imagination, playing games with me, but I must still take this evidence seriously.

His trident is now loose, struggling to get close to it, we both crawl on the, loamy, dirt as quickly as we can, but we both manage grab ahold of his Essence. I push it towards his face, as he is pinned to the ground. I shoot two spikes from my armor to the palms of his hands and one to his legs so that he is unable to shake free or better grasp his weapon, which I am holding at his neck. The tables have turned... It is taking all of my tremendous strength to keep him, somewhat, immobile.

Helpless, Satan continues to yell angrily, "SODOMA!"

His loud voice is heard echoing through the cobweb, but also pulsating in Sodoma's head. He does this so she can come and help him; yet, he never says the specific word, "help." He is too proud to do that!

She rushes back through the tunnel, limping, because of the wounds and debris that her master collapsed on her. Her footsteps splash through the puddles. She asks other rebels, to come and help her… These thirty-rebels are like nothing I have ever seen before; they seem to have the heads of fierce dogs on their shoulders… how odd! It must, just, be the faint light that makes me imagine this… The more the merrier, I guess!

From a far, I sense the many angels approaching. Before they were about to arrive to help, I knew they outnumbered me, and so I illuminate my body, trying to fly out of the cobweb, elevator, with his trident. Yes, I do not joke or deceive! I fly, using my wings… My wings have gradually grown and become much more functional, day-by-day, and I am sure it is for this instance. This is my debut, if you will!

Managing to get his now, purple-stained, hand on his trident, which I am about to take with me, Satan magically extends his weapon to the size of one of the pillars in the tunnel. Not just that, but it weighs a hell of a lot more, too! He does this by shooting the mysterious purple color, again, putting up a blinding barrier, and not allowing me to enter the elevator with his Essence.

I bounce, back and forth, like a fish hooked and stuck to a line of bait. What I am experiencing is like a security measure when the Trident finds itself solely in the hands of an unidentified subject, almost as if a protocol is compelling me to return it to its master. The trident has, significantly, increased in both size and weight, and continues to grow, which made some of the cobweb collapse, and so I have no choice now but to leave empty handed.

I was at the very brink of defeating and capturing him... At the very least, I could have taken his trident away from grasp, which I am pretty sure would have stopped all of this madness. Unfortunately, I too, leave with no trident trophy, which would have been a pivotal moment in our campaign… I was so close, but he was too strong and cunning.

For me, it is still a moral victory, to which I can, confidently, say, "The score is tied, **2 – 2**!" I had been looking for my chance to even things up, and now I have, but at this point, it is anybody's game…

The greatest lesson learned here is that he is not invincible, and that he is vulnerable. If I can beat him into submission, then so can the Archangels… My Gallants had thought he could possibly be invincible with three of the Essences. Still, we dare not imagine what he could accomplish with all four, which hopefully he doesn't already have. I pray to God that the purple fumes were all a cruel trick played by my imagination, and not the power of the staff of souls. Still, having uncovered vulnerability, I shall be the one to expose his weaknesses to everyone… After all, it was not as hard as I thought, dominating him in combat, and in his own tunnel! He had home field advantage!

The farther he is from the Lord, the more his powers seem to dwindle, even with more Essences in his custody. Boasting, he makes everyone believe that his powers have tripled, but instead, they have diminished! Our fight was not a display, worthy, of an Archangel.

Fortunately I leave unscathed, with the exception of a few bumps and bruises. Making a hole in the elevator with my, explosive, spikes, I quickly fly up the conduit, still managing to get my hands on the last bits of intelligence from within Satan's palace. The collapsed debris and his wounds did not permit him to follow me. I take advantage of this solitude, within his castle, because this could potentially be my last chance to be alone in his hall.

I gather many things, particularly a, curious, black parchment, with a drawing on it, it is almost like a schematic of a red snake that reads, *"Goliath,"* accompanied by Mammon's, platinum, signature. Interesting! Maybe this drawing is one of the original schematics for the creation of snakes. Although, it does not look like one of God's schematics, this one is different! This makes me remember what Satan had said to the serpent creatures about how he helped in their design, maybe Mammon also helped him and this is why the drawing bares her signature on it, but this snake also looks a little different, almost mechanic and not biological, not natural! How odd!

I press my ear onto his marble floor for two purposes, the first to thank God for this duel, this positive occasion to serve Him, and the second to attempt to listen to Satan's thoughts, to see if he crawls out of the rubble that I have tumbled on him. He is still alive! When Lucifer was in the clear, he thought to himself, "How could this be that Uriel can fly? And with such speed! Only Gallants can fly! Only I can teach them how to fly…"

Sodoma, finally, arrives to pick up Satan from the ground. He does not need her help and pushes her away.

Satan, fuming, says, "Now you show up, when you are no

longer needed!"

He humiliates her in front of the angels that accompanied her and they laugh. They would rather be on Sodoma's bad side than Lucifer's. She is getting sick of being degraded in front of her subordinates.

Sodoma, embarrassed, says, "Apologies! I came here as soon as I could, and ran my fastest… Who was that? Was that Michael flying?" Confusing me with my pal, whose traits are no doubt infused in my being.

He says, "No, it was Uriel…"

Sodoma, jealous that Lucifer would teach me how to fly and also worried, asks, "He can fly? Is this in the plan? Is he with us?"

Satan does not answer, simply vanishing from sight. I too slowly vanish out of Satan's palace above, but not before I see my new nemesis, the menacing but comical, Sweenie, running towards me at full speed. He had seen me gathering my last bits of information, here on the checkered floor, and had patiently been waiting, much like I had, for a moment to spring his attack.

Well played! Maybe we are not so different, he and I, but he is not quick enough! I stick out my tongue at him and when he reaches my spot, I disappear leaving him dumbfounded, angered even, and with an enduring image of my wacky face taunting him. He is knocked down on his backside, yet again, because of my now fading wings.

The Lord has seen it fit that I be elsewhere for now. Where is he sending me? I do not know... But, I will be back, and even more ready next time. I now realize that my one chance to make a difference was more figuratively speaking than an actual commandment. The Almighty ordered this of me so that I can focus all my strengths and preparations as if it were to be my one, only, and last chance. I hope I did not disappoint! Yet, this does not feel like my one shot! The Lord has something much bigger planned for me! Plus, the Lord cannot, possibly, hope for the first Gallant, Satan, to be defeated by the hands of a much lesser Cherub, me. Can he? Instead, I can tell that this experience is like a grain of sand that shall slowly grow and contribute to a mound, which, hopefully, should eventually collapse on Satan. I can see clearly that I will still have my calculated opportunities, and with the help of some luck, hopefully they shall be pivotal. But here I go doing whatever I feel like, again. Interpreting the Lord's words the way I want to. Shame on me!

Lucifer collects himself, slowly, and leaves to meet with Beelzy, who he hopes has finally changed his mind, especially after seeing Sodoma's continued incompetence. Just as it was hard for the Gallants to lose hope for him, it is hard for Satan to lose hope in Beelzy's paramount allegiance. It seems as though the odds are, and have always been stacked against her. He has been biased against her from the beginning, but has limited options for a decent commander. She seems to have negotiated a deal to assure her current status, and this cannot be fairing well with Lucifer…

Something big is coming… bigger than any dark prophecy can predict… bigger than the Essences and the Gallants… It shall be more than anyone can fathom and this sinister, "Goliath," whatever it is, shall play a quintessential role… What is worse is that I fear that the human earth is now in danger. ***"All that is material shall perish!"*** now reads a hidden inscription on the back of the Goliath parchment, which I have collected as evidence from the rebellious ones palace. This message begins to appear out of the blue as if magically emerging, barely legible. It is as though the red ink keeps secrets. The longer I hold it, the more secrets become unprotected and revealed to me. There are more words on the scroll that look as though they have been erased, traced over, and are dully faded, but for now, these menacing words are the only words I can read… I believe that little by little, just as my favorite mural in Paradise Palace changes, so shall all these sentences make themselves conspicuous, and this will, no doubt, be a key to unlocking Lucifer's strategies.

Still at this time there is something more troubling to me… My biggest concern, is that we have already failed God… all of us angels, myself included, granted, some worse than others… and perhaps what Satan has started is too late to mend…

Chapter 22

The Lunartic

I re-appear in a very dark place, wondering what I am meant to do here... I assume that my mission is to find out if what I saw in the tunnels was true. Does Lucifer really have the staff of souls in his possession? I am so eager to tell my Gallants of what I saw in the tunnels and also give them this Goliath parchment I found, with the almost prophetic words etched, *"**All that is material shall peris**h!"* I cannot help but ponder the meaning of these deep words and repeat them almost obsessively… But for now, I stay and obey here…

The ground is sandy and the environment dusky. The air is thin and the smell is metallic. I can see planet earth in the background. Evidently, I am on the earth's moon, which is closer to the earth than ever...

CHAPTER 22

I take a few steps over large dunes of gray sand. I feel weightless, bouncing on the surface. I don't know if it is because of my new gift of flight or because of the odd environment, probably both.

Then I see a dark angel landing on the surface, imprinting his feet onto the grainy sand. It is Lucifer! Now it is clear, this is why I have been transported here, to see him.

Judging by my surroundings, I can tell that the moon is a strategic outpost for the rebels to scope the earthly kingdom, like an observatory. The base they have established, looks like the Seraph training camp in Heaven, but is covertly hidden, vastly throughout the darkest valleys of the moon, but I can still locate their many garrisons with my gift of vision. They even have a name for this base of theirs, calling it the *"**Morning Star**,"* which is synonymous with Lucifer, and since from earth, it is the only object of light that is seen during the night, like a star. I think this name is suiting to him, very appropriate…

The only light that the moon emits, reflects off of the sun, therefore Satan is like the moon, and God is like the sun because Satan has no light of his own. There is not one original bone in his body, all he knows is God, therefore he is a phony copycat in all his tactics.

If Satan controls the moon, then he can control the amount

of light that reaches the earth during nighttime. Furthermore, if he should, let's say, destroy the moon, then the earth would be in complete darkness during the night, which will already be progress, or an accomplishment, in his mission to cover the material universe in darkness, one planet at a time, starting with what seems to be the most important one, the world! Then the rest, uninhabited, will be easy to opaque.

One of his biggest reasons for being here is to find clues about this human woman, which he had gazed upon, with hate and envy, in the screens of witchcraft. This woman, clothed with the stars, covered in a blue veil, and standing on top of the moon. This lady he has developed a hate for, *Mariam*. How curious that her praised nickname shall also be, *"Morning Star,"* the same as both his new lunar base and his, *"Lucifer,"* nickname. In fact, the nickname has partly stemmed from his obsession to know more about her. This not so coincidental namesake makes him rabid. Since she was depicted in his witchcraft vision, standing on the crescent moon, it only makes sense to begin his search for her here, and if she really exists, she will appear. If she is brave enough, she will show up, then she will duel him. This is one of his many plans; to find *Mariam* and see what the fuss is all about; provoke her into hand-to-hand combat, get a reaction out of her. He believes that if she is worthy to hold the title of

Queen of Heaven, then she will be skilled in combat. It shall be her powers against his Essences, and so he sweeps the moon incessantly with his scouts, searching for the location from the vision. Matching up the stars from her veil with the stars of the universe.

The image of this simple human has now become like a prophecy to him, way more important than any dark prophecy that has been announced by the choirs of angels. He has made *Mariam* his equal, even millennia before she is born into existence… The image of our Lady, *Mariam,* is engraved on another of his black parchments, which he holds tucked in with his many dark scrolls.

These scrolls seem to be just as prized to him as his Trident. I can tell this by the way he sheathes them, protecting them from almost everyone's sight and I have noticed how he refers to them, often, looking at them and following them to a tee, almost as if making sure that everything is going according to plan.

Even when searching for the golden tree in Eden, I was able to get a quick glance of the dark parchment and the red ink splattered on the canvas. No doubt these scrolls are his secret plans, they are the strategy of his rebellion, and unfortunately, I only have access to but a few of his visions and recollections of them. He keeps them completely confidential! What a hypocrite!

He does not share his plans, yet he thinks the many projects of his once Gallant brothers were too secretive, especially Gabe's project *Mariam*.

Now I know! The scroll that I gathered from his palace looks just like a missing piece from his collection of scrolls, and so it must be! Still, I wonder, what can the mechanical snake, etched on there, possibly mean? How do those ominous words on the back, coincide? ***"All that is material shall peris**h!"* Does he know the parchment is missing from his collection? Or has he shared this material, purposefully, with me as if I were his ally? But why would he do that? He does not seem to trust anyone, not even Beelzy, and I am no friend of his, not anymore!

Could it be that my new nemesis, Sweenie, had purposefully placed the scroll for me to find, which explains why he had been scoping me out, waiting for an ideal moment to pounce, as I was exiting the dark palace, just like bait! Just as Lucifer set a trap, for Seraphina, maybe this too was a trap for me, knowing that any piece of intelligence would interest me greatly! I am so confused! Which is understandable because this is what happens when I make it all about me and my understanding of Lucifer's plots, therefore undermining God's directives of non-intervention! Perhaps He gave me my mandates for my own benefit, so that I can maintain myself at peace!

CHAPTER 22

This particular picture, which he holds of *Mariam,* looks as if Satan has directly imprinted it from the screen of witchcraft. This vision of her on top of the moon, so innocent, haunts him. It is much worse that she is a human woman, which even by humans shall be treated as the weaker sex. This is a notion he would like to exploit, and will do all he can to keep her gender weak. One thing is sure, when they meet face to face, *Mariam* better watch out!

Right now his plan is to confront her, face to face, and end her, but everywhere he goes, the surrounding stars seem to be out of place when comparing them to the reproduction. They do not match up with his imprint, and this frustrates him immensely. Some of the stars do not even seem to be in the picture yet, and according to his calculations, will only come millions of years from now. He is too impatient to wait that long, so he anticipates, just as God has anticipated his rebellion with the contingency of *Mariam.* He even uses his superstitious and manipulative astrology methodologies to attempt to realign the stars, so that he can accelerate this prophetic occurrence, which he refuse to wait for... His trident disturbs the natural balance of everything using the darkness of fortune-telling and clairvoyance. Until the time comes when they meet, vis-à-vis, he is still ceaseless in his resolve to find this *Mariam…*

But how do I know of his plans? How can I so easily see and understand the schemes of the rebellious one? All considering that I barely know what I am meant to do… All be it, it seems as though, just as I am confused about everything, he seems to be the opposite. His plans never deviate and are extremely clear and precise. If a curveball is thrown at him, he stays on path, with great resolve. He seems to know what he wants… What is even more disturbing is that the peace that I have lost, he seems to have found…

Has he shared his plans with me in confidence, confusing me with his ally? I cannot help but to continue asking myself this. Am I being used by him? Which is something he seems to be very good at doing! As a Gallant, he is much better than I at reading thoughts and souls and knows how to push our buttons.

Perhaps something, so small, such as the stinging of the poisonous creatures on earth to the both of us, is where this bond comes from. I had forgotten about this, his head and my back. This might have formed a connection between the both of us.

Maybe after my attack to him in the cobweb, this solidified an idea in his mind, almost as if the attack had been a rehearsal, a tryout, and an audition for me to join his forces. NO! This cannot be! I love the Lord! I will not entertain his ideas! He will not persuade or entice me to go against my, one, true love!

Yet, I must admit, his incentives, which I can never reveal, are more than appealing. What I can say, about what he tempts me with on a daily basis, is that according to him, I am being allowed to follow him and spared of death for a reason. Still I cannot take to heart the now false promises of the new Lord of deception. The fulfillment, he once filled us with, has flailed away along with his beauty. Even still, I want you to understand with full clarity! Heed these very important words, which now come from God, and are proclaimed as a Godly decree to all:

"No matter how Satan has been depicted so far… Rest assured, he is NOT the hero, nor has he ever been, nor shall he ever be! Even if he has tried to tamper with your perception of him, getting you to like him, to sympathize with him, that is what he is good at...

"No matter how sentimental you may feel about him, as if fate has been against him from the beginning, or as though he is a victim of the circumstances, making him who he is… Amen, amen, I say to you, do not be fooled! He made his own luck! For all of what he has done has been premeditated from his beginning and I know that all the fond memories that you have of him, have always been a front, a theatrical farce, which he has fashioned for your deception and his delight…

"He is, unfortunately, the antagonistic decay of what I have created! There is something much darker and sinister hidden here that you will not understand until it plays itself out..."

These words are directly communicated to all angels, near and far, with the earnest and loving voice of God, and no one else's. I hear this announcement even on the moon. I know these words even reach the rebellious one, who now looks even more disturbed because his cover seems to have been blown. He laughs at the decree and spits to the ground in disgust. Nonetheless, he still ignores the broadcast, hitting his ear with a slap, having decided to no longer serve or heed the Almighties' words, blocking out any type of communication that may affect his resolve, his mission. I receive this decree, as it is, sincere and just, meant to unite us all once again with loving understanding...

At the same time he sees a sort of parchment, half-buried, in the sand. He picks it up, dusts it off, and reads what it says. It is my list of his seven capital and forbidden sins. It is as though we have traded one scroll for another. He has one of mine and I have one of his, see? I did not steal anything from him; it is an even trade! He folds it up and places it with the rest of his dark scrolls as a memento and just chuckles a bit.

CHAPTER 22

Even as he is covered with his cloak, the scars and scratches from my attack are apparent on Satan's face. After he is done scoping out his dark parchments, he puts them away, safely guarded in his armor.

Another angel lands on the surface, coming from the earth, via rainbow path. The odd friends, Beelzy and Lucifer, seem to be here to meet. Beelzebub's complexion is darker than ever! Or maybe it is just the darkness of space, which makes him look opaque. Beelzy walks toward him, who is now sitting on top of a large meteorite, in no rush to meet with him.

Lucifer goes straight to the point, moving fast, brusquely saying, "I will speak very clearly... I want you to mobilize the Cherubs and Seraphs, immediately, Beelzy.

"I want your Watchers to be my new troop in charge of abating this project Mariam, they shall alas be known, by their new code name, as *the Incubus or Incubus-Watchers* instead of this plain and ridiculous *Watcher* name. It should be you and I both, together, brothers in arms, joined in this worthy mission of defiance..."

Another of his crazy voices, silently says, "We need him! Use him…"

Satan hushes his own craziness, creepily singing under his breath, "Silence! Shut up! Shut up, be quiet, shut up!"

Clearing his voice, he points down to earth and continues saying, "You already have the allegiance of our very finest legions in Eden and on earth. If you are their true commander, turn their allegiance to me! Easy enough, right?

"They love you so much… If you would be thrown from here, the Watchers would catch you!" Implying menacingly that he could be the one to throw him from the face of the moon...

Then, his calmer self, clarifies, saying, "I would catch you too!"

Beelzebub, still not used to his friend's multiple personalities, says, "But…"

Lucifer, furious, growls, "NO BUTS... Just do it! Just do it! JUST DO IT!"

Beelzebub, now trembling, responds, "I c-c-cannot! All this s-said, I thought S-Sodoma was to be your General…"

"Sodoma is weak and she has already failed me, several times, throughout time… I no longer owe her anything!... I know she will ultimately let me down… You, on the other hand, are a strong and beautiful genius."

Satan uses his flattery to try and convince Beelzy. "You shall have a palace... That is what you want, is it not?"

He makes high-definition mirages of His temptations, for Beelzy to glance and reach after, visions of Beelzy and Dumah, happier than ever. His temptations, although grandiose, begin to sound like the empty ones he has enticed me with.

Lucifer shows him earth, temptingly saying, "All this I will give you, if you will bow down and worship me."

Beelzy timidly says, "W-Worship the L-L-Lord your God, and serve H-Him o-only! I d-d-do not want a-an-anything! Even if I were to a-accept, what am I to t-tell The W-Wa-Wa-Watchers?"

He is brave to stand up to his friend, just as I have.

Satan says, "Leave that up to me, we will tell them the truth... If you feel like taking the initiative, tell them you are their new General, their Gallant, and I am their new leader. Tell them God does not exist!"

A paranoid voice comes from Lucifer, correcting, "HE DOES EXIST!"

Beelzy agrees with the more reasonable voice, saying, "But God d-d-does exist, and you were a-a-always their l-leader! They have all seen the One, True, God, f-felt Him, and sh-shared with Him. You cannot f-fool them... So how can I t-t-tell them that H-H-He does not exist?"

Satan says, "How can you say that I was their leader? I was never their leader! God would like me to think I was their commander, but it has always been Him pulling all the strings…

"Yes, they know He exists, but God can be replaced with

many other things; with material possessions, pleasure, utopia, hate, passion, revenge, persuasion, sin! And these things will keep them just as busy as the Creator would!"

His creepy, evil, twin voice, again blurts out in chant, "That's what I like, that's what I like, that's what I like, SIN, SIN!"

When Beelzebub notices that his friend is being cold, he goes back to speaking militarily, like a soldier would speak to a General, loudly saying, "NO! THIS-IS NOT-RIGHT! I-CAN-NOT! NO-THING-CAN-RE-PLACE-GOD! YOU-WOULD-LIKE-THEM-TO-BE-LIEVE THAT-THESE-THINGS, THAT-YOU-LIST, CAN-RE-PLACE-GOD, BUT-THEY-CAN-NOT!"

His courage has been found; his stutter has been lost.

Satan, bothered, says, "No?!"

Beelzy literally plays devil's advocate. He is the first to ever do this, saying, "WHY-WOULD-THEY-LISTEN-TO-THOSE-LIES-FROM-ME?"

"I would make them listen to you!"

Beelzy objecting, again, says, "But…"

Satan cuts him off in a menacing way, saying, "NO?! BUT!? I DO NOT LIKE THESE WORDS, BEELZEBUB!"

The other, nicer Satan, tenderly says, "It's ok…" as he shakes nervously to his core.

Satan hates when people give excuses or use the words,

"But" or "No." Always getting what he wants, with the powers of persuasion and conscience, he is not used to the word, "No."

Lucifer breathes deeply to calm himself, giving in to ease the tension and says, "They do not have to serve me, they just have to follow me and I shall free them…"

Beelzebub says, "Free them, how? You would have nowhere to go, nowhere to hide… There is no place you can go where God will not see you!"

"That is not true! He would also like you to think that... I have managed to elude them thus far. I will let you in on a secret… I plan on staying in Heaven. I just wish to make a few minor command changes."

Seeing right through the wicked plan, Beelzebub says, "Minor changes? If you would change me as commander, then that would be a minor change… Attempting to overthrow God and the Gallants is not a minor change! It is a foolish and impossible endeavor, regardless of what weapons you think you may possess… The angels would never betray the Almighty."

Satan says, "As you know, I can be pretty persuasive. Even God can be persuaded."

He reiterates, "We can be pretty persuasive," referring to his developed alter ego of both his trident and himself, spinning it and staring at the tips.

Beelzy interjects, "If persuasion is your weapon, why do you not lead them yourself? If you think you can persuade God, you are wrong! As you just said, all the times you thought you persuaded God; maybe that is what He wanted you to believe..."

Satan, desperate, explains, "I will let you in on my plans... I need those legions and I need unlimited access to earth. The Incubus-Watchers are the only ones who can break the curfew. I need them to search for something on earth. As Watchers, they have sight that extends everywhere…"

Beelzy says, "Many have already broken the curfew. I am assuming they are your angels."

Satan, the proud, for once agrees, saying, "My angels? I don't have any of those! I have some angels sympathetic to my cause, but that is about it…

"And you know that all your Watchers are still loyal to God. Those who have broken the curfew, sympathetic to my cause, cannot enter Eden, and I need them there. This is where the Incubus-Watchers come in…"

Beelzebub asks, "What do you need the Watchers to look for anyway?"

Satan will reveal nothing more of his plan, and says, "I am a busy soul… I cannot do too many things at a time... It will be moralizing for them to see us, friends, united…

CHAPTER 22

Another one of his arrogant personalities, says, "I am doing nothing wrong… I am following God's example and attempting to do as little as possible, nothing! And treat others as slaves... If you wish to know the essence of what I seek on earth, a very specific artifact, then join me…"

He then sticks out his trident, and with a slithery tongue, says, "Join our cause!"

"You dare to say our Lord does nothing? I think you mean He does everything! God has created you, is that nothing? Are you nothing?

"Slaves? We are free! You have become the slave of your own passions," Beelzy says caringly.

Knowing that Beelzebub is right, but still not admitting it, Satan says, "The creator likes to control things, He is a control freak, I will give you that! I am growing sick of your questions! Stop it!" He hits his own head with his trident as if telling someone in his head also to shut up!

For once, the timid, Beelzy, stands up to Satan with all his might, resolutely putting his foot down, saying, "Well, my friend, this is where we part ways then because I too am sick of you and your plans!"

Fearing the worst, and afraid of losing his allegiance, Lucifer stands down a bit. Beelzy also calms down, wishing to not lose a good friend…

Satan, calmly and reassuringly, says, "And plus, I thought you knew... I already have my following, those who are tired of doing His bidding... Sick of all that Divine Providence, His plans, and of the tyranny. All I need is someone other than me to lead them, is this too much to ask?"

His followers, the ones he only calls, "sympathetic" to his cause, begin to ominously arise from the caves and valleys of the moon, numbering in the hundreds of thousands…

Desperately pleading and manipulatively alluding to Beelzy's compassion, Satan looks at Beelzebub with reproach. He also hopes that his large numbers will be convincing of his might, or at the very least, intimidating, forcing him to convert to his rebellious cause.

Beelzebub, regimentally, says, "I cannot! I WILL NOT! Those who are sick of serving, grow a sickness of their own…"

In a menacing way, Satan points his trident at him, and yells, "YOU WILL!"

Beelzebub yells back, "I WILL NOT! Have you thought about the consequences?"

The conversation has become a volatile screaming contest that seems like it could escalate pretty quickly.

"WHAT CONSEQUENCES? The Gallants are His power, His

Essences are His power, AND I AM THE NEW MASTER OF THE ESSENCES!

"His legions of Angelic Hosts, Cherubs and Seraphs, are His might, and soon I will be the master of the Angelic Hosts!

"If I take away all of that, He has no power. He lies idle in a golden box, pointing fingers. WELL, NO MORE!"

"Calm down," he loudly says to himself.

Beelzebub exclaims, "YOU ARE WRONG! THERE ARE CONSEQUENCES TO EVERYTHING! All He does is love us, and expects so little in return. I CANNOT!

"I never thought I would be the wisest between the two of us, but that day has now come…

"You do not have the staff of souls, so you are not the master of the Essences."

The once insecure Beelzy has now become the stable, secure, rock in the friendship. He has had enough, turning his back, paying his friend with the same medicine he paid God in the Palace, and now begins to leave…

As soon as Beelzebub turns his back, Satan, backed by his legions of rebels, uses his trident to cover himself in the enigmatic, purple mist. He engulfs himself in this, bright, purple, smog, I had seen arising from his being in the cobweb tunnels. Again it dawns on me, does he now have the staff of souls? How is the residue of the trident purple? But I cannot see the staff anywhere.

The mist is coming out from his trident and not from the staff, but maybe it is shrunk and hidden somewhere. I cannot discern this! This display of power is meant to be food for Beelzy's thought. This is probably his response to his friend's speculation, that he does not own all of the Essences.

As he walks away, Beelzebub thinks the same way I do, truly wondering if he now possesses the staff. He knows just as I do that if his friend truly is the master of the Essences, then he is a force to be reckoned with, and not many would dare oppose him. I know that Beelzebub would have to seriously reconsider joining him…

After the purple cloud has charged bright enough, he then uses his Essence to bring down a meteor shower from a near by comet onto his friend. With a simple circling wave of his trident, he forges chaos in the universe... If he cannot have his allegiance, then neither will God!

Beelzy runs and dodges many of the meteorites, as the surrounding rebels rejoice in this spectacle. This is a mistake on his part because I can tell that for the first time, Beelzy had actually seriously considered joining him, especially after seeing the raw, purple power, which is a sign that he is truly the master of the Essences. Lucifer's large numbers were also very convincing, but the fragments of rock, which rain down, do not help his cause. How can he join the one who attacks him for no good reason?

He continues to bring the debris tumbling down in hordes of thousands. Big and small, the first craters on the moon are created. Some of them fall with the force of enormous bombs. Many are even brought down to earth...

Since the meteors do not hit Beelzy, Satan tries harder, bringing small comets and asteroids to his position. Beelzy prays for his armor and so it appears, and he is now, stellarly, covered in it.

Lucifer screams, "SPIKE-ARMOR! GET IT AWAY FROM ME!" As if he were acutely allergic to being in its midst.

I look at his spike-armor and mine, realizing that if I look half as good as Beelzy, then I look really sharp. I do not know why I would be thinking such vain thoughts...

I am quickly awoken from my daydreaming and jump out of the way of an enormous rock that disintegrates, on the surface, after almost hitting me. I am now attentive, solely focused on the chaos that ensues, seeking cover and fighting off the falling fragments. One enormous piece grazes me, but because of my armor, I withstand the effects.

Both our spike-armor's illuminate to cover us in a luminous aura, much like the purple one Lucifer had just covered himself in. The aura protects us almost completely, pulverizing many of the rock particles, turning them into grainy sand, before they strike us.

One of the biggest asteroids hits the moon; it explodes and gouges out a truly enormous crater, in the South Pole, it even kills off a good portion of the rebels. Lucifer does not care about the loss of these souls. Some of his surviving subordinates disappear, into the depths, like ants into an anthill, continuing to search for traces of *Mariam,* taking cover from the chaos outside. Others stay at his side. The crater that is indented, is almost 1500 miles across and more than 5 miles deep.

After the asteroid hits, it bounces off the moon, bumping the moon closer to the earth, like a marble collision. Many of its smaller pieces now head down to the world, racing with ominous power.

Following several times of using our speed, diving to the side, and eluding, Beelzy and I manage to get away unscathed, although none of these projectiles were meant for me because I think they are unaware of my presence. With the unpredictability of his unstable, purple, power, one of the meteors now almost hits Satan; this makes him even madder.

Furious, he yells, "BEELZY! NO MORE OF THIS! JOIN ME!"

Then his more sensible personality, warns, "TAKE COVER, MY FRIEND, I WILL TRY AND STOP HIM!"

When enough room is between them, Beelzy illuminates his body and flies off, using his own wings, attempting to stop the asteroid that is accelerating on a collision path towards earth.

Chapter 23

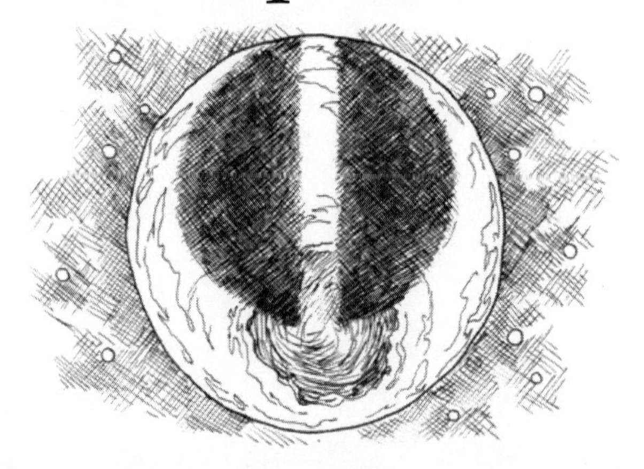

Settling the Score

When in flight, heading towards the earth, to stop the collision-bound asteroid, Beelzy quickly backtracks, and analyzes what Lucifer's more tame personality just said, "Who will Satan stop? From doing what? Who is he talking to?"

Lucifer is again mesmerized by the fact that Beelzy and I can use our wings to fly. He thinks to himself, "How can both Beelzy and Uriel do this? It must be the cursed spike-armor."

Then I can see a moment of clarity in his eyes, it makes sense to him and he smiles, but he is too far away for me to read his exact thoughts of pleasure. I knew that Beelzy and I had been changing together! I hope it is due to an upgrade from our matching spike-armors.

CHAPTER 23

Beelzy's train of thought is quickly changed as he jets down to meet the precipitating asteroid, beginning to race it hand in hand. When he approaches, even with the protection of his armor, he begins to burn, to combust...

Beelzy's plan of attack is to strike the asteroid, perpendicularly, with his armor, so as to deviate it from its trajectory. He does this repeatedly with incredible power and many small pieces break off, slowly, chipping away at the asteroid, heroically doing all he can do…

From earth, he sees many rainbows and many angels rising to meet the asteroid, eager to join him in his noble cause. It is the granite-looking Watchers, from Eden, who have come to help avert this disaster. They know that if the asteroid hits, it could kill all living things on earth. Thousands of them hit the asteroid and attempt to redirect it with their mirror-like weapons and armors...

Since the many deadly rocks did not allow me to get close to Satan, I too join in the effort to deviate this potentially deadly falling body. My presence inspires the Watchers as they notice in amazement my likeness to their commander. We use teamwork and unify our weapons to make them stronger. Some of them continue to follow the asteroid, using the rainbow paths as their propellers.

Lucifer sees this from afar, hovering above the moon, alongside his rebel minions, whose feet are planted on the craters, eager to intercept the Watchers and engage them in battle. But even if they wanted to attack, they cannot conjure rainbows to follow in flight. They are yearning to commence open warfare. Satan stops them from doing so, with his trident, as their stampede is halted. They thirst for death and destruction.

He says, "Not yet!"

They all stay put, dissatisfied and with dastardly smiles of elation. The evil one and his troops simply leave, certain that we will not be able to stop the imminent destruction that this asteroid brings with it.

The asteroid has been greatly diminished with the heroic acts of these Cherubs… Unfortunately, tragedy is still not completely averted…

As the space matter grows ever closer to the earth, the Watchers fly away as far as possible to not be caught in the ever-impending impact…

A few moments later, it indeed impacts with the force of thousands of atomic weapons. Much of earth is incinerated, but we manage to salvage the world in its entirety. A pole shift in the world, immediately, occurs, turning the world almost, completely, upside down.

The asteroid falls in what will be called, *the Yucatan peninsula,* in the country of Mexico. The asteroid crash shall trigger volcanic eruptions for hundreds of thousands of years. In time, because of the impact, beasts known as dinosaurs will become extinct…

Luckily Eden is not destroyed and left completely intact! The angels stationed in other places, throughout the world, had been preemptively evacuated by the resourceful Watchers. No angelic soul is left unaccounted for, sadly, the same cannot be said for so many species of innocent animals. So much biodiversity gone in a blink of an eye!

The continent separation begins. No longer is the earth united in the one continent of Pangea. Many dinosaurs and creatures of all types are painfully killed.

Satan looks from afar and is delighted. Now God will know the extent of his resolve and power. He is surprised he has not done this sooner. As a victory celebration, he covers the moon in fourths with the colors of the Essences, yes, even purple.

Then, soon after, the moon becomes mostly covered in darkness. From the earth, everyone can see the crescent moon taking over to reflect his trident as another banner of conquest.

After this, he thinks *Mariam* will appear, standing on the

moon, since this is how she is depicted in his prophetic vision, but she does not grace him with her presence.

"COWARD!" he yells to her, even though she cannot listen.

He speaks to my head only, proudly boasting, "The score is, **3 to 2**, Uriel! I am on fire! You cannot stop me!"

I know he will not give up until he has a commanding lead… But the game is not over…

Beelzy returns to Paradise Palace to report to the Gallants what just happened. This time he was acting as a spy for them. This makes him feel shameful, dishonest, and dishonorable. There is no reason to feel like this because he has done nothing wrong…

God, and the Gallants are extremely proud and grateful for what he has done, saving many lives. They tell him so, giving many praises. These accolades fall on deaf ears because the shame of his actions. The guilt that stems from his inability to stop the destruction of the world is overbearing.

Our Lord tells him to not worry… He did all he could… Something good always comes from this… ***"The earth will be reconstructed from the ashes, but this suspends the creation of humans until much of the earth is rebuilt."***

There is some potentially valuable intelligence that Beelzy holds onto and chooses not to disclose, what I am speaking of is the existence of Satan's multiple personalities… The various temperaments seem to be more prominent when he is with Beelzy, almost as if Lucifer is not afraid of showing who he truly is in front of his once friend.

Beelzy's report is followed by my own. I appear out of the blue, from the corner, hastily racing towards Raphael to try and inspect his staff, to determine if his Essence is real or if it is a decoy.

Raphael is extremely protective and nervous to see me so obsessed and worried about his Essence. This is my fault! I should have not approached so brusquely. My manners have indeed changed. It is as though I have become shameless in my actions, more confident in overstepping my boundaries. Raphael looks so defensive, as if he is ready to attack me, fearing that I have defected from their side and somehow been influenced by the rebels.

My vestments and darkening complexion contribute to the questioning of my allegiance, not to mention the new use of my beautiful wings. It is common angelic knowledge that only Satan can teach how to fly. The Gallants know this, for it was their big brother who transmitted the gift to them and no one else can fly but Satan's pal, Beelzy. They think maybe now, I am his best pal too.

Just that second, it dawns on me, what if this faint, "Goliath," project I heard Sodoma mention, is Lucifer's attempt to teach his loyal angels how to fly? The black parchment I have borrowed or stolen from his palace could refer to this. The schematics of the black snake on this scroll could very well be this, especially since serpents can mysteriously fly, even more impressively, with no wings. Maybe the snakes will try to teach his angels to fly and this is why he so desperately needs access into Eden. This would explain why he told Beelzy that he is a busy angel and cannot do too many things at a time, since he must teach them to fly personally. Perhaps he is studying the intricate schematic of that snake on the parchment to analyze the anatomy and physiology so that he can figure out how to help his troops fly.

Maybe these "Goliath" powers of flight inadvertently rubbed off on Beelzy and myself because of our constant proximity to him. This would explain why he was so surprised to see us fly because it was never his intention for this power to rub-off, especially not on us. But then, with his smile of realization, still on the moon, he understands why Beelzebub can fly…

After all, I am sure it is hard for him to control the overwhelming influx of all his new powers, brought on by God and his stolen Essences, and no doubt these powers are volatile.

What if he only teaches and grants this power to those who

join him, or those who will eventually join him? My heart drops! Rebels that can fly! This would be disastrous to our cause! My heart drops even further! But I also have another theory of what this Goliath project could be…

But first, I leave my Gallants minds at ease, reassuring them to worry not, as I am innocent of any treachery. I ask them to inspect my eyes, which have not changed. They remain blue and are in no ways a shade of red, but they understand that an eye color can easily be counterfeited. Still, a few moments ago, I was simply inspecting the staff to determine if it was the real one. I have no hidden agenda.

I explain to the Archangels how Satan had attacked me with purple gas, in the cobweb tunnels, and that the purple gas was twice as strong as his red gas. Even worse I tell them how the asteroid was conjured with this purple power, but Beelzy stays silent, failing to corroborate my story. I do not know why! I know he has seen the purple mist and is just as puzzled by it as I am.

I tell Raphael my other theory of what this mysterious Goliath rumor could be because my hypothesis is pertinent to him and his staff, I explain, "I have strong intelligence that suggests that Lucifer has stolen your staff during the rematch! What you have in your hand is a decoy! I believe the staff you have now is what Mammon and Gomorra have been constructing. They are calling it *"The Goliath,"* it is in the shape of a snake, very similar to your coiled staff. I have heard whispers of this plot in his faction. Mammon must have duplicated the appearance of your staff but could not have duplicated its powers. Test it out!"

The platinum signature of Mammon's inventions can easily be concealed with spells and trickery. But platinum would be significantly lighter than the unique materials God has fused in the staff of souls.

I show Raphael the black parchment with Mammon's signature as evidence of my theories, but all the proof in the world would not help the unbeliever, not to mention that the drawing of a platinum snake on a scroll is pretty vague and could mean anything to the uninformed eye.

Raphael still looks to the tabernacle in terror, worried that this might be true. He had felt his weapon much lighter lately, but thought it was because his brothers' Essences were missing and that perhaps, this had a profound effect of demoralizing even on his staff's weight.

Quiet consumes the room… He lifts it up and down, gripping it in different ways, to test its weight and grip; nothing feels extraordinarily different. He is too nervous to test this theory in front of everyone, especially God. As of late, he has been so careful with it, priding himself on not letting it out of sight, grasp or mind. Could he have failed at his most pivotal task of the moment? Keeping his Essence?

"Go ahead, try it!" I say, as I shine one of the purple gems, on the staff, with my robes, I do it just as I am used to doing with my master's sword. I probably should not have done that because he is not very comfortable with, but I did it more out of custom and to counter the callus awkwardness in the air, than anything else. But I understand how it looks, looking like an obsessed miser! He is still hesitant to follow my suggestion… But I have persuaded him!

He concentrates, points the staff to the air, placing it against his shoulder as if it were going to recoil back… Slowly… minutely… Purple gas, different to what Satan had conjured, and massive feelings of joy and love are expelled from the staff. This simple yet powerful display puts all our minds at ease.

I have never been so happy to be wrong! Everyone is overjoyed and satisfied with this authentication. After all, who knows the staff better than God and Raphael? But I can tell that Raphael still has his doubts. The authentication has worked for everyone except for him…

In horror, he drops his staff to the ground, almost as if it were contagious and unrecognizable to him. The staff bounces, clunking, very loudly, on the marble ground and echoing through the halls. This startles everyone…

After a few seconds, when he picks it up, he notices that it has chipped, and the dent looks platinum colored. He inspects the staff again, from top to bottom, and this time, there is no dent. It is only his vivid imagination playing games with him; after all, he has been through a lot of trauma recently, with a lot of responsibility riding on his shoulders… He looks perplexed… But feels an immediate and unfathomable reassurance by God that this is his true Essence. Alleluia, Amen!

As always, I realize that Satan had been playing tricks on my Gallant, Raphael, and on my mind too, still able to connect through their Gallant connection. His motives were simple, wishing for Raphael to discard his real Essence, so that he could retrieve it once it has been thrown away. With the inculcation of paranoia and false visions, he tried to convince that his staff was really a decoy and then the plan was to take it from him after he rejected it.

He knows how we all think and that with Raphael's propensity for dispensing-off coin in the game of dice, with no problem, this would not be a far stretch for him to do.

Since he was not able to get the staff from Raphael with this simple plan, no doubt Lucifer will still be after the staff of souls.

I can now accurately predict that he has another plan in motion to swindle the last Essence, but that is all I know for now... Forgive me, Lord, for ever doubting your words of confirmation!

The next question that burns in my mind is, how was the trident able to expel purple gas? Was this just one of Lucifer's many ploys? I also continue to sense that my Gallants still doubt the authenticity of my words... They think perhaps I made this up to get close to the staff. My request for him to test it out and my flawed hypothesis only further hinders my credibility. I can see where this disbelief comes from.

I guess I also had my hand in this, he used me, played me like a violin-trumpet. If I had not suggested that it was a decoy, then he would have not been able to plant this doubtful illusion into his mind. I must be more careful, not to intervene, because without even meaning to be, I can swiftly become a double agent. Lesson learned!

I have always remained silent, until then, never stating my opinion or chiming-in until this crucial moment. They wonder why all of the sudden, now, I speak after having been infiltrated in Lucifer's camp for a very long time. In their eyes, something has changed in me, not just my appearance, and I can see it too!

Among all this doubtful contempt, that I am currently experiencing, I now loosen my tongue, letting them know, saying, "I speak my mind, now, because God gave me my one chance to contribute and because I was just sick of standing, doing nothing. Can you blame me? Being in the lion's den and doing nothing?"

What runs through their minds about me is not true at all! I know what I saw, purple gas! I know that Beelzy saw it too, but he remains silent, just as I have in the past! It is a grudge he has been holding against me for some time now. I can sense it! It is payback for my silence and inaction in the steps of Paradise Palace when Lucifer stole the first two Essences. He still does not understand why I was unable to intervene in what we could have jointly stopped.

None of the Watchers, however, saw the purple power because they only aided after the asteroid shower was on its way to earth, making all my seemingly fragile cases dwindle today. Not even their witness shall help my cause of innocence, so there is no sense asking for corroboration from the pack of a dozen Watchers, standing, just outside the main hall, in the prestigious hall of fame.

More so, I know what I felt. The purple gas in the cobweb was nothing short of an Essential miracle. But how could this be?

I now receive some tabernacle inspiration. God seems to be the only ONE who believes me, knowing that my words are the truth, just as He is, who sent me. But He only leaves my mind at ease, explaining that the gas was purple because Satan had been using his trident and also channeling the powers of Michael's stolen sword against me.

Since the sword fires blue and his trident fires red, the mixing and combining of these two colors makes purple. This is also why the binding power that he emitted became stronger with the combined power of two Essences.

This is what I get for speculating and daydreaming without the help of the Almighty. I am lost without Him, as we all are! From now on, I shall try to go straight to the source; otherwise I am no better than Lucifer! I have been doing way too much speculating! For that I ask forgiveness! Lord, that I may see without speculating! Lord, that I may be docile without intervening!

Now it makes complete sense to me, but I do not think it makes sense to everyone else. I am very bummed! This means I was extremely close at obtaining both Essences in the cobweb, perhaps all three if he had the shield on him, which it is very likely that he did. The question still remains, what is this Goliath I keep hearing so faintly about? I must find out on my own!

I continue to disclose to all the many secrets of Lucifer's palace, and the cobweb below. I recount what happened in the cobweb, and how Seraphina's death was a premeditated ambush. This does not go well with Gabriel, who is rightfully still soar about the topic. I wonder if he thinks that it is my fault for not warning them! That would be way more guilt than what I need right now!

There is nothing I can say that will increase my credibility or lift the morale of the gathering. Still I hope all this information will serve the Gallants, well, in planning their counteroffensive.

Everyone listens to me but with reservations, not completely trusting what I have to say because of my apparent obsession with the staff of souls. They also continue to doubt as my mannerisms, composure, and voice continue to be displayed, and they are significantly different. They do not understand what I really saw, and why I needed to inspect the staff, but even if I were to explain, they would just see it as another excuse to try and get my hands on it again, or a tale of sorts.

In their eyes, they must be careful with what they heed from me because I have been so close to the master of persuasion, and his powers tend to rub-off. I seem to have lost a trust I must work hard to regain, which I know is not completely lost, otherwise they would probably not allow me to be in their midst.

Even my best friend, Michael, notices my alteration, but I

know his support towards me is always unconditional. I know he does not doubt me, even though I have changed. He cannot blame me for my alteration, and he actually relates to me because he too has changed without his Essence. He knows we must do what is necessary (under the laws of God) to fulfill our duties.

What saddens me is that he and I have not been able to bond lately. But we are apart for a reason! Perhaps it is good that I have not been tasked with following Michael, this probably means that the Lord does not question his loyalties because recently, it seems I have only been following those who deviate from God's plans; doing the dirty work. Nevertheless, we are both gloomy about being apart, but we understand that these are troubling times and for now, every angel must do what is needed of us. Still, we have not completely veered apart and shall have an eternity to make up for the lost time.

From a distance, I notice my favorite mural in the halls of the Palace has not further changed… at least not since the last time I saw it… or that I can remember… Maybe I have just been too busy to notice any minute fluctuations, or on the contrary, too preoccupied with the details to see the big picture. I cannot help but think that this mural is an artistic depiction of my documentary so far. Perhaps since the mural has not further changed, it is now complete…

Just when I say that, it changes…. It is pretty much the same, but I take a look at one of the biggest apples hanging from the golden branches, and it looks like a red Seraph. The juicy apple is bitten with two tooth marks indented in it. The apple's white interior is exposed. I think the bitten apple is the once gloriously white, Seraphina, overcome by the power of Satan's red…

After this painstaking gathering, I am again sent away by the Lord to a remote land… This is getting somewhat tiresome, being pulled in many directions at the beck and call of who knows what. I am a little bummed to have less and less trust placed in me, even slightly by my friend, Michael, whose facial expression of bewilderment, towards me, could not be any clearer. But it could just be that he is worried about regaining his sword, as he should be.

Just then, as if to only pass the Gallants previous inspection of my being, my eyes transform to become the brightest of reds. My eyes burn, just as they did when I struggled, entering the portico into Satan's palace, but it hurts ten times worse. What is this contagious virus of unsettling nature? Have I caught the sickness of conscience and persuasion without even knowing it? Without even wanting it! Are these the reaches of his infectious disease?

CHAPTER 23

With much of earth destroyed, with most of the Essences in his possession, with the creation of humans thwarted, and with legions of angelic support on his side, these darkening times seem to be turning for the worse...

The rebellion seems to be going in his favor and with little, to no, opposition. In fact I can see why it would be so appealing to join him, particularly, when all his schemes are fruitful and all that he sets out to attain seems to be getting accomplished. There cannot be much more that he wants to achieve, or obstacles for him thriving, is there?

The Gallants continue to be the scarce candle in the darkness… all we can do is continue to trust in the Lord because we can do nothing without Him who strengthens us…

I cannot help but think, what shall be my next move… what shall his be? But I know it is not up to me to decide, is it? As of late, I seem to have more freedom, a lot more! I like this freedom of mine, but has it come at a price? I hate having these warped and conflicting thoughts! It makes me feel corrupted… unlike me… confused… unstable, to say the least…

It is as though I grow closer and closer to the one I have been following, but also avoiding, and farther away from all the principles that I stand for. When there should be no doubt in my mind of my allegiance. It is as though Michael's tutelage has been suddenly traded for another's, and it has been done against my will, but the Lord's will is the only one that is important to me.

I have been spending so much time in the rebel's ranks, slowly swaying towards what seems to be an inevitable outcome, but what is the outcome? I also know that it is in Satan's best interest to make me feel this way, conflicted… Now I know how Beelzy feels… So many questions! Lord, that I may see, Lord, that I may be docile!

Peace has left me! God has commanded, so simply, that this not be about me, that I not make it about me, but how difficult it is to avoid pride! I must admit that I have become the insecure angel I once accused Beelzy of being. In essence, we have somewhat traded personalities, for he has become much more stable than me. But all my questions aside, who cares? I know the Almighty trusts me, and, I trust in Him! But do I trust myself?

The End.

ABOUT THE AUTHOR

Daniel A. Reyes is a young creative writer born in La Paz, Bolivia. Since 2004, he has been residing in Morgan Hill, California, a suburb of San Jose. Daniel or "Danny," as he is known by, graduated from Santa Clara University (SCU) with a bachelor's degree in Biology, but has always had a passion and an aptitude for creative writing. Danny is also a keen musician, occasionally performing in local venues throughout the Bay Area, alongside his siblings in their Alternative Rock band, "The Figureheads." He also has a passion for learning languages and more so, he is an avid Bay Area sports fan, having played several sports himself.

As a young professional, Daniel has had extensive experience with all types of research and sales, in both academia and industry. His experience helped him gather pertinent information to structure "The Essences series." With his knowledge of both science and Religion, he has fused a potential bestseller, modernizing the original antagonist and protagonist dynamic with a time-warping twist. The Essences first started as a movie script, which shows its potential for the big screen. With over ten years of planning and writing his initial drafts, Reyes puts forth a new understanding of angels and an epic of good and evil.

Edwards Brothers Malloy
Thorofare, NJ USA
November 29, 2016